Camilla Chance is the author of a number of books, including the best-selling *Wisdom Man*, which has been published in 5 languages.

Acknowledgment

My gratitude to all those who have helped me out of the most massive writers' block of all time, especially Emily Hanlon.

Camilla Chance

MELISSA AND KASHO

AUSTIN MACAULEY PUBLISHERS™

London • Cambridge • New York • Sharjah

Ordering Information:
Quantity sales: special discounts are available on quantity purchases by corporations, associations, and others. For details, contact the publisher at the address below.

Publisher's Cataloguing-in-Publication data
Chance, Camilla
Melissa and Kasho.

ISBN 9781947353909 (Paperback)
ISBN 9781947353916 (Hardback)
ISBN 9781947353923 (E-Book)

The main category of the book — Young Adult Fiction/Fantasy /General

www.austinmacauley.com

First Published (2018)
Austin Macauley Publishers LLC.
40 Wall Street, 28th Floor
New York, NY 10005
USA

mail-usa@austinmacauley.com
+1 (646) 5125767

Table of Content

Prologue
KASHO, June 1958

It is quite amusing to reflect on my mother and father, who tried to control every aspect of my life, sending me to this Italian finishing school, where they thought I would be transformed into a presentable daughter for the sons of their carefully chosen high society friends. Until that day in September 1957 when I left Australia, I had felt I was being watched on the flat earth riddled with insects outside our house by my parents, and their social circle, until I began to feel the whole world was flat like that.

But everything has changed since I came to Florence, even my yearning for Kimmie, my beloved brother. I feel relieved here because of Kasho with the magical heart, and because of my friends and what I'm experiencing.

I begin my tale after spending three months at this school. It is a week before I moved from my first bedroom to my tower that, with its austere walls stripped of plants, looks like a prison from the outside but, in reality, is the place that has set me free.

Chapter One
A New Life Begins, January 1958

In the palazzo's gigantic lower level where classes were held, every voice and footfall echoed across the marble floor. From the star-shaped wrought-iron lights hanging at cross-points in our vaulted ceiling, to the distant wide marble staircase, I drew a sense of both intimacy and space. We girls sat on a sofa and chairs around a hearth where black logs on broad metal supports divided flames that hovered lovingly over one another. I gave up counting the glass diamonds bursting out in multiple star-points from the ironwork light above my head and thought, without nostalgia, of the deep-pile sheepskin carpet on my parents' drawing room floor. The thin strip of cheap rug that crossed it was the only area in their room upon which I was allowed to tread. From there, I could glance at precious china busts, whose positions never changed, on furniture that was untouchable.

I was so glad when the somewhat plump, middle-aged Signorina Cecchi, our newly-hired Italian language teacher, interrupted my uncomfortable memories. Bustling around me and my friends, she began handing out books and paper, getting us ready for Professor Brunelleschi's class.

The Professor's job was to make classical works memorable to us. So memorable, in fact, that we would give the impression that we had actually read them, later in conversations at cocktail parties.

On loan from Florence University, the Professor was fond of saying, "It was wartime that made me grow up overnight, fighting in the Second World War where I got to know women very, very well—many kinds, in a hurry." As if that had been the point of the Second World War.

How different Professor Brunelleschi appeared to be from my father, whom I did not meet until I was four years old! My father returned home in his soldier's uniform, knelt in the snow, embraced me tightly, kissed my cheek and hissed in my ear, "You'll never be too big for me to give you a good beating." My relationship with my father was to be sealed in that instant. I'd learned too well from the attitude of the women and old men at home about Hitler and the Nazis—that whoever obeys a bully is a coward.

Unlike my father, who would often say, "There is no need for you to study—no daughter of mine could fail an exam," Professor Brunelleschi stressed his own view that environment, not heredity, molded character. Because I had learned from my brother Kim how to create a lively environment out of my own thoughts and the stories I told myself, and because I hoped I hadn't inherited my parents' coldness, the Professor's viewpoint made me content. I often tuned into this contentment as I noted that his head was big, his body long, and his legs bandy, yet he exuded a magnetism which made me think of wolves in the wild.

My thoughts were interrupted again, this time by Robin, as she brushed past my body. The bubbly *Signorina* looked in our direction. "Robin," she exclaimed, "You're late! Where on earth have you been all this time?"

"On the john."

"But where were you before that?"

"On the john." Robin turned her large clear eyes, looking innocent, onto the calculating look of the *Signorina.*

"Yes, but before—"

"On the *other* john!"

11

The *Signorina*'s full lips thinned momentarily.

Though others present were probably unaware, I knew Robin was telling the truth—something she hardly ever did. Every Tuesday—today—my friend took purges to 'clean' herself 'out'. But she was not about to admit this in public.

She plopped herself down on the sofa between Julie and Karen, immediately leaning her body, which was always without underwear, across Karen to where I sat on a high-backed wooden chair.

"I hope Signorina Cecchi has learned now," Robin whispered loudly, "that it is none of her business where I've been, and I won't tell her. Anyhow, if I'm late, the Professor's even later."

He was coming in now, but stopped when he saw attractive Signorina Cecchi, with her over-darkened eyebrows and large gold earrings. *"Buon giorno!"* he beamed, his voice booming— as all our words did—across the marble floor. "Did you enjoy your weekend in Paris? This *is* a lovely surprise. If only I could have gone with you."

"Are *you* familiar with Paris?" asked the *Signorina*. All well brought-up females, I thought, would have turned their heads away—as I would have—and ignored the Professor's remark, but the *Signorina* was different. She would often jokingly say to us pupils, as if asking for cooperation, how she hoped to steal some of the young men whom we would invite to the school—adding that she had not come here primarily to teach.

"I was only able to visit the city for half a day," the Professor admitted, with a pained expression. "It was really unfortunate because I wanted to spend more time there. Then, with the other touring lecturers, I went to New York. I had eighteen days free with lots of money which I didn't want to spend. But I had wanted so much to do so in Paris!"

"Whatever did you want to spend it on?" asked the *Signorina*, eying him coyly.

12

He leaned over and patted her five-bracelet arm.

"My dear," he said, "surely *you* understand?"

"Paris is full of *poules de luxe*—high class women of pleasure," the ash-blonde American heiress, Julie, mouthed to me from the sofa.

I didn't quite understand what Julie was talking about—but a person can be shocked without understanding something. I imagined a glacier and retreated into it emotionally—as I had from all sexually suggestive conversations since Mario invaded my hotel room three months ago, on my first night in Italy. While I had come to feel almost comfortable around Italian women, I still felt uncertain around men.

Signorina Cecchi was backing away, looking slightly embarrassed, so that Professor Brunelleschi's lesson might begin. Settling into an armchair, the Professor now turned to face us, his literature class of four. Only Nicole, from Monte Carlo, was absent today; she had attended this morning's lessons last year.

"Now," the Professor announced triumphantly, as if no words had passed between himself and Signorina Cecchi, "we got to that part of Dante Alighieri's *Divine Comedy* where Dante and his dead love, Beatrice, watch Church decay being symbolized by a giant making love to a prostitute on the back of a dragon. I have to admit, it must have been a jolly comfortable dragon. Of course, it would have had to be comfortable."

Surrounded by my iceberg, I retreated into the past. I recalled a verse I'd written long ago about Australia:

By someone who loves as no other,
Who wakes at the break of day
To the cascading call of the magpie
And the sweet smell of mown hay.
With peppermint trees all around her,
And dust rising from the track;

The heat creeps up and slaps her face
As she draws the curtain back.

Australia—how did my family come to live there? My blood is drawn from many European countries that I have not seen. But my mother and father were stuck in Britain when the Second World War was declared. Foreigners were totally mistrusted back then. My parents had overdone their self-protection by adopting customs from bygone eras, becoming more English than the English. They saw themselves as Victorian or Edwardian in behavior; but my night visitor, Kasho, later made me realize that my mother and father would actually have felt more at home in an earlier time.

I remembered too well what Britain felt like, both with and without my beloved brother, during the War—London in particular. I remembered the dusty, bare boards of the attic where, after Kim left, my parents shut me away every day, saying, "Other children play, but *you* are superior—you *imagine*. We can't have you roaming the streets like common children while their mothers stand for long hours in factories, making the outsides of bombs. And you're too grown up for toys."

Once Kim was sent away to boarding school, I was alone in that attic bare of furniture, and came to feel that God was my most true friend. I told Him, "I *love* other children. They know how to play. Why does mummy think they are no good for me?"

One morning I pulled back the blackout curtains, the purpose of which was to keep any light from showing at night and thus making our house a target for bombs. I saw an old man skipping along the road, holding the hand of a little girl like me. They jumped high. They made their own happiness, despite the bombed-out buildings. I understood that some grownups would do that for the sake of children. I also knew that sometimes children were left without parents after an air raid. Although I wouldn't want that, Kim would have looked after me then if he'd been here.

Once, Kim and I had been walking with our mother past the flattened house next door after a night when my bedroom windows were smashed, my bed was covered with glass and the cups swung to and fro on their hooks in the cupboard where my brother and I were confined.

A woman standing in the rubble that had been the house next door held out a box to my mother.

"I'm collecting for the family. They've lost everything," she said.

"I dislike having a box shoved under my nose," my mother replied haughtily. "How dare someone of your class and race accost me like that? You're nothing but a vulgar, busty woman."

The woman half smiled at me, but I looked down. I was too ashamed to meet her eyes.

"Why doesn't Kimmie come back from boarding school?" I asked God. "He must be dead. When people I've met go away for a while, they never come back. Oh, I love You, I love You with all of me, God—with my heart and arms and legs. Is it all right if I try to serve You greatly?"

My parents had told me God was like a father, but I didn't believe them. I felt that there was a good chance that God, unlike my parents, would love me back if I tried to please Him.

I knew I was a really lucky girl—I could draw pictures in the attic dust. Occasionally I drew pictures of Kim, or of Kim and me playing, or of an old man with a long beard who skipped with me in the sunshine. But I always wiped away my pictures before I was let out for a meal.

Until my brother Kimmie left our family, he and I experienced enchanted times together. But underneath them pain lurked, because I sometimes heard visitors to our terrace house whispering about Kim—with mysterious emphasis, words such as, "What a pity, to have a boy, and have something so wrong

15

with him!" I didn't know, couldn't understand, because Kimmie was so good to me in every way. But those words, *something so wrong with Kimmie,* haunted me, because they sounded like a threat. What was going to happen to him? I couldn't ask.

In my attic after Kim left, I remembered us standing on the flat roof over our sitting room, surrounded by a rounded wall, five inches high. We were laughing and swinging sticks that bent, sending the berries we'd fixed to their points flying through the air. The yellow-brown air, filled with smoke from factories, felt heavy on our skins, and we could not see where our berries landed—but it was as if our spirits soared within them far, far over oceans into the distance. Our mother usually put us out on this square flat roof for an hour immediately after lunch. We had access to it through a door-like window, beside which the rest of our house continued up, up to my bedroom. But on the day I most liked to remember, a dangerously big wind that could have blown me and my brother off the roof, had caused my mother to delay putting us out. When the storm died down, we were put out as usual, and to our delight, we found the wind had piled up stuff we could play with, such as sticks and berries, in a heap over the yellow pansies in the corner furthest from the house. My brother immediately said, "You stay there" in the middle of our flat roof, as he pounced on the berries and sticks.

I said warily, "We're not allowed to go near the edge."

"Our mother's crazy," said Kim daringly, his eyes extra big and bright. "Don't do what I'm doing now, but you need not listen to everything she says. If she cared about us, she wouldn't send us out here every day to get fresh air. It's stupid because, in this small space, it's easier to jump off the roof than not to, and the air makes the insides of our noses black."

He pushed the bundle of sticks in his arms into mine and poured berries onto my hand. We worked industriously, sharing our treasure, and jumped on the spot and giggled and sent our berries flying.

When I got tired, my brother cuddled me. We sat looking into each other's eyes, and—though I couldn't put it into words—I felt we knew each other's souls. My brother gave me a happy wink, and my bliss was complete. His body, despite the visitors' comments, felt powerful. Never did I want to use the word 'I' again. 'We' was the only truthful one.

"Mummy must be very unhappy without our daddy," I ventured.

Kim grew thoughtful. "I remember them together before the War," he said, "wearing such heavy clothes in winter that they could barely move, looking so miserable that I couldn't bear it. They'd sometimes say to each other, 'What's the good of living? We're getting nowhere.' They felt so sorry for themselves, they thought everything I did, like putting my ear to our mother's tummy when you were inside her, was aimed at hurting them. All the same, I wish our father would come back. But I don't believe he will. I don't think this war will ever end."

At this point Kim's arms around me tightened, and he added most intensely, "My sweet Melissa, I'm going to teach you how to deal with our mummy and daddy. We once had a servant girl who burst into tears every time our father spoke to her. Oh, he always shouted. He used to reduce me to tears too, though I've overcome that. But never ever let cruelty make you numb. Never ever stop feeling. Be my sister."

We sat together, hugging, looking at flowers. Just as I had felt that the sticks and berries wanted us to use them, so the pot of yellow pansies in the forbidden corner—almost the only color we ever saw—seemed to be willing my Kimmie to pick it up. At last he got to his feet, remarking, "It would be nice to see blue sky again." I stopped feeling warm, because he went slightly too far away, so close to the flat roof's edge. There, he lovingly stroked dust off the pansies' faces, laying his cheek firmly against their velvet petals. I thought, "Love is brave." And then my thinking said, "I want to be like that."

17

Kim returned, patted me reassuringly, and put the pot of pansies in my arms.

"Melissa, you're dreaming again!" I heard the Professor thunder. "What did I just say?"

"That it must have been a comfortable dragon," I absently repeated the last words I'd heard. "And then you added, 'Of course, it would have had to be comfortable.'"

Professor Brunelleschi laughed and laughed. The sight of his whole body shaking pulled me back into the wintry-looking basement walls, the precious glowing fireplace of the present. On recovering from his own reaction of delight, the Professor announced: "Dante was the greatest proponent of the *Dolce Stil Nuovo*, translatable as 'Sweet New Style', which springs from the heart. It sees woman as better than man, as an angel. Like you, Melissa.

"*Listen* to me. Listening is a virtue. I'm sure I could give you, my girl; and, if it comes to that, every one of you girls here, a huge bunch of white roses, so that all who wished to would know of your purity."

In embarrassment, I turned away from the man and the fire; but Julie answered, "We already know the difference between a '*buona ragazza*' and a '*brava ragazza*,' both of which can be translated as a 'good girl'."

"A '*brava ragazza*' is a virgin, but a '*buona ragazza*' does what I want," confirmed the Professor, appearing to pull back a little.

I began daydreaming again, thinking of how on Monday last week Signorina Cecchi, who was also our art teacher, had been taking us for our fortnightly trip to the Uffizi Gallery when she'd exclaimed, "Look! There is Professor Brunelleschi with his wife!" Sure enough, the couple was gazing into a shop window.

And during lessons the following day, Julie had mentioned to the Professor, "Yesterday we saw you with a most attractive woman on your arm—three or four years junior to you, I think."

He made no comment, but his usual belly laugh erupted from him a little uneasily.

After the lesson, Karen wondered, "Why didn't he *say* she was his wife?"

"He never gives *any* hint that he's married," Julie had responded. "He wants us to talk about him. He likes to picture himself always surrounded by loving young girls."

Plunging back into reality, I realized we were nearing the end of the Professor's lesson when he gave his diabolic chuckle again, telling us that the next work we would study was Boccaccio's *Decameron*, the full text of which had been banned in English.

The Professor had no notes to gather. He swept himself away, his blue-black hair sticking out in two tufts at the back, his pointed shoes ringing out on the spacious marble floor and stairs.

Signorina Cecchi must have been talking with the kitchen staff, possibly finalizing a suitable menu for the young men coming to lunch, because now she was descending the creaking wooden servants' staircase as she arrived to give us a class on the Italian language. Her high heeled shoes plip-plopped on the marble floor over to our group. When she had fully settled herself in the chair the Professor had just vacated, the first thing she did was ask me to read aloud, and I chose:

"Perivi, o tenerella. E non vedevi
il fior degli anni tuoi;"

Stumbling and stammering in nervousness, I went on:

"Non ti molceva il core
La dolce lode or delle negre chiome,
Or degli sguardi innamorati e schivi;
Ne teco le compagne ai di festivi
ragionavan d'amore."

Leopardi's words meant:

"You died, my tenderest one, and did not see
Your years flower, or feel your heart moved
By sweet praise of your black hair,
Your shy loving looks.
No friends talked with you,
On holidays, about love."

Signorina Cecchi was grimacing—apparently my Italian pronunciation caused her pain. Maybe the other girls felt similarly. Patting the chair beside her invitingly, the *signorina* said to me, "I know you came here, Melissa, and will probably leave, feeling that you are not attractive to boys. But it isn't so. You have all in your physical appearance to awaken love, longing, desire and passion. And yet your voice is everything that is the opposite of melodious. I've heard it harsh and brutal, like today, as if you were angry but I don't think you are. I think it's just that you are nervous and have difficulty in speaking. Are you really brutal? Or—"

"I *do* have difficulty in speaking."

"But I can't understand *why*. You have everything a girl can possess. Why on earth do you feel so inferior?"

"*I have told you so many times I am sick of it. Why* on earth don't *you speak up?*" my father had demanded.

I answered, "My voice always sounds to me as if I am speaking *very* loudly."

My father went on, "Well, you know now that you are not. I've told you *that* enough times. It's very rude to speak so that others can't hear you. Isn't it, *isn't it?*"

I'd answered, "Yes"—though I'd never thought anyone who spoke softly rude before then—and I felt my voice sounded insolent when I spoke loudly, when it seemed to me I was shouting.

My father now told a flat out lie, which he must have thought was the truth.

20

"I never have trouble hearing anyone else," he went on, "so it must be lack of consideration on your part. Do you *agree*?" He said this last sentence sharply.

I muttered, "I don't know," though I did know my problem wasn't lack of consideration, but simply fear. If only Kim had been with me… and suddenly I thought he was. I was certain I heard him whisper in my ear, *don't risk a beating. Be smart. Tell him what he wants to hear.* And so I did, but quietly.

In my father's face, the terrifying rage deepened. He leaned forward, his massive hand behind his ear.

"I'm sorry," I murmured, even more softly.

My father's face turned purple, and he leaned further forward. Behind his ear his hand curled, ready to grab my throat. It was far from the first time he had gestured with apparently murderous intent. That I am alive today is a credit to my father's agility in last-minute self-control.

I was too frightened to speak, but backed away with my eyes and mouth open, trying not to cry.

Immediately he changed.

"There," he muttered happily, in the tone of one massaging himself. "I like to see you cry."

I jerked my mind back to the *Signorina*, who was continuing: "I think I know how you can correct it. By singing—"

"*Signorina*, I *can't* sing!"

I waited for the other girls, knowingly nodding their heads, to burst out laughing. They did. So I continued triumphantly, "All my friends will tell you how awful my singing is."

"But *don't* sing in public. Just when you are walking alone with your dog."

The *Signorina* broke off because I had covered my face with my hands. To my shame, I could not stop myself from weeping.

"Sobbing your heart out indeed! Pull yourself together! You shouldn't be so sensitive."

"My dog is dead," I announced flatly. I had instantly stopped crying. The *Signorina*'s harshness had shocked me out of that. I recalled a true story my father once told me about the five-year old daughter of a ruling family. She made one lapse from protocol, by expressing herself emotionally. Her parents had ordered their servants to kill all her pets in front of her until she learned not to show her feelings.

"You will have another dog then," the *Signorina* assured me. "It is not betraying him to get another. Melissa," she continued very softly, "you know *why* you loved your dog so much, don't you?"

Big pause.

"It is because you are a loner."

"Hear, hear!" interjected Karen.

"And you must *not* be. Mix with other people, so there is no longer that emptiness in your life that can only be filled by a dog. Will you learn this lesson well for me?"

During the last few minutes of Signorina Cecchi's lesson, I struggled to recover my composure fully. "Socializing is not necessary," I kept telling myself savagely. "All you need, Melissa, is an oblong of earth the size of a grave, and solitude. Throw yourself on the ground, then; lay your bursting head on your arms and cry. That's all we do in life anyway. Cry."

For the first time in years, I felt Kim beside me and heard him say, *No! You must stop these terrible thoughts. Now is the time for you to live. Do it for me.*

I don't know if I was too startled by his closeness or too lost in my own despair, but I shook my head and closed myself off from him. I was still too much my parents' daughter, and too far away from the magic I once shared with Kim.

Finally, the bell rang, releasing us to make our way to the mid-level dining room, where two young men from fashionable society already sat drinking wine and waiting for us. Italian Ludovico and French Roland were the 'boys' whom our

Principal, normally known to us simply as *la Contessa,* or the Countess, had invited to lunch today.

In Europe as opposed to Britain, all children of aristocracy inherited their father's title, as had the Counts Roland and Ludovico. They were a couple of years older than us. Animated Roland was thin and—temporarily, we assumed—pimply with short mousy hair, heavy eyelids and a small mouth. By contrast, Ludovico's eyes looked huge and solemn; and one side of his face, distinctly sadder, never moved when the other side smiled. Sometimes, heavily-built Ludovico would murmur *"Senti!"* ("Listen!")—then, while we were all listening to him, he would lapse again into silence.

He looked up when we came in and smiled at me, as if I were a nervous child who had been confined to one room most of her life—which, of course, I was. "It's the storyteller," he exclaimed playfully, both to and about me, "and her eyes are shining like stars."

I felt confused by the trite praise and, muttering, "That's not very original," I sat down alone, facing the others.

Curving her body on the chair beside Roland, Julie nestled into him. "You've been too reserved," she whispered into his neck, "since you got back from the Sorbonne."

"I've learned to wear a sort of armor," Roland answered—playing, I felt, with words. "It is useless to show your feelings, it only makes people laugh at you. Now, I only show emotion when it is advantageous to do so. That is what I've learned at university in Paris."

"You are a coward." Julie turned her back—hard to do, when she was virtually sitting on Roland's knee. "I couldn't disagree more. I wish you'd go to hell."

Robin, who had been standing in the corner where only I could see her, sorting through a pile of records, put one on the record player but continued to stand there. Haunting jazz piano music began playing.

"If you want to damn me," Roland answered Julie, raising his voice a little, "there's only one way to do it."

"What?"

"By sinning with me."

"Why don't you sin with someone else at the school?"

"They would have to be willing. *I'm* not going to force myself on anyone. But would you be able to do it? Have you the courage?"

"I think it depends on how strong one's feelings are."

"What sort of feelings? 'Strong' means nothing. There is no love in the world. Only friendship—or passion."

Ludovico had been pressing his forefinger onto the ancient knife wounds between us in the old oak table. "Tell us a story, Melissa," he interrupted, also raising his voice. "Give us a treat."

"I want to know if you would have the courage to do it," Roland repeated to Julie very loudly.

"If it came to the point, I don't think I could."

"No, I don't think so either," mused Roland. "I tell you who could. *Melissa* could. With tears running down her cheeks all the time maybe, but she could."

Roland can see right through me, I thought.

"What is that record, Robin?" Karen asked sharply, turning in her chair.

"Prelude to a Kiss."

"Prelude to a Kiss," echoed Roland dreamily—measuring again, I felt his effect on us. "All life is prelude to a kiss," he pronounced. "And, sometimes, the kiss never comes. Of course, I'm not saying that men and women don't get a lot of kisses in their lifetime; but *they* don't mean anything. I mean a *real* contact—a kiss with Nature."

Looking at Roland with eyes that felt more open than usual, I saw what I considered tragedy—a young man who could not feel. The atmosphere of his character contrasted with the profound piano music I was hearing, and made me think that only

24

violins—or an obvious lack of them—could express the present death in his soul. I imagined him traveling with an empty, coffin-like violin case, and greeting villagers all around the world who loved music, telling them he was a famous violinist, although he had never tried to play a note.

He turned away from Julie towards me. "Melissa," he now said, "may I get to know you, the way the word is used in the Bible? So-and-so knew so-and-so and begat so-and-so?"

"How should I know?"

"Do you think I ever will? For I feel a great attraction to you—as a friend. Do you think I ever shall?"

"I don't suppose so. Why can't you see me as a human being, without always talking of sex?"

Ludovico leaned across the table and winked at me. "Make yourself ugly," he mouthed.

I was good at that. I rolled my eyes up, stared at the empty space between us, and hung my lips open to one side. Kim seemed to come back—I heard his wonderful laugh. I wanted to laugh with him, because making myself ugly was something he had taught me when we were children in London. But I didn't want to be anything but ugly for Ludovico in that moment.

Ludovico studied the doubtless scary sight. "Otherwise you'll never be free of men," he warned.

"Have you just seen a ghost, Melissa?" yelled Robin.

Much laughter. The boys turned towards her.

"Perhaps," I replied mysteriously.

Wide-eyed Ombretta, the *palazzo* cat, distracted us by coming in now—as always at lunch time. While the cat rubbed herself in and out among the chair legs, Julie bent to stroke her, murmuring, "And are you such a *naughty* cat? Are you so *naughty*?"

"What has poor Ombretta done, for you to call her bad?" I protested.

Under the table, Karen pressed her fingers into my knee, telling me that my reaction was too strong for the circumstances. "The cat feels happy anyway," she whispered.

I stared at her. Karen's perspective was new to me. How could anyone take for granted that an animal felt happy? In Australia, we lived way out in the country, and shooting animals was something my father did almost daily. Pointedly calling me "Little Misery," he'd always state, "I'm putting it out of its misery." Listening to my father, I believed that animals usually led miserable lives. I needed to think this out.

My parents did not limit their idea of mercy killing to animals. All my life I heard them say, "So-and-so ought to be committing suicide now. How can we convince him?" or "So-and-so *has* just committed suicide with her friends gathered round, and it was beautiful." They believed that anyone who happened to be physically weak, soft-hearted, loving or even artistic should be encouraged to die. And they'd say, "People like us are above morality."

"The trouble with the colored, the indigenous and the poor is that they breed so fast" was another of my parents' sayings. "It is a sin and a disgrace to bring a child into the world the way it is now."

Just before leaving Australia, I read a newspaper report about an Aboriginal man carrying back to civilization a helpless white farmer who had been lost in the bush. "You could have just let him die. His ancestors turned your tribe into pet meat!" the sympathetic white reporter had exclaimed. Weeping at the memory, the rescuer had nevertheless answered him proudly, "If I left that man to his fate, I would no longer be Aboriginal." I felt I had never encountered such love. My attraction to the Australian Aboriginal outlook as a result of that sentence felt beyond the ordinary, but I did not know why.

I grew up in a household where I never dared admit I did anything out of love, because it wasn't part of my parents'

26

world—they wouldn't understand. And yet I did everything out of love. My father directed a great many companies. Although I never knew which, because no one outside those companies did, I knew it sat all right with him that the international sale of armaments kept down those whom he saw as a nuisance. He was, like most people with power on Earth, one to reject universal love the way I understood it.

On the subject of the poor, my father would also say, "Common people brought their poverty on themselves, and therefore it is our duty to remind them at every opportunity of their low place. If they'd had any sense, their ancestors would have risen to power long ago."

Why did my parents always insist that I should lie? They said only poor people told the truth, that we had to be different. One truth that I believed in was that, when white settlers first came to Australia, Aboriginals were our hosts, and they went naked. I'm sure if an Aboriginal walked naked past our window in Australia now, my mother and father and many of their friends would still feel outraged, still want to kill him—just like many of the first white settlers.

But I also noticed how my father made all the people who worked for him, and whom he met in passing, quake. He was cruel to those in underling positions and never let them forget that they were lesser than him. He sneered when he spoke and it was as if he took pleasure in humiliating people whose lives were difficult. Every time he wounded a person in passing, it was as if the wound went into me. I knew deeply the pain these people felt as they were tossed aside.

When the Second World War ended, my parents had joined a huge number of Britons avoiding post-war hardship, and sailed with me, their only child by now, to Australia. I was six years old.

Eleven years later, it was still fashionable for so-called 'upper class' families like mine in Australia to send their daughters to finishing schools in cities such as Florence. These schools taught gracious conversation, and generally prepared girls for marriage, whether they wished it or not, to rich high society farmers back home or European noblemen. I most strongly did not wish to be tied to some insensitive snob or man who in any way would resemble my father.

When I was seventeen, my parents met a couple at a cocktail party whose daughter, Robin, was about to attend such a finishing school. As if they belonged to European feudal times, when, by law, rulers could wear purple though serfs had to wear brown, my parents had forbidden me to mingle with ordinary Australians. But Robin was a school friend. Her parents convinced mine to allow me to travel beyond their influence so long as I remained in Robin's company.

"*Why* don't you suppose so?" Roland was persisting. He had got up and was coming around the table to me. "Because I don't attract you? Or because you think *you* don't attract *me* enough?"

"Oh, stop it and go away! I think you're sick."

"I'm not touching you," he answered. "But you might at least tell me if the idea gives you pleasure, or revolts you. As for me, I like taking risks. Whatever is possible I count as done already, and as for what is impossible—let us do it! That is what a great man said to Marie Antoinette."

"Well, then, you've answered yourself," I replied. "Everything is logically possible."

"Yes, I have. *Anything* is possible. I'll kill you and then kill myself. Your friends will look up to you then, you who have been through the agony of violent death, and found out what lies beyond. *You* will know; *they*'ll be ignorant, thoroughly ignorant of the life beyond the grave; you and I will be the pioneers of our generation. Agreed?"

How did he know? Until recently, I'd have liked nothing better.

"But before I kill you I shall make love to you. I shall take you. Would you like that? I imagine you would. Yes, that would be too good an opportunity to miss."

I sighed to myself. All roads lead to Rome.

The dining room had three doors. I felt that lunch time was closer now that gossamer-scarfed Nicole came bursting breathlessly through one of the doors, planting a quick kiss on Robin's forehead. I assumed she had spent the morning in town.

Ludovico commented, "Hey, Nicole! Notice us. She kisses Robin, but she doesn't kiss us."

Roland's thoughts appeared to be returning from far away. "What?" he said.

The young Tuscan Count repeated it.

"Would *Melissa* let us kiss her?" Roland began bending over me. "Would you, Melissa?"

Robin, sounding jealous, yelled, "Why do you want to kiss her? She wouldn't like it."

I jumped out of my chair, shouting, "No!"

"Don't your parents kiss you?" Roland demanded.

"No," I admitted. "But it's not your business."

"Doesn't your brother kiss you?"

"My brother died long ago." My eyes began to burn.

"Well then, aren't I a brother to you now?"

"No!" I reiterated, longing for Kim's closeness but there was nothing of his presence in that moment.

"Why are you being so wretched?" Roland whined like a hurt animal. Then, "Why are you frightened?"

I couldn't tell him why. That, to my knowledge, I'd never yet had a dream that wasn't a nightmare. Unhappily, I often dreamed of Mario, the man who had terrified me in Rome the night before Robin and I had traveled, by train, to this *palazzo*. In my dream he would ask the way to our school because he had 'a date with a girl there'—me. Usually, I vomited when I awakened.

29

Almost filling the dining room entrance to my left, the Countess who ran our school appeared with purple-suited Signorina Cecchi. Our Countess wore black and carried an excessively ample purse. She, like Nicole, must have spent the morning in town, I thought. "Won't you step aside?" she came in saying to Signorina Cecchi. "I am squashed in this doorway when you take up so much room."

"It cannot be! I am as thin as a wire, a wire, I tell you!" protested Signorina Cecchi. "I am just like a wire."

Roland and Ludovico smiled benignly.

All hunger gone, I stood shaking where I'd jumped out of my chair. "I recognize that something in men desires to kill and to kiss," I told Roland fiercely. "And something in women might wish for it to be done. But the only important thing to me is a depth of feeling for all. For myself, I would like to be afraid of nothing. If we pass the point of no return and I am thrown—naked of help—out of a plane by my friends and enemies, I hope I will be at ease enough to admire the spectacular view on the interminable way down. But I'm not that kind of woman yet. I am scared of you, and scared of the reckless life you want to force me into."

In Rome, Robin had told me a story from her life that I couldn't think about just now—it revealed adult love to be mostly self-interest, little more than seeking physical enjoyment. I had thought love was more like a kookaburra bird I saw back home, sitting loyally beside his dead mate on a wire day after day.

By now I couldn't stop shuddering, as if Roland had, indeed, touched me in a forbidden place. I didn't want anyone to see me this way, so I backed out of the door behind me into the kitchen.

Chapter Two
Secrets Revealed

The heavy kitchen door slammed shut behind me as I retreated outside. I found a private place to sit on the long stone wall that sloped by our garden waterfall. I was terrified of becoming a moron like my friends. Would growing sexual feelings eventually dominate and twist *my* thoughts, as they seemed to have done to those from whom I'd just run away? I vowed before God that all my life I would hate any book or movie that tried to tell me sexual thoughts or practice occurred before true love. I would hate it—hate it—hate it.

Dangling my legs from the waterfall wall, struggling to control my trembling, my eyes half shut, I began to compose a verse that seemed to spring naturally from the dampened air:

"Snow is falling down,

Softer than the rain;

Blotting out the world,

Blotting out my pain."

Karen had told me shyly that her father was a big wheel in the American pop music industry, and could make or break an artist's career. I loved writing songs, wanting to create lyrics that would get people thinking, give them a new understanding of homelessness, hunger or grinding poverty, everything that my father denied. But I didn't see myself using 'the old school tie' to make my work popular. It just wasn't my nature.

Slow creaking interrupted my singing—the outside kitchen door behind me must have opened and then closed again. Someone had come out, inhibiting me from finishing the song in my heart.

Great silence enveloped us. "I *do* know who you are," I warbled in my head, as I felt my shoulders gripped tightly. I glimpsed black flapping material—someone was wrapping her musty jacket around me. Deep down, had I known that the *Contessa* would follow me out? Probably, I thought—and felt guilty for having taken advantage of her loving spirit.

My shivering gave way to sobbing. I couldn't stop. Hardly anyone had cared for me since Kim died.

Making a giant effort to speak Italian, the way the *Contessa* and I always spoke, I burst out, "You should *have* your lunch—you should have it!"

"I shared a cake with Nicole at Giacosa's—" (a fashionable café in Via Tornabuoni), the Countess replied in a voice so soft it would have angered my father. "I don't need any more."

Big silence.

My eyes, still half-shut, had turned the garden into twilight.

La Contessa insinuated her heavy body onto the waterfall wall, and gently pulled my head sideways onto her knees. After a while, she began to sing, "Melissa is a child—everybody loves her" over and over, like a comforting lullaby.

"You're safe here. Here is no pain," she eventually added. "You were very courageous to say what you said in the dining room."

"No—just bad mannered," I corrected her, lifting my head a little. I knew I truly would not have survived such an outburst at home. I visualized myself there, being thrown against the wall, and instantly dying.

"So brave; you trust me. There are more important things than manners. I wouldn't be able to sleep tonight, remembering you shaking and shaking, until I found out why. Therefore, it's purely for selfish reasons that I'm with you now. Forgive me—I am Italian, and curiosity is part of our culture. How often has it happened that you couldn't stop shuddering?"

"Many times since my first night in Italy." And every time, I added in my mind, that Roland makes overtures to me—which is maybe why he does that.

The Countess gasped, as if she were about to say something. But no words came. So I lifted my head higher, pressing it against her chest. Surely we made a very caring-looking picture.

La Contessa changed tactics. "You have a good imagination, I know," she said. "That must be so, because I think that as a child you spent a lot of time alone. And you write stories. I thought we could make a story together. Will you try with me?"

I assented uneasily.

"Let us begin. Imagine yourself as a very happy little girl."

"I can't," I objected, afraid that memories of me and Kim would return. He was too close now. Or was he too far away?

"Well, just imagine any happy little girl."

I thought of the fairies in the picture books that first Kim read to me and then I had read as a child. Wishing very much to do what the Countess asked, I decided to persevere. "Like a fairy, she is flying straight towards me on the back of a huge dove, giggling with excitement because of the ride."

"That's right. Children *should* live in a state of delight," the Countess encouraged me. "Children should spend their lives playing among trees in the humble, loving womb which is the earth," she went on dreamily. "At one with nature, feeling with every being in the universe that calls out its joy. Many of us adults have lost our joy—we are so split by fear. Your child is a magic child. She is going to lead you back into forests of Truth. There, in the haunting green, she has a present for you."

I could not believe how much I trusted this *Contessa*. I wondered if all her students felt the same way. In her presence, the vivid imagination I dared not show the world ceased to terrify me. Amazingly, I relaxed. Soon, in my head, I attempted the leafy journey, and *became* the child—wobbling forward with baby steps, my stomach smeared with dirt from past falls. I knew I was approaching the clearing that housed my present when the variegated leaves caressing me on all sides turned more golden. My excitement grew. Then I *saw* it. "My present is a huge warm pink shape. Its name is Joy!" I exclaimed to the *Contessa.* "It has come to bring me joy."

"That's right. The new form, the new life, is always greater than the old. You're walking a path that is wonderful, fulfilling, challenging, frightening. Let the wild part of you open her mouth to drink in life. You are walking barefoot on rocks and in grass and on soft wet earth. And you are going to tell me about your first night in Italy."

I did. I don't know how or why. I just did.

I began by gathering my thoughts together about everything that had happened when Robin and I arrived after our long flight to Rome from Australia. Our plane had landed in wet weather that quickly cleared, and I had left Robin sleeping at our hotel.

Wandering alone around cobbled alleyways, I crossed the road to talk with a hunchbacked old woman in black staring down a drain. In one hand she held coins, and in the other two large bags.

"Can I help you?" I asked eagerly, taking the bags. In my ignorance, I'd have done this just as enthusiastically had the woman been a man.

The old woman's eyes widened and she stared at my face. "I have lost a coin," she muttered.

I handed her two hundred lire.

"Oh, *signora,* you are so good!" the woman exclaimed. But any opportunity to give kindness back to people outside my family was, to me, a welcome delight. Although I did my best within my family, people outside it behaved so well.

The woman patted her heart. "We always say the heart shows itself in the face. Never have I seen one as beautiful as yours. Do you understand?"

"Yes, I understand," I assured the crone.

An invisible car sounded its horn. Immediately, the old one shivered and clutched me, pulling me behind her.

A few shocked seconds later, I found myself standing in the gutter while the car passed us. And the frightened woman, no longer crouching, had her arms spread, shielding my body.

Wonder flooded my being as I slowly came to realize that this woman, still trembling violently and whimpering, had been afraid for me. She had pushed me behind her out of caring! From now on, if she desired it, I would have broken my back carrying her bags.

"*Grazie mille, signora,* but it's all right," I said. "*Venga.*" So we continued our walk.

"If you went under that car your beauty would be lost forever. I was run over once and crippled, crippled."

Yes, the old woman was horribly bent. "*Mi dispiace,*" I replied. I felt great empathy for her. I, too, had been hurt in an accident involving my horse and a car.

The woman beside me stopped again to stare at my face, as if it were the rising sun. "I have seen so many radiant faces in the city today!" she exclaimed. "Are you married, *signora*?"

"No, I'm not married."

"How old can you be then, *signorina*?"—quickening her steps to catch up with me. I slowed and began wondering whether Robin, soundly asleep at the hotel where I'd left her, had awakened yet. Would she be annoyed that I'd gone out on my own?

"Seventeen," I replied.

"I was married at sixteen. I am now eighty-two."

"Where do you live? Can I carry your bags there?"

"No, no. I'm still young really. Let me take them."

But I noted, smiling, that her attempts to do so were half-hearted. We continued walking.

The old one soon halted again. She pointed to the sky. "Up there—God," she remarked. "Do you understand?"

"Yes."

"I pray. *Capisce*?"

"Sì."

We returned to walking. Though our route had grown more crowded, and passersby stared, we ignored them. At last we reached a house with great yellow sheets of paint peeling off its walls. Its windows were tiny, with green rain-stained shutters. Below them, sodden long black folded-over garments and pegged colorful children's dresses shared washing lines. The woman held her hands out to me for her bags. I released them; she then dumped them at the door and moved back to me in the road.

"I have to leave you now," I told her, feeling my worry grow that Robin might be angry. "I've got to run."

The old one drew a deep breath when I fully faced her.

I swung around and raced—then turned back to wave. The woman was still standing in the middle of the road, now calling *"Bella, bella, bella!"* as if I were a vision. Above her, clouds like playful puppies waved their legs.

How could anything like this have happened to me? Surely, I had reached a country full of miracles. I remembered my mother saying, "I need to change you into a pretty little girl, so I can love you." Whenever she saw me, she tried to fix my clothes or my hair. Every night, she'd pin hot metal clips into my curls with such tension that screams of hostility would burst from her if I moved. And every morning, after dutifully enduring a tormented night, I would be so embarrassed by the result that I would drench my head with water and sneak out to the school bus before either of my parents could notice. I knew it was important not to hurt them.

But that day in Rome, I needed the strange old woman with a beautiful soul to yell her opinion of my good looks loudly enough for my mother to hear—for me to hear. How loud might that be?

When I knocked on Robin's hotel room door, I found her putting on makeup. "Why haven't you changed for dinner?" she demanded.

I realized that, far from feeling angry, she hadn't even noticed I'd been gone. It occurred to me then how I tended to expect every person I knew to punish me if I actually *did* anything. "Welcome to your new life!" I told myself uncertainly.

Twenty minutes later, after changing my clothes, I was sitting opposite Robin, trying to eat in our hotel's dining room. As my friend talked continuously about how she never intended to wear again the slimming rubber underwear her mother used to make her put on, I maintained an exhausted silence. Only gradually did I realize that a pale man of about twenty-six at another table kept staring at me. His short curly hair seemed to be disappearing into the walls like clear water.

Robin at last abandoned her monologue. "Melissa, why aren't you talking or eating?"

"I can't," I protested. "I'm so tired that for me the room's spinning in circles. I just want to go to bed. Do you mind?"

Robin shrugged her shoulders, from which I concluded she couldn't care less. Having forgotten about the staring man, I rose and headed for the elevator.

I was just about to press the button when the man stepped out from the hall shadows, where he must have been waiting.

"All my life," I continued to the Countess, "I'll surely be able to see his eyes. They bulged from the sides of his face, like those of a fish—blue and cold, coming out of blackness. The stranger eyed me with a confusing expression of suppressed excitement. He said, in Cockney English with no trace of an Italian accent,

'I'm Mario—remember me from the plane? Come outside and stroll around a bit.'"

An amazed fearfulness washed over me, but I quickly rose above it. I'd had excellent practice, having focused throughout my adolescence on hiding both terror and pain from my father— whom I saw as not human at all, but a machine out of control.

"No," I snapped. "I haven't slept for four days and I want to go to bed."

I assumed that such words would cause any man to leave me alone—but, instead, they had an electric effect on *this* one. He walked into the elevator with me, and I felt my heart panic— irrationally, my head told me. But my fear increased when, throughout our ascent, the reflection of his bulging eyes stared relentlessly at me from the elevator's mirror. Finally, when we reached my floor, I jumped out—however, this man stepped out after me and accompanied me down the corridor to my bedroom. My bewilderment knew no bounds.

I still never imagined he would enter my room yet, when I unlocked my door and struggled to find the light switch, he pushed past me and sat on my bed. He pointed beside himself, "You sit there."

I obeyed, as always when I saw no moral reason not to do so. But for a long time I sat staring at the floor, wishing my visitor would go. I wanted to be polite; therefore, so long as he remained, I felt compelled to entertain him. I thought I had made it clear that I needed sleep, yet this man was paying no attention to my wishes.

Only half consciously did I notice that he turned out the overhead light and put on a dim one. As if from far away, I heard him say, "That's better."

He forced his arm around me and pulled me over against him. I didn't think anything like this could happen to *me!* He tried to kiss my mouth, waggling his tongue around, licking my face.

I pushed my arms up and shoved his chin away as hard as I could.

"Why?" he asked.

I tried but failed to make myself demand, "What are you doing?" It seemed so rude to answer, "Your tongue feels disgusting"—so I said nothing.

"Here in Italy," the Countess murmured softly, "we are so aware of sexuality that most of our young girls will not adopt the present worldwide craze for the hula hoop. They don't want to be seen wriggling their bodies."

"In contrast," I told her sadly, "the closest I've come to learning about sexuality from my parents was being summoned to my mother's bedroom, which was normally out of bounds to me. I remember my mother standing there, so beautiful and so icy. As always, I longed to be able to touch her. Instead, she began to speak:

'The time is soon coming when you'll never feel well again, though you won't officially be ill. And you'll find a little tiny drop of blood in your panties. It will enable you one day to bear healthy boys. You'd like that, wouldn't you? I know your father would have liked you better had you been a boy. And a healthy baby boy would have been such a grand present to give him when he was my valiant far-away soldier husband. You couldn't give your husband such a present if the blood didn't happen—you wouldn't be able to bear children. You'd be sad then, wouldn't you?'

'Yes, mummy,' I answered obediently, feeling as if she had just put a confusing spell on me which rendered me terrified of growing up.

"My mother replied, 'All right, you can go.'"

But, while with Mario, I wanted my mother. I believed it was my own fault that the things she said so often shocked me.

"Mario went on kissing the bits of me he could get to." After a few deep breaths, I continued telling my story to the thoughtful

39

Countess with more detachment, even slight amusement. "And I kept turning my face as far away as possible but, in general, my writhing had no effect.

"Some instinct made me plead: 'I wouldn't be any good for you.'

"'You'll be terrific,' exclaimed Mario, perhaps grateful that I at last understood.

"Suddenly he pulled my arms away and was holding my body down on the bed, with his legs on each side."

The Countess put her arms around me tightly as I went on:

"I could hear myself screaming for help—cries that drummed in my ears, and surely wound their way uselessly along all the corridors of the hotel."

"Did you know *nothing* about sex at all?" asked the Countess.

"The girls at my Australian school had hinted at what happens between a man and a woman. But I'd understood that a couple would only indulge in such a disgusting ritual when they desperately wanted children—perhaps during two or three nights in a lifetime. Until the American girls here were kind enough to disillusion me, I'd assumed that a baby always resulted."

The Countess explained, "Your mother's idea that a high society lady never feels well is very old-fashioned. It dates from when the dresses in fashion deformed women's bodies most cruelly. That doubtless made sex unpleasant, and childbirth terrifying.

"But we've left that time now. When a couple truly loves each other, the physical expression of that love brings them completion. It is a step closer to the great Mystery, which is God, the Unknowable. I was a rebel like you, and married a dying man much older than myself."

I did not feel free to question the Countess. Instead, I protested, "*I'm* not a *rebel!* I try so hard to fit in, but I always fail. Oh, let me be anybody but me!"

On our stone wall appeared a florescent green-and-brown lizard. Delightfully, it jerked towards me—then stopped still.

The Countess relaxed her arms. She studied my face. "You are not a rebel by choice," she breathed finally.

I scooped my hand under the lizard and lifted it. It looked complacent on my palm—very happy. "I won't eat meat," I told it. "Eating meat feels like being a cannibal."

The Countess threw in, more sharply than usual, "I wouldn't go that far. But, as you know, I respect your sticking to your ideals. That can't have been easy. What a happy day it will be when we no longer breed creatures for slaughter!"

"All I ever wanted," I lamented, "was to learn to be a human being. I was not brought up to be human. But I don't believe I'll *ever* get over the shock of knowing that love between adults is more than pure giving, more than sacrifice." I curled my lip in disgust, adding, "That it involves expecting a pleasant experience back."

The Countess moved her arm to tickle my face with a tendril of my hair, and the lizard jumped off my hand. I said to it in my mind, "Give me a message from your world." Immediately it snapped an insect out of the air.

After a while, deep humming came from my proxy mother's chest. When she stopped at last, she commented, "Emotionally, you are barely fifteen, if that. Though I love seeing you attract natural things like a child does, I want you to come alive, match your emotions to your age. We need to help you grow up. The yearnings of the soul take time to flower. It is very, very important that you and I make another story together."

I wasn't sure what she meant, so I went on with my own story.

"You're frightened, aren't you?" Mario had whispered when I ran out of breath.

"Yes," I gasped.

41

"If you let me do what I like, I won't hurt you," he said. "That's fair, isn't it?"

He stroked my breasts under my flimsy evening dress. My feeble arms flailed at his chest.

"No?" he whined. "What do you want to do?"

I repeated, miserably, "I want to go to bed."

"*You* want to go to bed," he bellowed with an emphasis I didn't understand. "You go to bed then, and I'll stay here and when you're *in* bed, I'll say 'Goodnight' and then perhaps I'll go."

"I wish you'd go now," I said tonelessly.

Never before had I been so deliberately rude.

Thankfully, Mario let me sit up. I was looking at the floor, but I felt him leave the bed. I heard him walk away. Where was he going? I couldn't believe the sound when my door closed softly. I looked around, looked in the bathroom, even under my bed. I was terrified he'd come back through the window before remembering it was nineteen stories above the ground. Eventually, when I felt satisfied that he was gone, I flung myself at the door and bolted it.

"You, my sweet bird, whose wings are folded in a straitjacket—you must have been in such a state of shock," reflected the Countess sympathetically.

Because the lizard had disappeared, I felt free to move slightly, to change the leg I was sitting on, which had pins and needles. "I knew I'd not heard the last of Mario," I responded.

I didn't dare leave my hotel room.

The telephone rang, interrupting me as I lay on the bed sobbing.

"Hello?" I heard my voice shake.

"Am I invited up again?"

"No!"

"Are you sure?"

"Yes!"

42

"You're lucky I'm not a few years younger. Girls didn't get away so easily then. I'll take you to the Colosseum tomorrow. I am very busy, but I am going to find time for *you*. I am going to do that for you, so you could at least do it for me. Good night."

"Good night."

I slammed down the receiver and changed into my night clothes. There was no way I'd let Mario enter my life again. I had no idea how to contact Robin—never ever having previously been in a hotel—so I lifted the telephone receiver once more, desperately hoping that Mario's voice would not come on.

"Hello?" a different male voice.

"Hello." I relaxed a little. "Could I please speak with Miss Robin Cragg? I think she's in the lounge."

Silence. Then, "Whom do you want?"

I repeated my request.

"Mr. Missrobincragga, or Mrs.?"

"Miss Robin Cragg."

"No one of that name resides here."

"Yes, she does!" I insisted, no longer worrying about courtesy. "And if she's not in the lounge, she must still be in the dining room."

After my overhearing great silence at the lobby desk, then a profusion of voices, someone said, "She is coming to your room."

Not long afterwards, I heard Robin's characteristic thump on my door.

"Well, it's happened at last, and you can thank your lucky stars it was no worse," Robin commented when she'd heard my tale. "You must admit you had it coming. A girl of your age can't go around with your head in the clouds without having a nasty awakening sooner or later. At least I hope it will teach you some sense. You behaved like a perfect brainless idiot throughout the whole thing."

I shriveled up inside, but was used to similar words. "Did anything like that ever happen to you?"

"Of course, you idiot," Robin had responded, "only much worse! But at least I had more sense than you. You know my parents are always shouting at each other? Maybe you don't. Well, they are. Anyway, once when they were arguing for the umpteenth time, I decided I was fed up with it. So I ran away. I put on my oldest clothes—jeans and a jersey – —and wore nothing underneath. I wore nothing on my feet, and let my long hair hang loosely over my face. I then went walking down the back streets of town, not knowing where I was going, but enjoying my liberty and asserting my independence!

"As I was going past him, a man caught my arm. I struggled and bit and kicked, but it had no effect. He put his hand over my mouth and dragged me after him for a long way, while I kicked and tried to bite him—past all the houses, until we got to a vacant block. Then he held me down, and he kept stroking my stomach. Did yours stroke your stomach?"

"No."

"You've no idea what feelings that can arouse. I almost couldn't bear it. Of course, he found out then that I had nothing on under my jeans and jersey. Then he raped me."

"I wasn't sure what this meant," I told the Countess. "But as you know, she goes around boasting about her 'experience' so that I don't feel wrong in telling you. However that night, seeing my absolute horror, Robin spared me details she had probably been about to give. She'd gone on hurriedly, 'Of course, I didn't let him without struggling and protesting—but when it happened, I enjoyed it. If you are a natural person, you can't help enjoying it.'"

Robin knew well how much it hurt me to be told I was a freak. But the normality she was describing sickened me.

"I never told my parents about my experience,' she went on. 'Indeed, I found it very strange to think of myself as having had such an experience. It seemed more a dream than reality. I felt disgusted with myself at first, and couldn't bear to look at my body in the mirror. But now I *know* God has forgiven me, because it wasn't my fault, and I tried to stop him. It wasn't my fault I enjoyed it in the end.'"

The *Contessa* had begun massaging my head. This was a new sensation, that I supposed I'd have to get used to before I could enjoy it. Certainty that she was sharing my pain—and, through me, Robin's too—made my pain flow away. Soon I grew aware of nothing other than the Countess's comforting, and sensed that she felt my feelings, but not her own. Our spirits, it felt, had flowed into each other.

"From the start of her period on," the *Contessa* remarked— so forcefully, running her fingers through my hair, that I knew she wanted me to remember her words forever, "a girl should be honored as an adult. Or, at least, she should be from the age of fifteen. From that age, boys, too, I believe. I promise you, Melissa, that growing up means coming alive, and making your own decisions. Growing up means having the maturity to achieve the goodness you might have been denied before. You are going to initiate yourself now, from child to maiden to womanhood. I am here to help you. We are going to make our last story together, before returning inside. In it, you are a nervous *brava ragazza* confronting your as yet unknown soul. You have never before seen your soul. She is a grieving woman, who has buried in sorrow many stillborn children—your writings and ideas on which your parents and their society clamped down. And she is pregnant with many more, being open to joy in the long run. But you are terrified by the black veil she wears over her face, right down to her feet.

"This wild powerful woman lights a candle before your eyes, and you can no longer see her," the *Contessa* went on. "You have a feeling she has lifted her long veil right up from her feet and flung it back, but you only see the dazzling candle's light. 'You don't know me,' she says, 'yet, I am your true self. You asked to be initiated into my ways. You think you didn't, but you did! However, first you have to confess the core of your problems.'

"What do you reply?"

I buried my head in the *Contessa*'s shoulder. I couldn't speak. Silence had been my problem, and naturally silence again overcame me. Gulping back tears, I remembered the tense atmosphere of childhood, when I had to be so careful never to attract attention. If I did, I would be punished. But, as I grew older, it soon became my duty to speak as loudly and clearly as possible if I was spoken to. "It's cold today," my father would often say. *"Melissaaa!"* How I dreaded my name, spoken in that tone, "what do you think would keep you warmer—a jersey or a good beating?"

This was always a trick question. I was likely to receive a beating no matter how I answered.

"They both keep you warm in different places," was one of my offerings, but I'd tried to vary them.

The *Contessa* interrupted my memories by repeating gently, "Melissa, what do you *say* to this woman who is your true self? As the sun nourishes the Earth, so she sustains you."

More than previously, the *Contessa*'s fingers pressed parts of my head, firmly but tenderly. For some reason, I couldn't help bursting into tears.

"I don't know," I gasped. I felt dreadfully embarrassed, hating myself for my sobs. I'd always tried to avoid weeping in front of others.

My thoughts unwillingly moved to my adolescent years, when my English teacher had demanded, "Writing such outstanding essays, how *dare* you not contribute to my lessons? You *have* to talk!" So I did talk—a little—in order to please him but by now I'd become my own worst enemy. I found saying anything I *wanted* to say impossible, as was asking anything I *wanted* to ask. I felt totally gagged.

The Countess now held my head up, kissed my moist eyelids and covered them with her cold rough hands. My life went dark. In my imagination, the tall fearful woman with the candle took over, ominously demanding, "You *have* to confess to something more basic than never expressing yourself. What is the *core* of your problems?"

"Please stop asking me," my silent depths pleaded. "But yes – the worst taboo was my period. At fourteen I wrote a short story mentioning it. I threw away my notes. The tale was about a woman who believed that the time just before her period was valuable, because it gave her understanding, and enabled forgiveness of those who habitually did or said terrible things under stress. And she believed that the pain which followed helped her grow, giving her unusual sensitivity. Her heart opened when she walked in her garden, and she heard with nature's ears. She heard the trees pray for rain.

"My father, while going through the garbage, noticed my crumpled notes for the story and smoothed them out to read. Storming into my bedroom, he demanded to see my final version. Then, watching my expression, he tore all my papers into tiny pieces, threw them in a bowl and set a match to them.

"'Don't you ever forget that I own you legally, body and soul, until you're twenty-one,' he raged, 'which means I'll own you forever. Because my aim will be to ensure that by adulthood you have no feelings at all. You are utterly immoral, and have no idea of right or wrong. I've always suspected that! No lady should ever admit to having a body. You have to spare us men from reading about such filthy women's business!'"

From then on I felt hurt that I was forbidden to express myself sincerely aloud *or* on paper, I explained to my true self. Though understanding my father a little bit, I felt his actions were unfair. Why *should* something that took up nine days of every month, which made me feel far more ill than pneumonia, measles or mumps, which caused me to want to vomit in people's faces

47

every time I opened my mouth, why should something so significant in my life be totally *unmentionable?*

I heard my true self object here, What's really happening, Melissa? Is your period a metaphor for the trials of growing up? You need to change your attitude, and stop feeling sorry for yourself. Everything your parents and their society have taught you about this great transition is wrong. And, in your heart, you know that. Menstruation has the potential of creation. Blood is life...and you've always resented pretending.

With sudden clarity, I saw my mother's lecture about being able to have children entirely differently—as conveying warmth. That, despite her icy words, blessings from a greater world had come through them. Could I really be human enough to bear a child? Would I, little Melissa, one day be given the wonderful opportunity of bringing him or her up in a totally new way? I experienced a flash of insight: surely nature had decreed that mothers would always be the first mentors of their children. Therefore, the education a girl received would have more ramifications than a boy's, determining the happiness and future greatness of generations to come.

Apparently satisfied that I'd recognized a truth, the tall woman in my vision blew out her candle. I knew I would die if I gazed up at her face—even the beams radiating down from it were so bright they hurt my eyes. Though I realized I would never be able to see my soul fully while in my body, I recognized that she—therefore I—was connected to a great spiritual reservoir of truth. No vision could take her in but she took in all vision, because she was an extension of God.

Gradually, I became aware, again, of the Countess' swooping rough hands, prodding my head. "It is the open Melissa that I want at my school," she confirmed. "Step out of your wounds, and laugh more at society. You can. You know what you know—if the rest of us seem foolish, feel no guilt for thinking so.

Anybody who loves you will love you for everything that you are."

The Countess kissed me on each cheek, and pressed my little body briefly against hers. Then she gave a laugh that reminded me of the kookaburra birds at home, a laugh that lacked the mocking note my parents' amusement always held.

"You are special, my child," she said. "Though you think you know nothing, you are so intuitive that, in the most confusing situations, at some level you still know exactly what is going on. You have more strength than you think. And how you have helped my girls! You have changed their relationships with each other, and brought us delight without their ever quite knowing that you were the catalyst."

Being unfamiliar to such physical closeness, I slid off the waterfall wall before asking her, "What do you mean?"

"A few days ago, when Nicole had hysterics at the sight of a spider, you cupped your bare hands around it most tenderly, and took it out. And you taught Julie, who was scared of our pool, to swim and float, just by showing her it could be fun."

"Yes—I still know how to have fun," I admitted. "Sometimes I feel like a dolphin, leaping in and out of waves, curving my back." I stopped, shocked at seeing such joy in myself.

"And, from my private quarters," the Countess went on, "I couldn't help but overhear you, once, in the little sitting room next to my bedroom, comforting Karen after Julie had been catty to her. Your perceptiveness helped those girls restore their usual friendly relationship. Even Nicole has told me she is impressed by your instinctive kindness. The world needs people like you."

I burst out, "Oh, I really want to *do* something for the world!" Reaching for the Countess' hands, I felt, for a moment, as if she and my true self were one. But I nearly fell. "And I've never been allowed," I went on. "Maybe that was *my* fault, but you can help me—I know it."

49

The Countess took my eager hands. "You are *so* afraid of growing up!" she breathed.

Wouldn't *you* be? I thought. My mother told me I'd never feel well again. And my father said that, to achieve maturity, I must no longer have feelings.

Then, another thought occurred to me. "Forgive me—I want to tell you this because it makes me feel so awful. My parents asked me to report Robin's words and actions to them by letter while I'm here. They said her mother and father want to know. But I would never, ever do that."

"You are to warn them, if she is making the 'wrong kinds' of friends?" The Countess' voice sounded sad.

"Yes—that's what I was asked to do," I said bitterly. "It's the custom in my parents' social group. Children and adolescents are trained to be each other's prison bars."

The Countess was silent for a long while. Then, she commented, "How can we *ever* have harmony in the world if we don't make an effort to get to know people of different temperaments, from a variety of backgrounds? Adolescence is a time for expansion, for choosing your own friends. The rule you mentioned is cruel, in my opinion. But, as far as counseling Robin goes, let *me* do it, you don't have to."

She stroked my forearm and, once again, I sensed the woman in veils nearby. She was lighting her candle, and I felt my body melting.

The very hairs on my arm seemed to be saying, "Just relax for a moment, and allow me to welcome you to the world of womanhood. From now on, you can rejoice in the rhythm of your life."

A whisper, soft as a kiss, added, "You will surely feel one with the cycles of the moon, the ocean tides, and the seasons of the earth..."

I am hearing my true self, I thought with a smile. How *could* she have been me or I her for so long, without my even suspecting that such intuition, wisdom or joy existed?

I sensed that the Countess and I had each become aware, again, of the other's feelings rather than our own. So I turned to her with a full heart; but all I could utter through tears of joy was, "Thank you—thank you."

Chapter Three
I Grow Bolder

That night I couldn't sleep. Although the day had drained me emotionally, I felt more alive than ever before. The Countess had opened my creative abilities again, and I lay composing something to give to her.

For hours my mind raced and rambled. Tonight I was too excited to feel my usual jealousy of Robin's contented snoring. At last I gave up trying to sleep. I got up, wrapped a blanket around myself, and fumbled in the dark for my clipboard and pen. I closed our door extra quietly, crept past the other girls' bedrooms and down the stairs.

The banisters were glowing in mellow light as I descended to the *palazzo*'s lower level where we had our lessons. I sat cross-legged on the plump cushions that adorned the sofa in front of the dead fireplace. I chose this area rather than the little sitting room, because the furnishings were more romantic and inspiring.

I wrote, crossed out, wrote, crossed out—and the story I wanted to give the Countess wouldn't come. Eventually, at about 3 a.m., I stretched my legs out, leaned back, shut my eyes—and experienced one of those visions that people have as a preliminary to falling asleep.

I am a child among other children at a magic party, keeping company with Kimmie, Emma, Jane, Jack, Susannah, Kylie, Colin, Clover and a girl in a dazzling white dress—taller than the rest of us—whose name I can't quite grasp. We are climbing trees higher than I've ever seen right to their tops. "I'm jumping off now!" Kim yells with amazing confidence above the abyss below, "Watch me!" He leaps into space and lands on one long-roped swing among nine. Adults beneath us, more gentle-eyed than I have ever seen, have rigged them up. Urged on by my brother's leap, we all jump now, making holes in the air. We never miss. We swing like mad, gripping the long double ropes. It's fun, and so wonderful to see Kimmie alive, healthy and strong!

My vision is momentarily interrupted as I remember the Countess' kindness and what she said about how helpful I had been to Nicole and the others, how much they like me. Away from Australia and my parents, I am free and loved again, I muse, as I find myself immersed in my vision once more.

"Come on!" yells Emma bossily. "Let's pretend we're opera singers. Sing!" But I can't sing in tune. She begins a song I've never heard: "The wind is passing through…" Loud-voiced Susannah joins in. Throwing caution to the winds, I join in too. We all sing mightily at the tops of our voices.

From our long waving swings, we shout to each other, delightedly making a rule that we each in turn have to invent a line of song. Songbirds are caroling around us. "Let's make up new tunes for the birds!" Colin suggests loudly. We do. Our childish notes echo around gardens that widen the more I look. All over the place, mostly melodiously, so freely… high and low… a few of us can sing in tune—but I certainly enjoy more those who cannot. We giggle merrily at each other's efforts. Now that I'm a child, even I take the gigantically brave step of singing a line alone, out of tune.

All at the same time—instinctively—we jump off our long swings to land in a central pool. A splash encircling us rises as high as treetops—first flowering outwards, with rainbows in its drops. But we will it to change direction—so then it arches over us, falling inwards. Its water, bath temperature, comforts our skins. We hug each other often, laughing.

Colorful wreaths appear—or I just notice them—lying on paving stones around our pool. Adults now toss them to us, and we, both boys and girls, take pleasure in arranging them beautifully around each other's necks.

"Children are kings and queens today," observes Kim. The adults graciously offer us ginger beer, then chocolate ice cream, which drips from our chins. We duck-dive to wash the mess off our faces. Surfacing, we hold our hands out, and immediately long spoon handles are placed in them. A huge bowl rises in our midst, full of minced apple topped with fluffy moist meringue, and we dip in our spoons. "This is a lot softer and nicer than meringue sold in shops," comments Colin with his mouth full. Fairy floss—cotton candy—comes next, which is sweet-tasting and melting into air.

More adults arrive, leading ponies with bridles but no saddles to the stones surrounding our pool. We are lifted onto the ponies' bare backs and we happily ride away, around a wild wide property, ducking under trees in the branches of which gauze-and-wire wings, with boxes of makeup, are loosely tied. We pull them down and hold them, cantering through.

A fence appears, snaking around the outer garden limits. We dismount, slip the bits out of our ponies' mouths so they can graze easily while we're gone, and tie their reins loosely to the fence wire and clamber through. In our neighboring meadow's center, I put down my wings and makeup box, and we dance ourselves silly with no adults watching. We sway, with our arms up, to rhythms newly invented, and do countless things I've never done before. Finding, in the meadow, a pair of abandoned red ballet shoes, I string them around my neck by buttoning the straps to each other. Dancing barefoot on grass as before, I sing "God bless the wild grass, God bless the wild grass!"

Kim nudges me, as spontaneous bell-like notes bubble over next to me from the girl wearing white. I had not known she was there. Obviously, Kim knew. He is grinning, as she touches my hand now, and she suggests—giggling that bell-like giggle again—"Let's build a house together with sticks and the grass, to show we were here!"

I try to invite Kim, but he deliberately turns away to play ball with Colin and Emma. I sense he wants me to be alone with this girl in white. As if she and I each know exactly what the other wants to do, we begin pulling the grass blades up and weaving them in and out around tougher ones still growing. We fashion a tiny hut. Our friends, tittering, are grotesquely painting each other's faces, screaming, chasing and scaring each other in fun— then they leave us one by one. Kimmie waves at me as if to say, "Stay with your new friend!" Then he runs after the others.

When my wonderful new-old best girlfriend and I get back to the party and the pool, will we be in trouble for staying here so late, working harmoniously and blissfully under a kindly sun? This precious moment is worth a punishment, I know. I stare at the sun unafraid, and remain here to create a small house with my friend.

Grass sticking out through our wild hair, and with rosy, cherubic cheeks from having had so much fun, we finally wriggle into our fairy wings and slash lipstick across each other's mouths. Giggling reassuringly, my friend gives me a 'leg up' onto my little horse and slaps its rump. Galloping out of my dream, I look back to glimpse the girl in white leading her own pony to where she can mount it with the help of a fallen log.

I woke up to find the servants had lit a roaring fire. I couldn't have slept for long after my waking dream, but it was time to get ready for breakfast—and I was ravenous.

When I went up the stairs to wash and opened my bedroom door, I was greeted by Robin, still in her pajamas. With wild tousled hair, out of sleepy eyes, she stared at me and exclaimed,

"Well! It was certainly nice to wake from sleep without you in the room. And where have you been?"

I said nothing, confused at her unkind words, because, underneath all our petty friction, I deeply enjoyed her company. After going down to join the other girls for breakfast, I continued to wrestle with my confusion. But, eventually, my powerful fantasy returned, to make me decide that Robin was Robin, and I was not going to let her thoughtless words spoil my morning. I never had wonderful dreams—usually my sleep was laced with bloody nightmares—and today I felt my experience on the sofa cushions in front of the fireplace increasingly lighten my mood.

Day became evening, then night, and finally bedtime in the room I shared with Robin. She found me, as usual, brushing my hair when she brushed hers, cleaning my teeth when she cleaned hers and planning to go to bed when she did so. She told me, as she often had, "I so enjoy you doing everything I do—behaving like a little dog I don't have to bother about or should I say 'monkey'?"

Previously, I'd shrugged without responding, thinking, "All right, she believes I'm imitative, but what's so bad about monkeys? Like any living thing, they have many qualities!" Robin didn't know, and I would never tell her, that if I went to bed before she did, and she switched on the light and banged the door, it would awaken me no matter how exhausted I might be. And, once I was woken up, I'd never manage to go back to sleep. This weakness may have originated during wartime, when I was awakened so often by the air raid siren's chilling wail. On most nights I'd then be bundled into the cupboard under the stairs— considered fairly safe because the houses around, flattened by bombs, would still have their staircases standing in the morning.

Of course, if Robin knew she had such power over me, she'd use it even more which was why, if she went with the other girls to the movies, I went too; if she remained at the *palazzo,* I remained; and, if she stayed up reading, I stayed up as well. This had gone on for three months, and—just as at home—I had increasingly felt I had no right to exist.

Tonight, however, was different. My routine of mimicking everything Robin did before bed felt stifling, as if I were clamping a lid on my soul.

I knew that the emotions whirling around inside me were not really caused by Robin. I alone was responsible for having been so submissive to her. Hadn't I once feared her anger because I went for a walk by myself? I was wrong about her that time, after we got off the plane in Rome, and might well be wrong now. I had to take a chance. So I asked, "Would you consider taking your things out of our room just tonight, as I want to go to bed early?"

"Just this night," I went on, a bit more meekly than I had planned, "I'd love it if you undressed and washed in the bathroom, and got to your bed without switching on the light."

Robin retorted in swift fury, "What are lights *for* if not to be switched on? What are basins *for* if not to wash in? It's *my* room, I tell you, and you're not turning me out of it!"

With the self-deception I'd been brought up to use, I thought, 'Of course I'm not turning you out of it.' Then I faced the truth, 'Well, only for an hour or so.'

Robin snatched up her things, spread out all over the room, and left. I went to bed.

Not long afterwards I heard her regaling the other girls with, "The poor little precious couldn't sleep, and was afraid it would ruin her precious health," and "She wants to fall asleep—yet she talks half the night!"

"Untrue," I muttered to myself. "I talk for two minutes, because after that, Robin, you're asleep. Or perhaps you only pretend to be?"

The shame of realizing that Robin hadn't enjoyed our nightly dialogues blocked my ability to say this out loud to her. Instead, I called out to whoever would hear, "I'm sorry I talked!"

Then I acknowledged to myself that much of my wakefulness had, indeed, sprung from excitement at sharing a room with someone after spending most of my life alone. In Australia I'd been so desperately lonely that, while studying Milton's *Samson Agonistes* for my matriculation exams, I'd written in the middle of one night: "'Dark, dark, dark,' cried Milton's Samson. He was blind; he could see no people around him—just voices from nowhere, footsteps from nowhere, laughter from the darkness of nowhere, shadows that loomed up to stare at him and passed and died away. To Samson they might have felt like ghosts, and I am a ghost to members of my household here. They mostly leave me alone, facing the unknown alone."

Somehow, in Italy, after meeting the old woman in Rome, and after my hour in the garden with the Countess, I felt for the first time that I could see and be seen. Therefore, hearing Robin yell, as she did, "Melissa is impossible to share with!" upset me doubly because it was probably true.

"Oh, she's odd," contributed someone in the corridor, and I heard a good deal of giggling.

I lay awake for hours, believing that my fellow Australian had raised hatred against me in the other girls.

For what felt like all night long, I heard Robin stomping on the same spot outside my door—sometimes fast, sometimes slowly and deliberately. She banged my door, too, several times, to keep me awake. I lay pondering; I've never crossed her before. So this is how she reacts. Well, I thought, poor Robin! This situation is as intolerable to her as it is to me and it needs to be resolved.

The *Contessa*'s bedroom being on the ground floor, I never thought she'd overhear our upstairs drama.

But, one way or another, she knew all about it in the morning. I assumed the other girls had told her, because she caught me when I descended for breakfast and, touching my shoulder gently, she said, "I'm so sorry I'll have to move you to another room, Melissa, since you're such a light sleeper. The trouble is, the only unoccupied one is the tower room. Nobody chooses to sleep there, because it's supposed to be haunted. But *I* don't believe in ghosts—do you?"

"It wouldn't excite *me* at all to sleep in the tower," announced Roland, delicately sipping black coffee. We had gathered together in the little sitting room after lunch. "It doesn't even have a ghost."

"I'm told there is one," commented Robin, sprawled across the chaise longue to his right. Now I was officially out of her room, and I had the feeling she was satisfied. It had always been a great relief to me that, as far as I knew, Robin and I never bore each other grudges for long.

"Nobody has ever seen it," Roland persisted provocatively, probably not believing his own words.

"I was told four people had," returned Karen mildly, moving to the side table to pour from a ribbed jug on a silver tray. "Around town, once people know where I'm living, they have actually told me that a lot."

"The worst thing about believing in ghosts is the expectation of becoming one yourself, after death," said Ludovico on the sofa who came out of one of his frequent trance-like states. "The loneliness! People who scream and run away when you approach them. The fear! Why are people afraid of you, when you're so much more frightened of them? They certainly feel like ghosts to you. You can walk through them as if they were nothing, and you walk through walls as if they were ghost walls. But—bad luck— *you* are really the ghost, having no part in the lives around you, and deprived of the warmest joys of life: drinking, eating, loving and being loved."

"Very true, Ludovico," said Roland sarcastically, putting his cup down on the smaller table to his left and staring at it. "But *I* want to know about Melissa. Melissa," he said, looking at me and beginning to get up, "wouldn't you like a handsome young ghost to be up there with you? *I* wouldn't mind flirting with a ghost."

I was tempted to tell them about Kim, and how I'd felt him extra close to me since I'd been in Florence, but of course I didn't. Instead, I answered primly, "It might be a female ghost."

"Oh —then, *I* must go and sleep up there, too."

I winced briefly at the "too," but saw Roland's word was logical. I countered again, "She's obviously very old."

"I don't care *what* she is, so long as she's female," replied Roland, just to shock us, I presume.

During the pause that followed this conversation, I cleared used cups and stacked them on the tray. I was attempting to make the servants who would come in later feel we cared about them. I sat down again. Roland then added, even more meaningfully, "Hey, just suppose it *is* a male ghost, and you'll have him watching you *all the time*?"

I threw a cushion at him. A month ago I'd have been overcome by embarrassment, but I was getting used to him now. So what if it was a male ghost? He might be worth knowing.

Chapter Four
My Ghost

My first night in my tower room, no one could have found me. I sank deeply into the middle of a large four poster bed and stretched out under a blissfully comfortable red continental quilt. Above me, slits for windows, now glassed in, imitated those in castles from which arrows used to be shot.

During the day, I'd briefly tried out the bed. From my pillow, the window-slits had revealed blank sky—but when I stood close, and looked down, I'd seen long, distant, low, serene clouds stretched over hills and olive groves, cypress treetops, the *palazzo* driveway and the tips of roofs.

My bed was in the center of a big, almost empty room. On my right, if I sat up in bed to do my homework or write in my diary, because this tower had no desk, I faced a wooden staircase which led through a hatch in my ceiling to a very noisy water tank above. Under the staircase was a deep basin, with a goose-necked pipe below. In contrast to where my friends slept, I had no bathroom nearby. There was also a large fat supportive column in the very middle of the room.

Ahead, on my left, a welcome door stood open. It led downstairs to civilization, and the rest of the building. Never would I shut that door, I decided, not wanting to feel totally alone.

As my first night progressed without my even dozing, I so wished Kim would make his presence known—but I was alone.

I slowly became afraid that Karen's and Robin's words about the other ghost might be true. If I so much as breathed a little more loudly than usual, my breathing echoed. I only had to lift my head and shoulders for my still-empty cupboards to rumble. And beyond my stone walls, rainy gusts occasionally sang a descant of "Ooooooooooh!"

Always one to meet terror head-on, I sang "Ooooooooooh!" back out of tune.

Each time I shut my eyes, the water dripping in the tank above my ceiling sounded like footfalls. With so many unusual things happening, I had no trouble imagining the wind outside to be an angry sea roaring, thundering and smashing at my tower's perpendicular walls—throwing spray at my high windows.

The more exhausted I became, the louder the water tank's drops became. Louder and louder. Eventually, the stone steps that led downwards from my tower room to the outside world began, I thought, to resound with loud crashes as if a person half-dead, with rasping breath, was striving to climb them.

I was just about to scream when a guttural voice came into my head, "It's traditional in Florence—do you know the legend?—That if I, a ghost, don't visit a sleeper on her first night in this tower, then I won't visit her at all. That would be sad for us both, wouldn't it? I hope you will enjoy my visits. I'm going to like visiting you. I have so many plans to help you. And I'm very sorry that you had to fight with your friend to get here."

My first reaction—to call for help—subsided. Although, consciously, I'd never before heard the voice, something deep in my guts told me I'd always known it, just the way a person, if normal-sighted, recognizes that red is red. And a strange thing happened. The water tank's clip-clopping plopping noise started to annoy rather than scare me. It was interrupting a voice to which my limbs responded by relaxing. I was shocked to find that the speaker's rasping tones neither surprised nor frightened me, but caught me up in an unknown yet familiar empathy.

As if this weren't strange enough, I was suddenly drawn into the memory of an incident I realized must have happened before my birth, when I was gathered with a million spirits under an enchanted tree made of light. I felt at home there, remembering. Someone was giving us names, someone great who had told me that my soul-name was Little Mystery. Then a being beside me who seemed larger than life, who radiated compassion, turned to me and, in a voice with the same feel as my present visitor's, said, "Such a name is older than creation, and contains universes, all worlds."

I guessed that this same spirit must have just now punched a hole in eternity to be with me. A new landscape curled, like loving misty arms, around me. I looked into both non-existence and existence, knowing that my ghost would take whatever I said or thought deep into him and respect it, seeing directly into my heart. It was the most wonderful thing that had ever happened to me—having an entity perceive my heart totally. It meant I no longer had to struggle to express myself. I sensed, too, that he was used to communicating with silence.

But I kept my eyes tightly shut. Consciously, I refused to see a ghost. Roland's scary words came into my head, "You'll have him watching you *all the time*!" And I heard again Ludovico's idea of ghostly experience, "People who scream and run away when you approach them." *Suddenly*, I wasn't at all sure I *wanted* to believe in this intruder. Fear washed over me once more. I began to see my situation the way others might. But that only meant I needed to be bold.

As a small child, alone after Kim abandoned me during the Second World War, I trained myself to be attracted to anything really terrifying. I tugged with all my might at the blackout curtains, each side of my bedroom window, but could never get them to meet. Nobody checked my handiwork. My mother told me simply that bombs would fall on our house if I left a chink between the drapes. And so I believed that, because of me, death for us both was forever imminent.

In the middle of air raid nights—only common people, my mother had said, went to shelters—I made a resolution I've kept all my life: if I was ever really terrified of doing something, I would do it. Otherwise, I reasoned, I'd be unable to live truly, because I would be terrified of almost everything. Throughout the night, if my mother didn't come to push me into the cupboard under the stairs, I'd keep getting out of bed and walking into the bent-over giant shadow that my nightlight made on the far wall. But my plan to conquer my fear never worked. Every time I returned to bed, that terrifying giant's shadow was back.

"Where do you come from?" the depths of me asked my ghost without my wish.

"Just now, my love?" I felt him inquire without really speaking.

My guts replied, "Of course."

"I'd rather talk about *you*," I sensed my visitor object, in a tone both directive and light. "Little Mystery, it turns out you're my soulmate." I heard a soft chuckle. "I can tell you're a bit down tonight, and I want to cheer you up. If I dance on one leg, both arms waving, would that work? But you'd have to look at me. Forget where I've come from. I've been haunting this tower room for nearly two decades, expecting your arrival. Think of me as a rock that has waited, relaxed in the grass, for thousands of years for you to trip over. Having hovered around you in Australia off and on, I knew you'd turn up here in the end. Be bold—that is my advice to you. You, yourself, are the one you've been looking for. I learned endurance partly from observing yours. So stop apologizing for your existence. And for what others have done to you.

"Do you realize that some parts of your personality are entirely new?" my strange visitor went on. "I want to make you

64

as happy as possible on Earth. You and I belong to each other. Our relationship crosses worlds."

For many minutes, I pondered the meaning and beauty of what my phantom had just said. This was utterly different from anything that had transpired between Kimmie and me. How could I take it in? I felt overwhelmed. Questions and likely facts zigzagged through me like lightning bolts, and vanished as quickly. For a few seconds, I felt as if my visitor had bared his soul to my mental gaze. As I looked with my mind's eyes, I decided he contained the best qualities of both men and women. Not knowing where it came from, I had a vision of him when a child, in trouble for drinking a dangerous plant's juice that his elders had left in partly empty cups on the breakfast table after a night of carousing. Beautiful songs from forest flying creatures that I'd never seen echoed in the background, as his elders severely lectured him. This being's use of my soul-name now evoked so much that it called me, plunging me into a world of strong feelings, where the spiritual realm felt closer than my life vein.

Eventually, after we shared a happy but fruitful silence, I realized who he was. I recalled a moment of my life that I'd forgotten till now when my spirit, in despair, had gone straight to this same being for comfort. Now I remembered. As a little girl, I'd infuriated my own elders by refusing to eat meat. I dearly loved all animals. At meals when I was not at school, I'd sit all day in front of gristle, with instructions not to move until I'd eaten it. Vomit would rise into my cheeks, and I'd swallow it. Those who noticed told me how disgustingly naughty I was, so after I'd sat there till nightfall, I was regularly beaten.

But once, when I was eleven, the punishment had been more savage than usual. "Your mother has given you up as a bad job!" my father exclaimed, thrashing me. "Even the servants have given you up! From now on, they have orders to serve you *only* meat, and it's your choice if you starve! You just shamed us in front of our good friends when we were all out to dinner, and a couple asked, 'Is your duck all right?' You answered, out of loyalty to *ducks*, 'I haven't tasted it yet' instead of 'It's delicious, thank you.' Quack-quack!" he bellowed. "Quack-quack, you wicked, ungrateful girl. And you refused to wear the expensive fur your mother tried to put on you. Manners are among the important things that distinguish us from the lower classes, and you have none! But we'll make sure you acquire them. From now on, you'll eat what's put before you." Then he muttered, as if to himself, in a tone of frustration, "I came home from war to find your mother with you—a child I had never seen, with her character fully formed. And I could never get through to you."

"I live in the dark ages," I kept telling myself as my father's blows threatened to take me beyond pain, *"I live in the dark ages. But I'd rather not live."* My spirit must have left my body because, while my father hit me, I found myself lying in semi-darkness in stinking sludge on pockmarked stones. That was when I heard the selfsame voice I heard tonight, asking, "You all right, my girl?" Though the voice had caused my heart to perk up, I met it with silence then—unlike now. Fetid air told me I was in some sort of middle ages dungeon, and I heard a whooshing of waters that I instinctively interpreted as a threat. A stone gothic, virtual grave with a slushy floor, from the blowhole in the middle of which wandering droplets lingered on my naked face, arms and legs. The voice came again, saying, "Would you like us to groan together? Here I am stuck too, being unfairly hurt. Groaning could bring us much relief."

Despite my injuries, I laughed heartily. But I failed to remember what happened next. I knew I had encountered selfless kindness in my pain but did not recall returning to my own body.

Why had I blotted out that experience till tonight? Because it hadn't related to my everyday life? Because I had blocked out the beating? There was no point in trying to decipher why.

"I *know* where you've come from!" I insisted, picturing my ghost's dungeon clearly now. "When I visited you as a girl, I saw movement in the gloom! You are chained to a massive pillar in some medieval prison!"

"Yes. But my physical self is nowhere near that pillar at present," my visitor corrected me. "By day I am led elsewhere."

"Where?" I pressed. "I don't believe it's to somewhere better!"

"I don't want to make a big deal of things," my phantom sighed. "But I've left my body behind in a building on a planet beyond your world's present knowledge, not even in your galaxy."

"Ah! I should have realized, way back tonight when the wind was crying," the depths of me communicated cheekily. "You're not really the ghost of someone dead, but a live person's visiting spirit!"

"Very clever. That's true." My guest sounded amused. "But you can call me a ghost if you want. I know that's what your friends call me."

From my long-ago sojourn in his dungeon, I recalled a slithery creature.

"Oh, yes—you are right," my ghost confirmed. "Twice a day, it works its way slowly past me, without legs, through the rubbish. Keeps me company."

Another striking memory came—of more animals. When I'd visited him, there'd been unnatural movement high up on his body.

He tuned into my thought again. "Don't worry about my rodents," he laughed. "They're making nests for their babies. I've named them all. They help keep me clean, pulling hair from my chest. I play jokes on them. In my best moments, they remind me of your world's puppies! Even they have families! Even they can touch each other! They have as much right as I to live and be loved."

I couldn't help asking, "Were you once loved, even though you have such a horrible life?"

Surprisingly, he corrected me with, "I do *not* have a horrible life. I used to be addicted to a certain plant's liquid that, since we were conquered, has been the scourge of my people, mercifully shortening our lives, dulling our pain and helping us sleep. Mossiface III, my jailer, brought it to me, but the authorities cut his tongue out in punishment, to my everlasting guilt. But my tribe never needed such medication, and I've found I don't either. We've always been able to send our spirits wherever they were needed—it happens naturally because of our intense caring for everyone, without our trying. Leaving my body chained to the pillar, my spirit soars like a once-caged bird whenever I wish among colorful treetops swaying in the breeze. With so much new stuff stimulating it, such a freed bird's feelings, like my spirit's, will become even more powerful, its perceptions greater, and its happiness increased.

"And I still am greatly loved! A certain hunger remains in me from times long ago, before I was thrust into prison. If I received all the love in the world, my thirst for my own family's love would not be quenched."

Fleetingly, I imagined my visitor with a tender human face, looking down through his eyelashes while remembering his family, and smiling. "By God, my family longs for me!" he went on. "And, by God, I repay their love with a yearning that comes from the whole of myself. Though we visit each other in spirit, we cannot touch. The family I came from is physically lost to me while I am imprisoned."

I felt my head soaking in a pool of water. Tears were streaming out of my screwed-up eyes, matting my hair and flowing down each side into my ears. Horror I felt, yes. But deeper than any pain was my great distress. My ghost's suffering mattered to me, terribly. I knew I loved him to distraction, because I knew well the pain of someone you love being lost.

What he said was true; we were soulmates. But just then I couldn't focus on what that might mean. "I am sure you are a good, good man," my heart was crying out. "How could *anyone* do this to you?"

"I will try to explain. I weep for my devastated land, on my far-away planet that is very like yours, you know," my visitor confessed. "But it has certainly known better times.

"My own people used to be nomadic. They lived close to nature. To us, a person's heart was everything—we didn't think of separation. I suppose we were pretty vulnerable that way! But we have been overrun by unnaturally cold people from the only other continent on our planet, overrun by folk constantly squabbling among themselves, with the crazy desire to dominate. My ruler, and those who rule the provinces surrounding him, have set up frigid hierarchies similar in some ways to your middle ages.

"The trouble is, my tribal folk don't have the slightest idea of how our rulers think. We tend to be as deeply shocked as I know you have been by your parents. Sometimes we refer to our invaders as 'insects', because we have such difficulty understanding them—though, deep down, they must be worthy creatures. Poor things, they don't seem to have human feelings. They behave with the soulless regularity of machines, and we know that pretending to be stupid is the way for us to keep them as happy as possible. But it would be nice if we could just brush them away like insects."

I wondered what it had cost this seemingly gentle, loving spirit, who squeezed my heart so much, to come visit me. Was he still in terrible pain, even without his flesh? I worried that he must be. His ruler did, indeed, sound just like my parents who, during my teen years, had impressed me as being left over from a period of hell on Earth. The only act they saw as a virtue was instilling terror into others, and 'showing them who has the mastery'. My parents needed me to be their clone, I understood, in order to

69

perpetuate an extreme hierarchy that had long ago outlived its function. Of course, no bad times in my life had been as ghastly as what I realized my ghost was going through. But they were enough to make me feel I partly understood him.

"Tell me more about where you live," my heart was pleading. "And what you did to be treated so cruelly."

"In our galaxy," he said, "just like yours, many civilizations have risen and fallen, leaving no physical trace, so altruistically focused were they. And their outlook still lives on in the way *my* people see things. But it was during what we call the 'Era of the Earthquakes' that the 'insects', if you like, managed to build boats, and finally crossed the treacherous marshes that had isolated them. But they had become selfish and inbred. I don't want to talk about what they did to my people. We are all *one* soul, and feel each other's feelings. As we suffered and died, we pitied the 'Insect Folk' for having forgotten the compassion our mutual ancestors used to learn at their mothers' knees. Our cold conquerors have now imposed on our whole planet the kind of dishonest hierarchy that your world is at present pretty much discarding. They have pushed what was left of my people to a remote corner of our former land, so that the general populace can forget we exist.

"In that remote corner, 'insect' henchmen hang around the youngsters of my village when they play in our forest, or swim in our ponds full of soulful-eyed creatures. The henchmen keep telling our children, 'Wait till you're older! We'll get you.' There is no hope. I managed to leave our settlement as a young man and go far north, where I joined a band of strolling players and tried to bring happiness with music. Everyone we entertained said what a good actor I was, and that if my skin had not looked like dark wild honey, I'd have been a star. But there are not many roles for Forgotten People. The officials in the area our band covered stopped me—which was inevitable—because they saw me riding a particularly beautiful furry beast. 'Forgotten People don't own beasts like that!' they said. 'You must have stolen it.'

My beloved ghost paused so long here, with such obvious unease, that I felt I had to help him. "Please continue, my dear friend!" I exclaimed.

"Of course, I'd bought the beast with my recent earnings. The officials beat me anyway until that familiar, terrible moment when my bodily control gave way.

"Then they smeared my feces all over me and turned me out of doors," he went on. "After healing, I returned to my homeland to teach the little kids drama and music and offer them hope, self-expression—maybe even give them a future. The decreed punishment for such behavior is death. I thumbed my nose at the law. Inevitably, my ruler's henchmen caught me. They hated people who returned after seeing the rest of our planet. They called us 'stirrers'. I had come back telling my people how to survive outside, how our conquerors think, all of which made my ruler feel insecure. Basically, I didn't see bad people—only unhappy people. And, sadly, it is the nature of your and my present eras that many perfectly ordinary, everyday folk feel they have to take their essential misery out on someone—but one person will often do. My ruler kept me alive for his own purposes. I mean, he's glad to know I'm there."

I reached my arm out in my soulmate's direction. Dismayed, I realized it probably went through him. I was filled with a great longing to help him. Would my spirit ever visit his planet again?

"Time to change the subject," he said. "I was thrown into a dungeon, and that's the end of my story. You have lovely shiny hair, somewhat sodden by tears at present."

His words made me think that he was trying to stroke my hair—in which case he failed. I felt no physical sensation whatsoever. I made a vow then: that one day my courageous visitor, chained forever, as far as I knew, in degrading conditions simply for trying to bring joy to people, and I would orchestrate

71

a situation where we could feel each other's touch. I could imagine his people living so close to the earth that they held lively dances to raise precious shells, or whatever they used, to pay for their funerals. Every part of me was aware that meeting such an exciting person tonight—one who, I sensed, felt other people's emotions more strongly than his own, who was never bored though his body seldom left his pillar—had been a great and deep gift, and the realization saddened me that, walking outside tomorrow, I'd feel the tiniest leaf that the wind might blow on my face, yet fail to feel this very human-sounding ghost. Meanwhile, gratitude overwhelmed me for what we did have.

"How do we *do* this?" I asked. "How do we leave our bodies? Send our spirits so quickly, so far, from one galaxy to another?"

"That's easy," my amazing visitor answered warmly. "Natural. Space and time have nothing to do with it. Strength of feeling can cause spirit travel in an instant—through any material barrier. Just as it has for you and me."

I protested indignantly, "If we are soulmates, why were we born at different times so that I am barely more than a child, while you sound quite old? Why do we spend our lives on different planets, in different galaxies, you being of an indigenous conquered race, and I belonging to parents with high society pretensions?"

"What difference, really?" he retorted. "All that truly matters is that, while we're both alive, we've found each other!"

"I was hurt so often, why didn't I go to you a lot of times?"

"Indeed you *were* profoundly hurt. Guests at your house didn't know how you survived such cruelty, how you kept your heart. I myself respect you greatly for surviving, for remaining compassionate despite the upside-down values that have been drilled into you. But the one moment you did visit me, don't you recall how difficult it was for me to persuade you to return to your body? You were angry at me for that, too angry for us to be together. You fervently desired to escape your life at that time but I knew you had important things to do. So had I, though only God knows how much I wanted you with me! I watched from a distance, ready to intervene drastically if need be. Later, I tried to visit you; but your heart had closed down towards me. But I did have my offsider, as you say in Australia—my partner!" He chuckled.

I pictured, for a moment, my phantom having beautiful eyes, gleaming with delight. I knew his partner was Kim.

"Indeed!" Kim's voice filtered happily into my head. I imagined him taking a bow then.

"Does my brother know you? I mean personally," I asked.

"Suffice to say the devotion between you and Kim sustained you. I had to wait, in deep sorrow, for you to meet me beyond your parents' influence."

I pulled the continental quilt around my shoulders, and sat up in bed. Though my ghost might have looked monstrous, I knew by now that I would not find him so. For the first time, I opened my eyes. Even so, I was relieved to discover I still could not see him in the darkness. "Thank you for Kim and for waiting," I said.

"Nonsense. I had little to do with anything between you and Kim. It was the love between you. It always comes down to that," he said.

"Yes," I replied, understanding for the first time what he meant. Love was beyond words and held the meaning of all that made existence beautiful, no matter what the pain.

"Love is the underlying reason for everything that happens in your and my universe," my phantom explained. "It causes planets to attract, and atoms to cling together. I visit different parts of your world so often; I'll tell you something about it. Your Russians have just performed an experiment which proves that material barriers cannot stop an animal mother's unity with her babies. A scientist wired a mother rabbit to a machine in a submarine and sank with her to a tremendous depth far away over the ocean. Back on land in a laboratory, a second scientist killed

73

her babies at random intervals and noted the exact times. The machine in the submarine recorded the moments that a sudden change in the mother's blood signaled acute distress, and the split seconds on land and under the ocean turned out to be the same."

I wasn't sure that my own mother would feel my own distress, since she never seemed to. But I felt deeply sad about the mother rabbit's suffering, though knew it was just a drop in the ocean of cruelty that existed in my present world. Russia had, after all, recently launched a trusting little dog into space. So I turned my attention back to the main point of our discussion. "If I see you as family," I concluded, "the gap between your and my dates of birth is no problem. You could be my spiritual brother, my uncle or even my grandfather. You don't have to be a sweetheart. But why the racial things that hold us apart? Why the physically impenetrable space? Why the class difference? And," I whispered nervously, "maybe a difference in species? I really don't understand. You've got to explain from the beginning."

"First of all, you must realize," he replied earnestly, still near my bed—possibly sitting on it—"that you and I meant an infinite amount to each other before we were born, so it was impossible to say goodbye! You must understand what it cost us to go in different directions. We both knew devotion, heavenly wisdom and compassion before we entered the physical realm. And if we go on feeling the same way you and I will be together through all the worlds of God.

"Do you recall," my ghost continued, "that time when we stood together, preparing to jump into a universe of stars and planets? I saw a big problem in one galaxy, resulting in the slaughter and torment of children. I had to go there."

"Did I hang back?" I asked, dimly seeing us at that moment. "Did I let go of you and send floods of tears through infinite space after your disappearing figure? And I'm still too innocent! Even now, I've been kept away from the outside world. I beg you, I

74

beg you to help me toughen up enough to *do* something, like you did, for the world!"

"You said 'I wish I were brave enough to go too,'" my visitor told me gently. "And I replied, 'Your situation has nothing to do with courage. You will know when it's your time. And, when it is, I have the feeling, your life will be great. Also, though it won't be easy, there is no doubt we *will* meet again one day.'

"But back to present practicalities," he went on. "You need to get some sleep. Next time I come, I'll try to make it during your daylight. Let's visit your Boboli Gardens together here in Florence. My spirit sometimes likes to lie on the grass there. It's because my bodily eyes have been deprived for years from seeing greenery. My own planet's greenery is more sparse anyway, and bluish. I revel in the majesty of your earthly foliage."

"You must enjoy our *palazzo* gardens too," I said.

I thought I heard a smile in his voice, when he replied simply, "These days, I wander about outside my body wherever love takes me. I linger by the bedsides of children all over *your* planet, *and* mine, trying to give them happy dreams. Children make me strong—I adore little children. I remember they used to run through my village in hordes, giggling, laughing. We older ones starved ourselves, saving our food for them. We'd never let our kids go hungry if we could help it. Bringing out compassion is what *I* try to do in *your* world's children's dreams, encouraging the kids to put their whole selves into everything they start."

I was hanging onto self-control, but only just stifling sobs. "I had great need of good dreams," I said. "Why did you leave me out? Why didn't you come to me?"

"I've told you why," my ghost said with infinite sadness. "Almost from birth, you were like an animal being amateurishly slaughtered—overwhelmed, struggling to please those you could not. You wouldn't let me in; you were too stressed. But it was by attempting to visit you that I discovered I could whisper to so many other children at night.

75

"But enough of bitterness, my Little Mystery. Don't worry about what *was* anymore. I'm here with you—I'm here with you now. God, I've missed you so. One wonderful day, if you wish, you and I will be completely together again. What a great day that will be!"

My beloved's use of my soul-name once more evoked so much that called to me, immersing me into a world where the spiritual realm felt closer than my life-vein. The yearning to remain there made me ask desperately, "What you mean, 'completely'?"

"Well, let me begin where I left off. Nineteen years ago, a while after I'd left you for my present galaxy, you volunteered to be born to the powerful couple who became your parents. They didn't like each other much, and felt that only they and their kind were worthy of living well. In fact, of living at all. The common folk were dispensable in your parents' worldview and, with all their money and connections, this attitude is dangerous. You wanted them to take their anger out on you instead of doing a lot of harm on Earth—"

My thoughts began whirling. Had I really chosen my own parents? Had Kim? And, if so, had we truly known how bad our lives would be? Perhaps. Though my visitor would deny it, insisting that we acted from our own strength and courage, I could imagine myself and Kim wanting to imitate his nobility.

Yes, his information was beginning to make sense. For a long time, I'd felt as if others were stifling a great cry down my throat—as if the world of my parents and the culture around me were squashing me under a giant snow-like blanket. In any social milieu, I seemed to be the only person who believed that hatred, humiliation, cruelty, shallowness, murder, fighting, greed, disrespect and desire for power were insanity. So I felt like a freak.

A voice inside me, that I'd ignored practically all my life, was telling me more and more that my ghost spoke the truth. I *had* chosen to be my parents' child, and for good reasons, one of which involved imitating *him.*

"May I continue my explanation?" he inquired.

"Sorry," I said.

"Oh, don't apologize for *that*—what you've just been thinking!" he laughed. "But you'll also want to know about the others. Because I've noticed, on my bedside rounds, that in these crucial times, many kids similar to you are being born. And so has Kim noticed. You know, one day he will move on, completely throwing himself into the mission. But not to worry. You will be ready, and happy for him. It is all beautiful and good. You and others in spirit like Kim are working to help your Earth become one tribe—where individuals put the tribe's welfare before their own in everything they plan to do."

"How can I find the others?" I asked wildly. "I think I can be as brave as they are. How will I know them?"

My visitor's answer didn't sound helpful. "I'll do my best to guide you, but you'll need to use your intuition. Here's a big hint, however: never, ever listen to anyone who hankers after the past. As far as the future goes, certain of your planet's most recent prophets have foretold your coming era—when you'll witness the death throes of your old world order and the birth pangs of the new; when many folk will behave worse than they ever have, but others will do better things than they ever have. You can have the world being one family the easy way or the hard way. Either you change your hearts now at the grassroots level—because it's no use changing institutions until your hearts change—or you will suffer an enormous calamity that will chasten you and you'll all want to have different priorities; you'll just *want* to. World peace is inevitable. Among most people of your world, first there were tribes, then city-states, then nations, so anyone looking at it from outside can tell that the next step is an international government that keeps the richness of local culture. It's your job to start a process that puts soul into that upcoming government, so it has a *selfless* solution to the world's economic problems, transporting food rapidly from one end of your Earth to the other. Above all, for the sake of the children. I adore children."

"Please stop!" I yelled defensively. "You are going too fast!"

My ghost laughed again, and then pointed out with great sweetness, "You, my girl, have a strong sense of what is kind and what is cruel. Many people on your planet and mine do not. In my galaxy, in fact, the situation happens to be far worse than in yours. So it was important that I volunteered to enter life there, and get in my ruler's way. He is nobler than most of the rulers around him, so taking out his frequent rages on me in my dungeon fulfills him deeply, and frees him to govern his subjects fairly well."

I felt stunned. My visitor had just made everything clear to me. He had volunteered to help a far-away race in a distant place by receiving all of their tyrant's sadism. So, now I saw I had chosen to tread in the footsteps of his magnificent gesture. But did his great sacrifice have a time limit? Does any service?

"Human beings are not naturally cruel," my guest went on to explain. "When we are, we go against our own natures, to prove our loyalty to something outdated, that we think we believe."

"So you *are* human?" I queried. "I thought you were."

"Yes, we're quite human on my planet. As human as can be." He sounded amused. "May I introduce myself? My name is Kasho."

Chapter Five
I Write a Play About a Prisoner and a Painter

Two nights after I met Kasho in my tower room, I had a dream that shocked me. I was surrounded by a dazzling white prison cell echoing with a voice like Mario's, but exaggerated. It said, "Me mother died when I was very young, and me Auntie showed her body to me. Me Auntie would often say, 'I did the right thing—the kid understood what 'appened an' 'e never asked for 'is mother again.' Me mother was beautiful, so beautiful on the outside, but she 'ad a 'ole in 'er 'eart."

Of course, upon awakening, I immediately took pen and paper from under my pillow, and allowed inspiration to dictate the play I wrote. Perhaps my near-rape stimulated it, or my over-demanding sense of justice. Or neither of these. After all, part of my everyday experience used to involve going into dark places within myself and coming back with a story or poem that caused me to wonder, how did I know that?

SCENE ONE, I wrote. *Dazzling white prison cell.*
Evening.
White ceiling, white walls, two white beds, white floor. White from top to bottom. White table and chair at back between beds. There are no headboards. Slop bucket at back in right hand corner.

One drunken prisoner, looking like a seal, entirely wrapped up in gray-white blanket on left hand bed. It wriggles around every so often throughout this scene and the next, but no head or limbs visible.

Second prisoner sits on right hand bed.

Seated prisoner—Rapist—getting up and coming forward:

I'm the only person in the world what's got feelin's. I know that. Other people, specially girls, try to trick me by all that screamin' an' carryin' on into thinkin' they feel pain. Makes no difference to me. I know it's a trick.

Lightly, almost in a falsetto voice, nodding his head in rhythm to his words:

I just keep on doin' whatever I'm doin'.

Sits on floor and takes a drink from chipped cup. This cup is filled with alcohol, and Rapist's words become more slurred as play continues.

Waving hands toward left and right hand walls:

You see, a young prisoner what was shut in 'ere before me 'ad all these walls covered like windows. Shapes an' colors everywhere, from ceilin' to floor. Yep, the prisoner before me put paintin's all over these walls. 'e must've thought we wanted windows 'ere, to look out, feel free, lose ourselves in 'is work. Or look in. 'e was a tricky one, that earlier young prisoner, no doubt about it. But I'm tough. I don't need windows. I asked the warden for whitewash an' poured it all over these walls. I made this cell white from top to toe. Ha ha! Gleamin' white.

Crossing arms over breast, looks up with wicked gleam:

I covered that first prisoner's spirit with white from top to toe.

Yep, an' I laughed with the warden about that poor young feller. Must of been cuckoo. Turns out 'e was a gentle feller, waitin' for 'is trial. They found 'im innocent when 'is case come to court.

80

I knew from the moment I was shut in 'ere, with all that stuff 'e done, that 'e was innocent. Unbroken spirit. 'Is spirit was a wild unbroken stallion, not like mine. Reckon it might be guilt what breaks you, long before they put the walls around you. 'Is spirit made some sort of agony in me come alive, made me think.

Takes another drink, then gets up and goes to pat body on other bed.

Rapist:

Not like this older feller 'ere. 'e's in jail for life. 'e's a lifer.

Shape on other bed lets out three snores. One medium-loud, next louder, last VERY loud.

Rapist removes the gray blanket from his own bed and puts it very firmly on top of the other prisoner, paying particular attention to his mate's head, like wrapping up a parcel.

He takes immense trouble over this, because it is an expression of hostility that he cannot put into words. He wears a grim smile, his movements are extremely tense, and he presses down the folds as if the head were inanimate and could not feel pain.

The head does not cry out.

Rapist sits heavily on blanket-covered legs of other prisoner. A blanket-covered knee comes up.

Rapist (patting an ankle, which kicks up through bedding):

Very few murderers would do it again. Like this feller 'ere.

Rapist strokes other prisoner's body as if he were an animal, with one gesture and considerable pressure, from head right down the length of it, several times.

Rapist:

Not that I care, but there's blokes 'ere should never be in. I'm told the big neighbor bloke drank methylated spirits an' wine an' was always pickin' on this little feller sleepin' 'ere. One night the big neighbor followed 'im into 'is 'ouse—'e could of sent 'im flyin' with one 'and. 'e's only tiny, like I said, this feller.

(Patting body)

81

An' 'e was fuckin' terrified. Picked up the nearest big thing an' 'it out.

(Continues punctuating his words with patting):

But the authorities wouldn't 'ear that 'e spent 'is life in terror of the neighbor. An' so 'e became the lifer 'ere what thinks the world of me. I tell 'im funny stories—sometimes 'e laugh an' don't stop.

(Changes tone, looking up):

But you know what that young painter feller done what painted these bloody walls?

Gesturing widely:

Made a picture of this murderer's enemy,

(Pats body, then looks to right)

Of the big neighbor bloke, made it like the murderer feller 'ere described 'im. *Gesturing toward right hand wall:*

In the picture the big dead bloke was wavin' cheerfully as if 'e was surrounded by mates in a bar. As if 'is violent death, an' the feud between the two 'ad been a big joke.

Well, things might be easy for that neighbor bloke, wherever 'e might be, but it's no joke for the little feller 'ere left be'ind.

(Patting body)

'e got life. Not that I care. An' not that 'e cares much, if it come to that. Nobody really feels except me.

Coming forward, sits on floor and drinks again from cup.
Rapist:

Aaah!

(Musing):

Grinnin' an' wavin' in that picture over there,

(Gesturing again toward right hand wall)

That big bloke was.

Stares at audience and states solemnly:

From real close up.

Gets up, goes to right back corner and picks up slop bucket.
Brings it forward and heaves it onto his shoulder:

Ha! Ha! But I murdered that big bully all over again. I put whitewash *all over* 'is body spread-eagled on our walls. This is *our* place, *our* cage. 'ow dare 'e be 'ere? Pretendin' to be our friend. I threw white paint just like this!

Splashes dirty slops onto right hand wall, which immediately glows with an intense orange light. Part of picture of big neighbor, grinning serenely and waving, appears.

Rapist's body jerks back, as if flung. Lands on his knees, his back against the left hand wall. Head has jerked forward and arms are raised, like a man executed by a firing squad. His shock is obviously extreme. He yells in a strangled voice:

Go away! I don't give a stuff about your love!

SCENE TWO: On the back wall, between swathes of snowy whiteness, large areas of a fire-colored painting have appeared, lit yellow-orange from behind.

Furniture and sleeping body are as before.

This is the painting:

Near ceiling, in top left hand corner of back wall, a row of angular artists' manikins have their right arms stuck out like swords at an angle. They are sexless, identical, and have bits of white showing through their severely outlined 'wooden' bodies.

Their right arms touch with severity a young girl's head, over which a net of thick knotted rope has been thrown. The girl has been drawn with fluid, voluptuous strokes. Through the net's holes, she looks out at her tormentors with a gentle smile and defiant eyes full of pain.

In contrast to how the girl seems outwardly—trapped—there is indication of total freedom in her feelings. Within her body silhouette are painted beautiful wild landscapes, waterfalls, trees, clouds, planets and human beings comforting one another.

I, the creator of this play, see the manikins who are outside this young girl, on the other hand, as imprisoned by their own lack of feeling. I think people who fear the present and the future can practice sadism, especially to children, without being natural sadists. But our innocent prisoner has had a wonderful vision. The young girl in his picture is open in her mind to the harmony and unity of the future, which she desires to help create.

Figures on the painted side walls are less distinguishable.

Jerkily, Rapist is twirling on his heels, frantically hurling slops at the paintings, wanting to blot them out. Where slops hit, paintings reveal themselves more and more.

Rapist:

I'm crazy! I'm goin' insane.

Light flashes behind the identical manikins painted on top left corner of back wall, and they speak.

Manikins:

We have news for you. You've actually been insane for years. We are the Rapists of Mother Earth. We are you split up, so we know. We are cold, like you. We have deprived *ourselves*. There's a reason for us taking up only a small space in this painting. It's because, even if the world admires us, we are not important until we find our hearts again.

Rapist shakes head, wearing silly grin.

Rapist (dropping empty bucket, still grinning), in pleased falsetto voice:

I'm goin' crazy! I'm goin' insane!

Hands over ears, Rapist flops down in foreground. Rests elbows on floor.

Keeps head lowered for a while.

Raises and moves head in semi-circles, still clutching it.

Rapist:

I'm rememberin' what I don't want to.

I'm goin' insane.

Musing:

I'm rememberin' bein' a little boy. Me Auntie was always 'ittin' me real 'ard.

Rapist tips cup upside-down and looks at it in disgust.

Pause.

Rapist:

But she didn't know what she was doin', did she? It was drink what got 'er. She reared me up when I was little. Sometimes as a boy I would scream all night, but now I don't feel pain—mine or anybody else's. I look on everybody as me toy. Knowin' that animals an' women are not important is a sign of bein' real grown up.

The best thing in me baby'ood was when I was three. One of me Auntie's drunken men friends picked me up an' bit the back of me neck quite savagely. For days I kept jerkin' me 'ead back with a scream every few minutes. When I recovered, I thought 'I can be'ave like that too!' Taught me a good lesson, that bloke did.

Gets up, goes between beds, fishes bottle out from under his bed and refills cup. Puts bottle and cup on floor, stage center.

Rapist:

That prisoner before me was a funny one all right. 'e 'ad to be innocent, of course. Reckon 'is spirit was a wild unbroken stallion. An' 'e splashed that free gallopin' spirit all over these walls in 'is paintin's. They raised some sort of agony in me.

Sits on floor in front of bottle and cup.

Bowing head, takes a drink.

Silence.

At last Rapist looks up with a full-bodied wicked grin.

Rapist:

I covered 'is spirit with white from top to toe, didn't I.

More dreamily:

But when I get drunk, the images that *were* 'ere still 'aunt me. When I sleep they come in my dreams. Even sober, the way these victims of violence 'ere are right outside of each other—no, that's not what I mean, they get outside of each other; they get outside of *themselves* an' into each other some'ow… yeah, the way they do that makes somethin' in me come alive that I thought was dead.

Waving hands purposefully toward left and right walls, as if outlining shapes:

I could cheerfully murder that innocent prisoner, that's for sure. 'is spirit is callin' out for me to murder 'im. If ever I meet 'im in the world outside this jail,

Shakes hands, looking sincerely into eyes of imaginary person:

'e will greet me cheerfully an' with trust, 'cos 'e's too innocent—me record will mean nothin' to 'im.

Yeah, when I meet 'im I will say to meself, 'Ha! Ha! I already murdered your soft spirit, I put whitewash *all over* where you exposed yourself on our walls.'

Sadly, looking at bottle as if it can hear him:

But the white paint seems to be comin' off now.

Recovering:

God knows *I've* committed violence. The neighbors testified that they...

(Nodding and speaking in falsetto again)

...''eard the poor girl cryin' all night an' all mornin'.'

Normal voice:

But they didn't go to 'er, did they, so they're just as bad as me. An' 'er landlady said she...

(Falsetto)

...'can't bear to go into that bedroom no more.'

(Normal voice)

She...

(Falsetto)

...still feels me 'orrible presence there,

(Normal voice)

...that's what she said.

Musing:

Was it worth it, I wonder? Well, I must admit I 'ad fun. Power brings its own ecstasy, don't it? It goes to yer 'ead, provided you leave yer 'eart out of it.

Forcin' that girl was me initiation, a *good* thing—like steppin' through a doorway into the world of adults. Provin' that I was a 'ard, 'ard character an' proud of it.

I was a famous king layin' a conquered country waste, deaf to 'is subjects' entreaties.

Drinks from bottle.

Wistfully:

But sometimes me stomach churns over as if I'm feelin' 'er screams there in the depths of me, an' then I get deeply ashamed.

Recovering:

Like I said, *I've* been cruel an' violent—so much so that witnesses 'ave said they can feel in the air where I did it, 'ear the girl's cries for mercy long after they stopped, feel every turnin' point of me time with 'er. Come to think of it, I'm not sure whether I 'urt 'er or meself more. But, like I said, nothin' I ever done 'as the power of what this so-called innocent young painter feller done.

Supposed to be innocent.

'e knew a thing or two, I reckon—an' that's a fact.

Opens arms wide and looks toward left and right hand walls.

Rapist:

That young feller 'as imprinted the soul of all the world's victims on *me.*

Blackout.

Two people begin to give a loud variety of snores through microphone.

Chapter Six
An Out of Body Experience

Six whole days and nights had dragged by since I'd written my disturbing play—without any sign from Kasho! I knew that he and I were as one in our mission, and in our belief in the future, so why was he absent? What possible good or terrible thing could be taking his time? Suppose he were no longer alive? Was my play, if he knew of it, so dark that it pushed him away? Had I imagined him?

These thoughts were tormenting me one morning when Robin and I arrived first at the breakfast table. We sat opposite each other, the window to her right and my left. Between us on the oak table lay a bread loaf in a leaf-shaped wooden platter, among glowing glass dishes of unsalted butter, runny honey and jams.

Robin opened the conversation with, "I'm sorry to say, Melissa, that in my dream last night you were murdered. People held up your dripping corpse."

I laughed. I was used to being seen as victim material. Robin's nightmare didn't worry me at first—then I wondered in a moment of panic if Kasho might be in his grave.

Robin glanced at me penetratingly, then added, "I always seem to have had lone wolves for friends rather than people who mix well."

"Because you can't get the others?" I asked sharply, before I could stop myself.

"I was afraid you'd take it that way. No, because I've liked them more. Lone wolves have character, are usually more interesting than girls who form cliques like sheep. And they are normally more intelligent. But I am not thinking of *anyone* in particular."

She was silent for a minute, then picked up the knife beside the bread platter and waved it in front of my face. "I dare you to make a hole in your hand big enough for blood to flow."

"Do you really want me to?"

"I hope you have more sense. I bet you wouldn't dare. I don't suppose you would. In fact, I *know* you wouldn't."

"Do you want me to or not?"

"I know you wouldn't dare."

"All right." I held out my hand casually thinking that, if Kasho were dead, I'd be happy to die too. I'd always intended to make ending my life, if I did it, look unintentional. Perhaps this way, out of carelessness. I would thus free my parents to talk about me with appropriate conventional regret at cocktail parties.

Robin snatched the knife back.

"Not on your life!" she said. "What makes you *do* such things?"

A door swung open. The maids Bruna and Giovanna burst in.

"Good morning, young ladies," exclaimed matter-of-fact Giovanna as she bustled through from the kitchen, placing heavily grooved fresh white rolls in a basket on the table. "Oh! How beautiful you are looking! How beautiful this dining room feels, having the world's loveliest young ladies inside it!"

"This exact moment is actually the loveliest in the room's life," I observed, glad of the distraction. "Because it has inside it the two most beautiful maids who have ever brought us coffee."

89

"Oh, am I really beautiful?" asked Bruna eagerly, holding the coffee pot out sideways and pushing her face into mine. "Tell me honestly, am I more beautiful than Giovanna?"

"Yes, am I more beautiful than Bruna?" asked Giovanna. "Tell us, *signorina*."

"You both look like old witches," Robin snapped. "And that's the truth."

I wanted to say something kind to the women but my brain suddenly felt foggy, as if I were being tugged away. I knew I had a choice: to go or stay but everything within me needed to leave. I waited, however, having no idea of where I was supposed to go.

I noticed both women glare at Robin then Giovanna turned towards me. "You sleep better alone, don't you, *signorina*?" she asked. "We have just come from cleaning your bedroom. We could feel how happy you are now."

"Giovanna means you sleep better without a husband, or someone else, in your bed," contributed Bruna.

"No, I didn't at all! I meant without *la signorina* Robin—" began Giovanna.

"That's even worse!" said Bruna.

"I meant sharing her bedroom, *not* her bed!"

Their voices grew dim. I longed to say something to Robin on Giovanna and Bruna's behalf but, instead, I was immediately and truly 'up there'.

Where?

Squashed against the ceiling. Trapped. At a flat circle of light's edge, as if that had been my place always. The circle was haloing a garish twisted glass chandelier. My left eye in light, my right in shadow, I flattened myself into the right hand ceiling corner as I used often to do in childhood nightmares, when dodging my father's elastic arms that reached everywhere. In real life, though, this new situation gave me a *good* feeling. Happily, I trod air above my body which continued to converse merrily with Giovanna, Bruna and Robin without my control. The fact that even my body seemed not to notice I wasn't there amused me mightily.

The chandelier's brightness did not hurt my eyes. I could see beyond the window, beyond walls, far across the world. Horizons disappeared. Grass blades in the garden outside beckoned me individually. I longed to be out there in the great sun which had become the day, and immediately I was.

One by one, the lights in the grass made by sunshine on dew went out. I found myself wheeling bird-like, soaring high, falling backwards into wind I could not feel, somersaulting through tree trunks as though they had no mass. But I did not feel dizzy. To my great relief, I had a joyful sense of Kasho's presence at last. Vivid colors thrilled me, and I heard sounds that didn't come through my ears.

I saw the light particles around me slowly come together to form Kasho. So he wasn't dead. He hadn't left me! Sunshine was haloing his white mane, and shadows of leaves dappled his chest and white beard. He was sitting on a high branch, his ravaged features smiling like a child confident of being loved. He gazed straight at me, out of eyes that seemed to reach back into the earth.

In his spirit's presence, I felt a pang of fear. But it was the terror you feel when your life is about to be changed by something enormous and good—when a whole world, of which you know you are not worthy, is ready to welcome you.

Kasho and I had never met this way, and I could see he felt as overwhelmed as I was. I pulled out my handkerchief to wipe his luminous gray eyes, and then wipe my own. "Oh! It's been so long," I said—my heart, rather than my consciousness, speaking.

As I hovered in front of my Kasho, who moved forward to receive my handkerchief's touch as if that was all he'd ever wanted, air swirled through me. I managed to distinguish every leaf's outline—leaves behind leaves. They caressed me delicately, though I felt nothing. The important thing was that I

91

could feel *him.* He gently held my elbow, and I joyfully felt once again that I was on the verge of understanding his whole character.

"May I join you on your branch?" I asked, and instantly did. It felt like sitting on clouds, more than precarious. I could sense nothing under me. We were balanced on nothing.

Kasho and I were now spirits in the day, not the night. We had both left our bodies behind—to their own suffering, their own devices. "The trees outside your school were calling me," he pointed out, "and they got the better of me. I like normality and quiet. I like being outside.

"Almost a week has passed since I visited you," he went on. "Were you happy during it?"

"Not very," I admitted. "Truth to tell, it's been more than a week. I wrote a play that left me in shock. But then, what my pen produces usually surprises me. Maybe we writers—and presumably not only writers—tap into knowledge of everything when we're inspired. I certainly couldn't understand what I'd written or why—"

"Oh, *that!*" Kasho interrupted, chuckling. "Had you been alert to them, you would have sensed human arms the color of wild honey coming over your shoulders, and rather heavy hands clasping yours as you held your pen. I used to teach drama, after all. I said I'd help you with your request to toughen up! We created that play together, and in time you'll come to understand it."

"Why not now? Because I honestly don't know where I'm going!"

"Where would you like to go this minute?" Kasho inquired, changing my meaning to something more mundane.

"Capri might be fun," I replied, as if we'd always had such conversations.

"It's been raining there for days," he objected. "Although we wouldn't feel the rain, we wouldn't see much. I have a better idea.

92

Almost from birth, I've been taught about ever-multiplying galaxies, ever-multiplying worlds, and ever-multiplying dimensions. I'd like to take you to a secluded corner of the planet I wish we'd visit for much longer, if you want to, in a future time. I get to go there in spirit occasionally. Come, follow me."

Kasho stepped forward, then turned around to add, "Whenever yearning for you overwhelms me, I find myself inside your feelings. My people often have that kind of experience, but it's still a gift from God. The qualities we have so little trouble in expressing are there, latent, in all human beings. When my spirit is outside my body, I feel fully alive, much more alive than in day-to-day life. And in your presence, I feel peace." He sent an enormous wink my way, and I caught a glimpse of him young again. Gone were his beard and white hair spread out like creative hands. Gone was his ravaged face. He no longer seemed the least bit old. He was young and beautiful. His warm honeyed skin looked smoother. Red-gold hair, flowing almost to his shoulders, reminding me of ferns in the way it curled, and his gray eyes shone brilliant and deep as enchanted caves.

"Yes, yes. This is me before I was put in prison. I think you like what you see." He laughed heartily. The landscape behind him was also renovating itself, opening more to wind and sky, though I paid little attention.

"I was loving you how you were," I said, distracted now by the changing landscape but also embarrassed by the way his youth filled me with wonder. "You didn't have to change for me."

"I am much closer to your age than you think. Currently, with my white hair and all my broken bones, in your mind I could be at least sixty. Right? Am I right?" He roared with laughter. "But prison did that to me. However, don't be the least concerned. Very little worries me. I'd take back my healthy young body, if I could—but that's water under the bridge, as you on Earth say.

93

Come, we're here for a bit of fun!" He took off running and—for a moment—all I could do was watch the grace of his movements.

"Little Mystery, are you coming?" his voice rang out.

In my spirit state, I found catching up with him easier than I expected. As we neared our goal, some small creatures, brightly colored wings flapping, were giving themselves dust-baths in our path. They were enjoying themselves so thoroughly that they obviously didn't want to move, but expected us to run around them. My Kasho picked one up, and looked as if he were squirting a refreshing drink from its mouth into his own. He turned to squirt a drink into *my* mouth, but I couldn't feel it.

Our first port of call was a gorge-like sandy hollow filled with children. Kasho said he had missed the laughter of little children more than anything in his gloomy dungeon.

We decided to perch among the scattered remains of the fire around which these children sat. It failed to burn us. I giggled with joy at being able to sit on hot coals without feeling them. Bare-legged children squatted and sprawled in a circle, eating something like a fish, cooked in wide leaves, evidently scooped out of what had been their deep covered sand oven. Now, all that was left of that oven were the hot coals under me and Kasho. The kids laughed plenty, with full mouths.

Kasho crouched, then jumped sideways. Arms and legs flailing, he dug up sand flurries, teasing. They whirled around the children, like a spirit wind.

A little girl with black ringlets exclaimed—I could not hear her words, but *felt* them in my core—"Hey! Let's take turns running up this dune and sliding down faster and faster, pushing a small amount of sand onto the dying fire each time with our bare toes. To put it out slowly."

Up the yellow slope the kids ran, leapt and danced, patches of sunlight in their hair. When a boy below them with a protruding tummy danced on one leg, Kasho imitated him.

The children above the boy struggled to the sheer dune's top, where they gathered, turned and pushed themselves off. Sand clouds pouring below them, they descended fast, sliding between patches of grass. Down they plummeted, creating grooves as smooth as giant fingers. Kasho himself crashed into the kids, big like a polar bear mother playing with her cubs. He rolled onto his back into the ash-filled bottom, like a white-haired mother bear saying, "Enough of play. I love you. Feeding time!"

Bumping their bodies against each other, the children fell through his skin and bones to land on crunchy, hollowed out ashy sand below. Kasho was constantly changing shape—sometimes the man with white hair and beard and other times the handsome young warrior. I loved it best when the children crawled through Kasho as the emaciated mature man.

Arching the back of his neck, Kasho gazed with more tender eyes than I had ever seen at the tops of the children's velvet heads, while they appeared to feed from him. To me he had become Mother Earth. Lowering his head among the boys and girls, he moved it from side to side like the great mother bear nuzzling her cubs.

A group of what seemed to be gulls flew overhead—some mysterious sense told me the exact note range of their screeches, without my actually having heard them. The apparent birds' slow disappearance through the sky made me feel it was time to move on.

As I turned to go, however, there burst from me a laugh like that of a surprised child—because out through my stomach hurtled a cup. It must have been kicked into my back. I swung around, to catch sight of a little boy who looked so much like my brother the last time I'd seen him physically that I wanted to play with him.

"Kimmie!" I shouted. But nobody answered. To my dismay, I saw the boy wasn't Kim.

I sensed Kasho feeling my disappointment more intensely than he would in his everyday state, and suspected that emotions coming from groups of people or me were to him so overwhelmingly strong that his naked spirit could focus on nothing else while he experienced them. I realized I had been totally unaware of the drama of my own thoughts, and that my thoughts, to one like Kasho who was pure spirit, would always feel much larger outside me than in, reverberating relentlessly around buildings or trees. "Don't worry, my Little Mystery," Kasho reassured me, laughing. "If a person is giving out thoughts of war, I can still oppose them by stronger thoughts of peace. My self-effacement is not extreme." I could feel his love filling me with calm. "And you know that Kim's happy now. Although he's sometimes with you, you need him less now. Isn't that so?" he pursued. "You understand that now?"

I nodded, hopeful once again.

"Then go on, kick back the cup!"

By concentrating my will, I returned the cup—though my foot went through it. Wonderful! The boy's face lit up. Maybe he'd felt my presence fleetingly. Grinning like a sliced watermelon, his nose softly contoured in the sharp light, he kicked the object happily back; and the cup—that I kicked again—returned to him in a curve, as if its movements were caused by the wind.

"This place of fun and childhood laughter will always be sacred to me," Kasho explained. "When I come upon any scene, I feel it throbbing with life. Ancestors reach out to me from every sand dune, rock, winged animal and tree. Every flower has depth and speaks to me," he continued. "Let's return to this place during the future I envision for us together." He grasped my hand, and took on his youthful appearance once more.

"How do you *do* that?" I asked.

"Oh, it's not hard. No harder than you abandoning your body actually. But now let us leave," he prompted.

"Tell me what the adults are like on this planet," I demanded. Kasho's expression grew serious. "Every pore of their bodies intones God's praise and vibrates to His remembrance," he said. "The people here integrate greater truths into their daily lives than your planet yet knows. They feel happier than all your nations put together, because absorbing universal truths and laws has brought them freedom and joy."

Then Kasho let go of my hand and, like a cub trying to keep up with a furry adult of its species, I bounded after him over and through a smooth sand plain with sudden valleys and serrations. Eventually, my Kasho scrabbled sideways as if he had tripped, and rolled lazily onto his back. He was an old man again. As he lifted one white-haired arm invitingly, I dove through transparent hillocks into his ribs. He gave me a brief bear hug. Brief, but enough to stay with me forever. "Eeee!" he exclaimed, pretending to squeeze me as hard as he could. "To me today you are my sister, and innocent child."

"Can you feel the grit of the sand?" I asked when I rolled off his bare chest.

"Well enough. When I want to. It takes a huge effort of will, of course."

"But changing shape doesn't?" I persisted.

He laughed again. "You take this far too seriously, my Little Mystery. But there's something I want you to understand. Sometimes indigenous people get powers that they know haven't come from them, or terrible feelings because they know a bad thing is happening. Nobody has told them, but they know. And they don't know if they are dying, or if someone else is. But, even in that extremity, they realize it's their spirit that got the message. And the fact that it's their spirit brings them joy, because everything of the spirit is joy. And they feel more alive at those times than any other." Lying fully on his back once more, Kasho gripped his toes with ease. "I'm so comfortable, I don't want to

97

get up!" he announced, winking playfully. He yawned blissfully like an animal; then closed his sensitive, luminous eyes.

I looked freely at his scarred face. While my eyes fully devoured that feast of which they had been deprived on the two nights he had visited, I heard screaming inside myself.

"Every bone in your face has been broken," I observed aloud. Through his tight translucent skin, tiny cracks were picked out by the sun. Between the white side hairs flowing back into the sand, I saw a lifetime of suffering, forgiveness—I fancied—and beauty.

Forcing myself to sit cross-legged on the cloud-like sand, I drew Kasho's head onto my knees. My fingers touched his beautiful broken cheekbones, his vulnerable mouth. His eyes still closed, Kasho grinned at me, and he moved his transparent-skinned fingers—through which the white bones showed—to tickle my ribs.

I brought my head down to my beloved, and kissed his sunken tear-filled eyelids.

His wise gray eyes flew open, searching my face, as I straightened.

"What do you see?" I asked.

He was deathly silent for a while. I imagined this barely living man chained to a pillar in the depths of a water-filled dungeon, rodents pulling out strands of his hair to make their babies' nests and cockroach-like creatures crawling over his sunken cheeks. "I see someone who's had practically no childhood," Kasho finally concluded. "It's time for you and me to enjoy rough-and-tumble, time to be silly!"

Against my will, his words recalled my brother begging my father to chase him around in the way a normal father would play with his son. My father had spat out in reply "You're too delicate. You disgust me. I can't bear to look at you! You're worse than a girl. Your bones are like chalk. And, to add insult to injury, every time I try to punish your sister you stand between us."

"Come back to our present, Little Mystery," I heard Kasho whisper. Little Mystery. I so loved it when he called me that! "Kim is fine, really," he went on. "It does you no good to think about the past. Sad thoughts take us away from this precious time."

"Yes, yes!" I brightened. "I'm sorry."

"No apologies; not now, not ever." Seemingly without effort, my Kasho, his white hair flowing, leapt onto a tall cliff face far away, and stood gleaming on a ledge there, stretching his whole body. Then he was by my side again. I understood that he still had the strength and sure-footedness of the young tribal man he'd been, working in the open air, possibly spearing his kind of fish for his family. "Let us play a game of tag," he said. "What is better than being silly together? But whoever loses has to say something wise, invent a story or sing a song of their own making."

"I long to write songs," I lamented. "But it's so frustrating— I don't yet know how to write music. The tunes in my head come out differently when I try to sing them."

"Not anymore," Kasho laughed. "*I* would hear your tunes perfectly on every occasion, the way they are in your head. However, you'll find you are pure spirit now. Your voice can soar any way you want it to. This is freedom. This will be fun."

"Fun," I repeated dubiously. Darting from his side, I found that my legs enjoyed moving one after the other—running and climbing on nothing. Though I'd ridden on horses, I'd never done this before. But it felt natural.

Kasho was racing after me in the joy of the sunshine, pretending he couldn't catch me.

I wish my brother had been able to do this, I thought wistfully, then remembered I'd promised Kasho not to think about sad events. But running and laughing with my beloved, who appeared frailer than even Kimmie had been, brought me back to a memorable day in London during the War, when my

99

parents ordered my brother to go outside for a walk. This command sounded strange, even to me aged four. And my brother, who had never been obedient, immediately ducked back into the house, into the kitchen, where my parents had begun lecturing me.

"Your brother is incredibly frustrating, with all the care he needs," my mother said, her back to the door.

I pointed to where my brother was listening, behind them, but both my parents ignored the gesture.

"We have no choice but to send him to boarding school," contributed my father.

"Oh, darling! That will be death for a boy in his weak condition," my mother murmured in a rehearsed tone.

"For God's sake, woman! Let's get it over with. That's the way of the world. The weakest to the wall, I always say. All young lads who are destined to gain the mastery of others start at boarding school. Such institutions sort the men from the boys. It will do him a world of good."

My brother piped up from behind them, "I'm obviously a terrible nuisance."

My parents turned, and the three of us answered at once, "Yes, you are." And I, in great distress, with my arms flung out as if to keep him home, cried, "No, no, you're not!"

"I've already made arrangements," my father finally said. "He can take the train next week."

That way, my eight year-old brother left us.

He wrote home from boarding school, "I have arrived safely." Naturally, he could not be visited. Petrol was rationed.

He wrote home, "I hope Melissa is giving you no end of trouble." I realized he felt angry that he could no longer look after me. Yet my parents showed no shame when reading his words aloud. My mother threw in that having and bringing up children was a nightmare.

Other letters came weekly, but the one I remember most was postmarked from the hospital, "I am learning to be a man. Father would be proud of me. I haven't shed a tear, but I do have a few broken bones. They've promised to patch me up in time for school next term."

The letters ceased and Kim was never mentioned again, except for my talking about him every night to God while my mother sat with pursed lips on my bed. (Over those months, I asked for help in composing letters to my brother—because I'd only just learned to read and write—but my parents, jeering, simply took my efforts away.) Eventually, after two long years, my despair got the better of me, and I burst out in the middle of lunch, "Oh, I *wish* Kim would come back from boarding school!"

Temporarily, he *had* come back, though, but not in a way I could mention. I had learned the difference already between the true things I experienced and what adults could accept. One evening, when I'd been alone and hungry because my parents had gone out all day, he'd brought me a thick warm piece of wartime bread, and the sun and the birds and the whole outside had come into that attic and we'd played with the wind. Kim even cuddled me, which no one else ever did. I could trust Kimmie not to tell me I was an idiot or that the walls were full of goblins that would pickle my eyes; I could trust him not to beat me. After that, every time my brother came, I patted his chest and the air stood still. The air felt full of wonder, and my heart full of happiness.

In response to my outburst at lunch, my mother said airily, "Oh, didn't I tell you? Kim's dead. Children with bones like chalk can only die. It's a well-known disease called *osteogenesis imperfecta.* These children are a liability. I expect one of his bigger friends was trying to carry him and dropped him." My father concentrated on helping himself to more food.

I half smiled, because I knew better than my mother. Even as I sat there now unable to eat, listening to mummy, I was reliving Kimmie's and my special place, where no one could see us or hurt us. I experienced Kimmie's passionate loving eyes, the bliss of his touch, his laughter and above all the coarse, warm, health-giving taste of the bread he gave me.

But what was my body really recalling? A daydream? A ghost? Of course not—I could even hear Kim's voice now, helping me get through my mealtime conversation with my mother. *"Go on eating your lunch as if nothing has happened. Show no emotion. They think that children who show emotion are a nuisance, just as I was."* And then he laughed and added, exactly as I remembered him telling me that day on the roof, *"Do it to protect yourself—but never, never stop caring. You are my sister."*

Even though I was having fun now on a strange planet that might even be in another dimension, I would never ever forget my brother.

To steady my thoughts, I tried to return—and managed for a few instants—to my eighteen-year-old self whom I'd left sitting, now much more relaxed than usual, at breakfast in the Florentine *palazzo.* I saw that self of me, ignoring the angry voices across the table, stuffing a roll into her mouth.

"Please tell me a story?" I asked, coming back because I couldn't help it to Kasho playing with me here in this other world.

"Last night," he said, sitting upright on a small transparent dune, his shiny gray eyes melting with love in the sun, "I dreamed that I took you to meet my tribal ancestors. They were so pleased to see you. They looked into your heart and told me I should have brought you to my village in the physical world long ago; that you were one of us. You understand caring and sharing.

"They took us to their spirit village in the middle of an island. And in the middle of their village they showed us a magnificently handsome great whale in a little pond. The whale kept flapping up an incredibly steep hill immediately ahead, balanced on his tail, but eventually collapsed back into water. A wise aunt ancestor said, 'He cannot get to freedom in this way, the way that nobody gets hurt. What way can he go? It is a riddle.'

"To our left, a sharp-pronged fence rose out of the water. And if the whale went over, under or through it he would hurt himself so badly that his life in the ocean could not be free; he would be crippled. To our right stretched a sandbar crowded with people with whom we sensed the whale was angry. But he did not want to hurt them, and if he went that way he surely would. They were the hunters who had captured him. And his last choice would mean barging into you and me. He would hurt us. What should he do?"

A pregnant silence engulfed me and my beloved, but at last I broke it. "Thank you for letting me know your ancestors accept me. That is a relief," I admitted. "And I look forward to meeting them when I die. To conversing with them, spirit to spirit. It would be great. But I don't understand your dream."

"That's all right, my girl, I don't either," Kasho laughed.

I don't believe you, the thought welled from my gut, surprising me.

Kasho said penetratingly, "So, what do *you* think the dream means? Come, sit by me." He lifted one arm, encircling me, and hinted, "Remember that my ancestors *truly* love you, with no ulterior motive. Unlike the way some living people love."

I flopped down beside him onto the unfelt sand, and confessed, "I have no idea what your dream means. Is your whale supposed to symbolize me? I guess, in that case, he should forget the natural way things used to be, and make a huge effort to grow wings and fly!"

"Yes, very good. And now, my girl, I sense that *you* have a dream you want to tell me. You'll begin healing if you do." Kasho looked at me from under lowered eyebrows.

I did have a dream, one that I hated. But, while my beloved told the tale of the whale, thoughts of this terrible dream had returned and I knew I had to tell him. "Yes, all right," I said, "I do have a dream. It's a recurring nightmare that my family is as young as before my brother went away." I tried hard to keep the awful feelings that always came with the dream at bay. "And yet we are in Australia. We are driving in a car when my father mentions that he thinks my brother's skin is itchy, so he stops the car and skins Kim 'to make him feel better.' My brother, skinless and looking horrific, staggers away towards the beach, and my father says he'll let him 'go for a run.' He then drives us many miles down the coast to a place where he says, 'We'll wait for Kim to arrive.' After we've waited an hour, my father drives us back to the beach where we originally left my brother.

"Ashamed of my father's callousness, I go around asking various people who are having picnics among the bushes, or relaxing in tents, 'Have you seen a skinned boy?' A man dressed as a nursing sister tells me, 'The insects are eating his corpse in the next clearing, behind those bushes.'

"My father's voice suddenly booms in my ears. 'I manage my family very well.'

"I lie face down on the ground and cry and cry for the cruelty of the situation that surely I could have done something to change. 'I'm sorry, Kimmie—I'm sorry,' I moan. I do not care who sees me.

"I continue to cry after I awaken."

The sunshine on Kasho's broad forehead was making him blink. "I'd like you to stop judging yourself," he said. "I happened to be there while you and Kim were playing. You were a good, fearlessly loving, creative girl, and he was a good boy. He was the love of your life. He gave your life love and fun and the only sense of freedom you had as a child. He was the one you felt could save you. You were so young when he died that you still hold onto the good. His memory, representing truth, protection and rebellion against cruelty, has kept you going. Neither of you deserved what your parents did."

"You are so bad for me, Kasho!" I cried out. "You are telling me not to blame myself when I need to. I need to throw out those happy memories of Kim after he died. They weren't real. They were made up! Imagined. The stupid imagination of a very bad child. I should be punished all the time, because it was my fault he was sent away."

"Whatever makes you think that?" Kasho asked. "Because he tried to protect you? No, no, my girl. That was not the issue. I was there when your parents sent Kim to his death. They were ashamed of him because he was sickly—which made them ashamed of themselves—and let him die alone and kept you in chains. They were embarrassed by him, and pretended he'd never existed and, once they reached Australia, no one knew he had. Your mother and father wiped his life out of history. They sent him away to be bullied, and tortured you by never letting you speak of him. I can feel your anger rising up, my Little Mystery. That's all right. Go ahead and rage at them, but not at yourself. I will not let you throw away what you and Kim had. And does it really matter if those things were real or imagined? They were joy. Your joy. And, I am certain of this, his joy too. He wanted to protect you and give you hope in his short life on your Earth and even after. So yes, rage, shout, blame—but not yourself. Rage at your parents. Maybe then you will have your freedom. Their cruelty was beyond belief."

I felt confused and frightened. Kasho was compassionate, so why did he want me to rage? As if I had spoken out loud, he said, "Anger can be cleansing, you know, like a forest fire burning away undergrowth. A young girl in my tribe once had herself tied to a tree so she could harm no one, and beat the ground all day because she was angry. Perhaps, afterwards, you will be able to forgive."

"There is nothing to forgive, and you know it," I said. "My parents did what they believed was correct, and that is that. All right, they can never bear to see the truth but that is their way.

And," I added stubbornly, in a mutter, "they brought me up to believe that anger was presumptuous and sinful in everyone but their godlike selves, and that they had a right to do anything they liked to me. I cannot eradicate the outlook I'm left with."

My beloved Kasho lowered his voice to a sober tone. "Even if they thought they were doing the right thing, God bless them," he said, "they tormented you and Kim. I saw it all. I saw, too, that your beatings were not totally inevitable. Occasionally, you went without. You were given just enough leeway to cause you tremendous stress. Besides, I wasn't thinking of you forgiving *them,* at least not yet. Only of you forgiving yourself."

I felt assaulted by his words, and persisted, "I have to take into account my own inexcusable crimes."

Kasho faced forward, as if informing an imaginary audience. "Ah! Now we're getting somewhere," he grinned. Then he turned aside to me. "What crimes, for goodness' sake?" he asked gently.

"Being born. Becoming a terrible burden on my parents. Failing to pretend. That makes me dangerous."

"Yes, thank God you are dangerous!" he burst out, with a force I'd never encountered in him before. "Or you *will* be when you and others call people to their true selves. Call them to leave the comforting winter of hypocrisy for the springtime of an honest life. I believe that during the next decades on your planet, people will find it harder and harder to lie. You know, once a lie about history is told, people try to get back to the truth and can't. So they just tell lots more lies to try to get back to the truth."

"Why do you talk in riddles?" I protested, annoyed. "You're not helping, Kasho. You're only confusing me."

Falling silent, he chewed his beard meditatively for a while. Then he said, sounding tolerant, "All right. Maybe this will help. The moment that you and I met again, we recognized in each other the existence of a love that embraces everyone and everything. The kind of love that your parents would have felt at least for their children if they'd been true to themselves. I composed something that expresses it. You can use the song in *your* world if you want:

"Selfless love—selfless love—selfless love—selfless love—
People are a symphony, and people are the sea;
I am the dust beneath their feet.
Beauty, peace and agony are what they bring to me,
The dust beneath their feet.
Like waves they beat upon me—but my spirit sings out free:
'Past the size of dreaming, *sacrifice for one another* is sweet!'"

With enormous relief, I exclaimed, "That's something you *do* understand, my Kasho! Why doesn't anyone else? The sweetness of serving others is beyond what anyone can imagine, even if it involves cleaning up their vomit when they have over-eaten. My parents enjoy ruling, but I desire to serve. I want to be a servant of servants. In the mornings at home, wild birds used to feed from my hands. It was a delight. Serving them was sweet! How much more, human beings—"

"I can help you write many more songs, if you need me to," Kasho assured me, "and I can teach you the very different music of my planet. My tribe's music usually turns out to be wordless but profoundly soulful, because we can get into trouble from our conquerors for expressing our thoughts that way. Our rulers are never quite sure what we are saying in a tune, though they often can be when we tell stories, act in plays or paint." Then he pointed out, "The most popular lyrics in your world seem to be about love between a man and woman."

"I can't write about that," I protested.

"Oh, yes, you can," Kasho insisted.

"How?"

"Just imagine that you'll never hear from *me* again."

"Ah, I would be so lonely again," I realized. And I began singing to a keening tune, almost entirely on one high anguished note:

"Kasho the Silent, oh my own darling,
Before I met you my heart knew some gladness.
Now how I wish I could be just as careless,
Wish I could leave you without this sadness.
How do you think I shall be without you?
You who have put into my sober heart madness?

"Kasho who loves me, I'm in your power;
Before I met you there was no tomorrow.
Now you dismiss me—but how to obey you
Unless this power of yours I can borrow?
How do you think I shall be without you?
You who have put into my carefree heart sorrow?"

"You see?" whispered Kasho, gently patting my shoulder. "You can do anything! But, if you and I were really meant to part, God would be contradicting Himself."

I found myself back, sitting at table, where Robin, Bruna and Giovanna were still arguing. Their disagreement sounded so petty that I got up to leave. My companions barely appeared to notice. My body, seated in front of a plate full of crumbs, had obviously long ago stopped talking, and I looked with fresh eyes on the knife that I had wanted to drive into my hand. A great deal had happened since then. So much I still didn't understand. Or was I not *wanting* to understand, I wondered? I needed to be alone to think all these matters over.

Back in my body, my spirit quietly asked Kasho, not expecting him to say yes, "Are you coming to my room with me?"

"No, that's enough adventure for today," he said.

But suddenly I couldn't bear leaving him, not knowing when he'd return. I demanded, "How long will you be gone? I was so worried last time that something terrible had happened to you."

I thought he patted my shoulder again. "Circumstances kept me away. I don't want to go into it. But I promise that I'll never again be gone so long." I felt too happy to have thoughts of pushing the subject further.

Chapter Seven
I Meet Daisy

I was walking down the hill from our school on a glorious Italian spring morning. I felt that the trees and birds present in this moment were my kin and home. For some reason, I believed that I would have family responsibility for everyone I would meet from now on, and that everyone I met from now on would be responsible for me. My mood had something to do with having been out of my body for so many hours yesterday, on an unknown planet or in another dimension that boded well for Kasho's and my future. And with having been blissful during a large part of that short eternity.

From today on, before doing anything, I would check what the spiritual realm wanted me to do. I longed to tune into the guidance of the great ones who had passed on, as Kasho's people did routinely. "God's Executives," I called them. I believed that they would protect me through my commonsense, so long as I tried to do the right thing. They would warn me intuitively of danger. On this I could rely, and therefore live without worry, even when I returned where I least wanted to be—home with my parents.

Pigeons fluttered everywhere, as usual, while I walked down the hill towards Florence city; and I exclaimed, very tenderly, to them, "Hello, my friends!"

Immediately a pigeon flew low and brushed my hair.

I laughed out loud with delight.

A teenager with slicked-back hair rode up my hill on a motor scooter and turned to whizz down past me. A weird feeling in my body told me to pay him no attention. So I coldly stared ahead and walked straight on. But my reaction made me unhappy, and just then I realized how much being outside my body had changed me. What was wrong with me now, my old self accused, that I should commune harmoniously with nature yet not a human being?

The young fellow zoomed up once more, stole a good look at my face and whizzed down again, circling closer. I noted that he wore a shiny leather jacket.

The motor scooter rider roared up past me a third time. On his descent, he swerved across into the wall beside me, cutting off my path. Now I absolutely could not avoid speaking with him.

"Dove vai?" he asked.

I shrugged my shoulders, though being so rude distressed me. My intuition was telling me to behave that way. Had this young man been a woman, I thought resentfully, we might have had a friendly conversation. Meetings between strangers of different sexes should not be potentially dangerous. I wanted to help create a future where the most beautiful woman ever, covered with jewels, could walk anywhere in the world with total safety.

But all I replied, vaguely, to the man was *"In città."*

"Ma dove in città?"

I would not tell him where in the city I intended to go.

"Would you like to sit behind me, and I will give you a ride?"

I'd have loved to try sitting on a motor scooter, but felt myself warned, mostly by the play Kasho and I had created together, to be wary of its rider. "No, thank you."

Till recently, I'd believed that being afraid of something was a good reason for doing it, and this had always meant denying my intuition. I'd actually been taught to despise intuition; my

111

parents had looked upon that divine receptor as belonging to the inferior, to the ruled. To womanly women, who were without power. To races that made my parents' flesh crawl. To the so-called stupid lower classes.

"*Perchè?*"

"*Non voglio, grazie. Preferisco camminare.*"

"Don't tell me *that*. How *could* you prefer to walk? Come on, *I'll* take you into town."

"*Mi piace camminare*—I truly *like* walking. *Non voglio andare con lei.* I don't want to go with you." The word I used for 'you' contrasted with his. It was coldly formal.

"*Allora, buon divertimento.* Enjoy yourself then. *Arrivederci!*" And the greasy-haired fellow was gone.

Sadness filled me as I watched him leave; and I thought of how, if we'd both been children playing in snow, we'd have shared a toboggan and arrived at the bottom of the hill bright-eyed and laughing. I longed so much for the world to be innocent, and profoundly resented the fact that I couldn't be equally friendly to everyone. Remembering Kasho, who, I realized, was always uneasy if he couldn't feel part of his surroundings, I resolved to try to help foster a wise innocence, like his, wherever possible.

I was moving along Via Maggio now, heading into town to meet with the Countess and my friends. We girls were planning to try on dresses for a ball that would be held three months from now in our *palazzo*. By walking instead of taking a taxi, I hoped to give the other girls time to choose their gowns before I arrived. I didn't want to be part of the silly giggling, fuss and insincerity that I expected to occur in the dress shop.

I didn't care much about dresses and balls. To me, clothes were little more than a necessity.

I crossed the river Arno, then Piazza Santa Trinità, going towards Via Tornabuoni. There I heard a familiar voice call my name. Standing near Via Tornabuoni's corner, in front of the

Renaissance building where I was headed, Nicole came into my line of vision. She was shifting her weight from one leg to the other, hand on hip, in a stance that seemed to express unwilling patience. Forgetting my selfish concerns, I hurried to her. The moment I arrived, her other hand, behind her back, tugged open a creaking, iron-studded wooden door, to reveal steps winding upwards through dark, damp air.

'You're late!" Nicole accused. "We've chosen our original dresses already, and have all been measured for copies. The sewing lady will take a while to make them, of course. I should let you know, there are no nice gowns left. So you might as well go home. And we *saw* you. Oh, don't deny it—yes, *la Contessa* and I *saw* you from our taxi talking with that bikey.

"Melissina, your obsession with getting to know common folk will hurt us all," elegant Nicole went on scolding. "If powerful multimillionaires hear of your wandering the streets, they will stop sending their daughters to our school. And think of the effect your behavior will have on this ball! It happens every year. An entertainment committee, elected by Florence high society, chooses our school as the very best place to hold it, and our Countess usually makes a lot of money from their decision. Why do you *do* what you do? How *could* you cheapen yourself like that? Don't you *care*? Your parents sent you here to be polished for high society." Checked by my grimace, for I'm a natural rebel—as the Countess once observed—Nicole suddenly met my feelings halfway, in a lowered tone. "Whether our *Contessa* is actually a snob or not, she has to attract parents and people who *think* she's a snob. Otherwise she'll lose money. You could hurt her beyond belief—"

"I'm very sorry," I admitted, staring dumbly at the bumpy stonework near the door. "The last thing I ever want is to harm anyone, much less our Countess."

I climbed the stone-walled winding steps in confusion, following Nicole. At the top, two unpainted wooden doors faced

113

each other. I heard a loud belly-laugh come from behind the left-hand one, hinged on the right. I couldn't believe it. I'd expected this dress-choosing occasion to be stuffy. Nicole tugged the door open, and held it for me.

The room we walked into had been made round by burgundy velvet curtains hanging from ceiling to floor. A few plump balloons, firm as ripe fruit, bobbed against the ceiling, their strings taut like stalks. I became aware that the Countess, seated on my left, was in such a sunny mood as to render inappropriate the apology I'd planned to offer.

But more noticeable than anything was the white wavy waist-length hair flowing down each side of a tall young woman's soft-featured face. Previously preoccupied with the Countess, its owner turned to flash a smile at me. "Welcome, welcome to my daytime castle!" she laughed, making a deep curtsey. A bubbling quality in her laughter made me feel I'd known this girl before, but how?

I looked towards the Countess again, but she was absorbed in fingering this tall girl's fluffy green skirt. So I turned to take in other details of the room. Robin and Karen sat with their hands over their eyes. As I watched, Karen shifted her fingers and returned my glance. Her flushed cheeks and merry expression made me realize, with a pang of envy, that a good time had been enjoyed here without me.

An untidily fallen magazine lay at Robin's feet. She and Karen were squashed beside Julie into a curved sofa on my right. At this sofa's further end a small chair, shaped like a woman of gold, seemed to beckon me so thoroughly that I concluded it had been placed there deliberately for me.

Settling on this chair—the golden woman's knees—I tried to understand the atmosphere here. Only Julie seemed detached—but then, she always was.

"No, no, it will never do for Melissa," the Countess remarked good-humoredly.

"Sì, davvero," the model cheerfully replied with an American accent. "Now that I've met your pupil, I know the perfect dress for her."

"What! I thought we'd seen all the good dresses," Nicole, now perched beside the Countess, cut in. "Did you deliberately hide one?"

The Countess shot her a reproving look. Karen began staring at the floor, probably embarrassed by Nicole's accusation. Robin picked up the fallen magazine and leaned back, reading. Julie stared over Robin's shoulders at its pages.

I remarked to the model, the white-haired girl, "The dress you're wearing at present will do. What does it matter?"

"Oh, yes!" was her reaction. "It matters very much!" She sounded charming. *"Signora la Contessa,"* she added, "I've done my best for your other pupils, parading for them in dresses that I felt expressed their personalities. But there's something mysterious about your Melissa, which the gown I must show you can bring out."

With that, the tall young woman moved slowly to the burgundy curtains on my far right, divided them and disappeared.

"What are all these balloons doing here?" I asked the Countess.

"Oh, the girl modeling for us bought a bunch from a boy on her way to work. Miraculously, her boss allowed her to release them into the room. He has a great sense of humor, I gather. She explained to us that she wanted to lighten our mood today."

After a few minutes of pensively playing with a balloon, I looked to my right again, and was rewarded by the curtains shifting. The girl appeared in a magical gown. I guessed its top must be put on separately from the skirt, the heavy satin of which cascaded to the ground. A wide tight-fitting oriental sash of tinselly material cleverly covered the join. Everything embroidered and sequined.

Blue usually doesn't suit me, I thought. And, anyway, how can I possibly take the dress? The way Nicole said, "Did you deliberately hide one?" made me think this girl was saving it for herself. She must be practically in love with it!

The young woman took a few steps, then stood in front of me with lowered arms forward and her fingers curled, palms facing heavenward, as if offering a gift. I glimpsed black ink marks on one palm. A gasp went up from all of us. "Pale, pale blue," I couldn't help speaking the words dreamily, out loud, "blue—blue—blue—with gold embroidery." Looking up at the girl's face, I struggled to express the inexpressible, being very impressed, "But without the chalky effect of ordinary pale blue. Rather, as if an artist has taken some dark, deep, rich blue, and spread it in a thin, thin film over the material. To make, not a light *shade* of blue, but a light *suggestion* of a dark shade."

The white-haired model smiled, pleased. Thank you for being born, my soul seemed to be saying to her.

When I go back to Australia, I decided, just remembering what happened in this room would help me.

The young woman, still standing in front of me, drew her arms back gracefully and began to twirl slowly, chanting under her breath, *"Gonna fight to live even if I can't breathe. Gonna fight the dark even if I can't see."*

Her words, so blatantly taking for granted that an individual has the *right* to survive in spirit—which I hadn't known, and still didn't really believe—were fingering my soul in a way that made me feel exposed to everyone here. I started wondering, what do *I* fight for? What do I stand for?

The model rhythmically moved her hands, almost hiding the black ink marks on her palm.

"Would you tell me your name?" I pressed.

"Daisy." Her cheeks made bronze apples as she smiled faintly, still moving.

"Well, Daisy, I've never heard that song before."

She stopped twirling, her hand to her mouth. I had been twisting my head first one way, then the other, trying to make out what she'd written. Now that her palm was hidden, my plans were foiled.

"I didn't know I was singing." Daisy's dark round eyes searched mine for understanding. "But I always need music in this room. I made the song up."

"The tune too?"

She nodded. Karen raised her head, elbows on knees, and startled me by asking her, "Do you accompany yourself at all on an instrument?"

"Yes," Daisy answered. "I have a guitar."

"That's unusual," Karen mused, "though my dad expects female guitarists to become more common. Knowing all the trends in the pop song industry is his business. You have a pioneering spirit. There's something about a girl playing that instrument. It's so rare—but even the most delicate guitar style, accompanying a soft female voice, can give off a powerful feeling."

Nicole excused herself to go to the bathroom, which she said must be somewhere behind the door across the landing.

"Though I come from America, my family is of Italian ancestry," Daisy responded to Karen. "Rhythm is in our bones. My parents see music as the language of the heart. Two of my brothers and I have been traveling the world, playing and singing. But when I inconveniently fell in love with Florence, they left me here alone..."

The wistful way in which she spoke her last word, 'alone', made me sense a need in her that I might miraculously be able to fill. She continued, "...and went on to Cambridge, England where they're now studying. Myself, I've deferred a university course at home for a year or two. Only six weeks ago"—my hopes for friendship with this wonderful girl increased—"my brothers and I were sitting on the cobblestones in a Brazilian village street, playing music with Indian friends. Without our having any words in common, our music brought us all to a unity, a new world to come, that even embraced the spirit world. We saw beautiful lights dancing around and above each other's heads."

I felt as if I were standing in cold rain beside a stranger who'd just remarked "My country is sunny." Daisy had experienced reality, sitting on the ground with local people, seeing heaven and earth overlap, just as Kasho believed. I, in contrast, brought trauma from my past, where my mother would have forbidden our acquaintance. What chance did I have of getting to know this girl better? And yet, I longed to try.

Having begged the spiritual realm, whose ever-present powers I now believed in, to give me eloquence and courage, I said, "Daisy, your song was exactly what I needed to hear. Your words could even change my life. They express a freedom I've never known in my everyday world—"

Daisy looked as though she saw right into me. "Actually, I seldom hear such a detailed reaction to my singing," she murmured, her warm eyes still on mine. "Official audiences usually just say 'Beautiful'—which could mean almost anything..."

I had been temporarily unaware of the other girls who, I now realized, had begun tittering; but at that moment the Countess brought Daisy's and my awareness back into the room. "I hate to say it," she interrupted us, "but now we have to talk about Melissa's dress. Just the same, we'd love it if you'd lunch sometime with us in our *palazzo*, Daisy. Any day that suits you— maybe next week? We have a good chef. I'll send a car for you. You could play and sing for us afterwards while we have coffee in our little sitting room. I suspect Karen would like to hear more of your work, and it looks as if you and Melissa are already bosom pals. I'll invite a few young men also."

"Thank you, *Signora la Contessa,* from the bottom of my heart," Daisy breathed. "I must admit, I'm not sure when I can be free in the next couple of weeks, but I'll ask my boss." Beaming, gazing around at us all, she explained, "Yesterday, I knew no one here my age. I even bought a ball so I could play with any lone dog I came across. And now, I have a whole family!"

She paused, allowing her bell-like voice to become professional. And the change in it gave me sudden awareness of what I'd previously been hearing. I recognized the voice as that of the white-haired child beside whom I'd ridden a pony in the waking dream I had downstairs at our *palazzo,* after everyone was asleep. Holding out the blue satin skirt, she intoned, "This gown was designed by Christian Dior, the world's top fashion designer."

Daisy looked around above our heads this time, I guessed, and went on, "The model before me paraded in it all last season—so my boss says that we are treating it as shop-soiled. If you want the original you can have it at a discount instead of a copy made to measure."

The Countess rose to her feet, stretched her spine and strode across to feel the slippery material. "I'd like to see Melissa in it," she said. "Why don't you accompany Daisy to the changing room, Melissa?"

Daisy smiled delightedly, weaving her arm into mine.

This girl is *happening* to me, I thought. Aloud, I couldn't resist telling her, "I won't take the dress. It's not worth it, just for one night. The gown fits you perfectly already. Clothes don't mean much to me."

Glancing at me sideways through lowered lashes, Daisy acknowledged, with a serious nod, my understanding that she herself loved the gown. But she cried out, "When would *I* be invited to a ball like yours? This is just a dress to dream over. When would I—of course, the gown fits me perfectly. All the clothes here were made to fit me—or changed, for me to model

119

them. But I want *you* to have this one. *You* can afford it and I can't. I've already worn it more than anyone would, who is not a model. And been admired in it plenty, as you will be too. Just a few well-placed pins will have it ready for our seamstress to fix for you."

"Daisy, if you find you enjoy our company, I'll arrange an invitation to the ball for you," the Countess promised.

"Thank you again, *signora,*" replied Daisy, returning to her formal tone. "I have a simple but adequate outfit I can use for dancing."

Coming back, Nicole pulled the noisy door shut behind her, and stood tapping her high heeled toe. "You came here to buy a dress, Melissina," she stated, jerking a high-up string and hitting its balloon with her other hand. "Maybe the rest of us should leave. We haven't got all day."

As if on cue, Robin ostentatiously yawned. Julie buttoned her coat. A look passed between her and Nicole which I suspected meant that, although they had witnessed an honest soul-to-soul meeting between Daisy and me, they would talk critically about it back at the school.

I didn't care. Having a more important thing on which to focus, I suggested to Daisy, "When your sewing woman takes in the Dior dress, then, please ask her to do it temporarily, so that we can let it out again later without spoiling."

Had I said the wrong thing? Most women, in my experience, become deeply offended when offered cast-off clothes.

But, with jubilation, Daisy responded, "Sharing! I love sharing! Sharing brings me back to sitting in the street with my Indian friends."

Ducking under the curtain that my new friend pulled back, I overheard our Countess dismiss my fellows from the *palazzo* with, "There's no need for the rest of you to stay. I'll see you at dinner."

Days later, I stood in that same Florentine Street, pressing the big brass bell on one side of the building's door. From the window sill on the other side, a pigeon looked at me calmly. I wriggled my fingers in front of its face. A distant dog barked. Long moments passed. Then I heard rapid feminine-sounding footfalls. The iron-studded door opened to reveal Daisy, her white-blonde hair pinned back, her big dark eyes smiling, and her high cheekbones flushed and clear. Her warmth and beauty were heightened by the frame of a gray scarf. After thrusting a brown paper parcel into my arms, she hugged me.

"Why did you bother walking all the way down?" I whispered in her ear. "I could easily have come up to get the dress."

Daisy answered with a soft laugh, and said, "I couldn't wait for you to come up, sister, because I had the most marvelous idea. *You* could take a job like mine, you're beautiful enough. You could be my sister in the clothing industry. This is the best job in the world!" she went on. "How can I convince you? I get to meet people like you, and the modeling season—the tourist season—is very short. Then, the rest of the year, I can do what I want, as you could too. Myself, I plan to write music and lyrics to my heart's content."

Her enveloping warmth, which I could hardly believe, tempted me to say "Yes." But then I thought of my parents' disapproval, and of my duty to return to Australia. Anyway, I decided, I was probably too tiny to model.

I tried to tear open the paper in my arms but Daisy exclaimed, "No! Don't spoil my wrapping! You'll find that the dress has been perfectly taken in for you, and we've had it dry cleaned. Our seamstress is so clever, amazingly she hasn't cut off any material; it can still be let out again easily. But, if you find something wrong with the gown, I'm here. And I'd love to join you for a cup of coffee in a café some time. Just us."

She brushed a tear off her cheek. "Forgive me," she added. "Tears come easily when I feel truly alive. A whole lot of emotions are welling up in me at once."

Alive! That was it! Entering Daisy's world had brought me life, the way I'd never felt before in the everyday world. I brushed away my own tears.

"Yes!" I agreed, feeling incredibly dizzy. "Let's have coffee together sometime."

"I am lonely here," Daisy said. "I miss my family and playing music. It would be wonderful, if we could meet and share together. Don't you think?"

I nodded, with tears now in my own eyes.

Chapter Eight
Friendship Awakens My Soul

At sunrise a few days later, I felt so excited at being about to join Daisy in a café that my enthusiasm could only find expression in creativity—in a story. I had not finished writing it when the time came for me to leave our *palazzo*. So I walked down our hill praying that Daisy would be late.

And late she was. I sat in Caffe Giacosa, writing fervently, at a small table. Making my last notes, I gave thanks that, like an ocean, love from the spiritual world had swelled around me, inspiring my little story as well as, I sensed, greater works the world over. My feeling was strong that many invisible beings like Kasho were involved in the lives of all of us on earth. But, unlike Kasho, they did not have bodies. Loving back the entities who loved me, I knew that my true community embraced more than the male café customers who had stared at me going alone to my table when I'd walked in, more than the loud woman in a straight red dress with a small matching jacket standing at the café bar, more than the woman in an advanced stage of pregnancy who was leaning against it—in fact, more than anyone I could see, hear or touch. The universe was blowing through me like a huge wind, wiping out everything petty.

I heard a throaty girl's voice, "Get someone to telephone me when your baby's born!" Looking up from my scribbled-on papers, which depicted another world and covered my table surface, I noticed the young speaker at the Caffe Giacosa bar, wearing a brown circle skirt with a soft off-white top, talking to the pregnant woman.

"Sì, sì," her impatient listener replied, then remarked, "We wanted our baby for ages, but the doctors said we were not likely to manage. We'd given up hope. I'm so excited! And now our baby will be born in late spring! What could be better?" Though the pregnant woman was small, her bulge enclosing her baby looked gigantic, almost fully round. Her flesh hugged her baby, and mysteriously I myself felt the embrace. How could this be?

Suddenly Kasho's voice in my head came as a surprise. "Most of the time, my people experience the unity you're feeling now. We make the spirit world happy, because they know we never forget them. And if anyone belonging to us has died, is ill or injured, my people know. But, my dearest Little Mystery, many over-civilized folk on your planet and mine have blocked these kinds of messages. When non-tribal friends visit with my tribe, they invariably marvel at how things that never happened to them elsewhere begin to happen, coincidences and so forth. There's an atmosphere among us where the spirit world is much closer and more active, even sometimes causing food to materialize in our children's hands when they are starving. Soon, if I whisper in enough of your kids' dreams, life will be like that all over your own world. Your people will feel invisible, protective arms around them wherever they go in the blackest night. And this feeling will unite you so deeply, you will always want to behave sincerely with each other. If you accept me as a teacher, my Little Mystery, you will probably help create that situation."

It felt wonderful to have Kasho believe in me this way. His presence tended to throw glamor over my environment wherever I was, blotting out the ugly. "From the moment I left our *palazzo* this morning, I have felt your spirit protecting me," I pointed out.

"That's true," Kasho confirmed. "I'm always watching over you. But I'm not the only one. Recently, I notice, you've tuned into my tribe's outlook. As naturally as breathing, we, the members of my tribe, allow the spirit world to guide every move we make.

"The spirit world, through intuition, has stimulated in your scientists your own world's marvelous material inventions, and it's essential to use those. But it's also important never to forget the more direct, often tangibly expressed love from the spirit world surrounding you. The community you dwell in is not just the visible one, as you now realize. Whatever befalls you, you'll always feel deep contentment if you never forget that the other— the Divine Protection—is there too."

"Kasho," I asked in my head, "does that woman at the bar, about to be a mother, symbolize something for me? A budding relationship with Daisy that will flower, for example? A re-shaping of society? Because I feel almost as excited today as that woman says she is. Or am I overdoing my obsession with symbolism? You would know, because I suspect you've been helping me with the story I am writing."

A big grin seemed to spread inside me, and I felt Kasho say, "Others in the spirit realm have been helping you, not I and, as you know, unlike me, they do not have bodies."

"Why are you in my head, anyway?" I asked.

"I thought that visiting in your head would be handy," I sensed him say, "Because your intuition wants me to let you know what's going on beneath the surface of things. You really don't need to see me now. My body is still chained, at present saturated with urine, in my gloomy dungeon. Twice a day, I glimpse one shaft of sunlight from a distant high window. The light reminds me of you, of your colorful clothes, and of our fun in the sand dunes. But, as always, I'm overwhelmingly grateful to my jailer, Mossiface III. Poor fellow, as I mentioned, he's had his tongue cut out, but he knows his way to me even in total blackness, tips water on me occasionally and brings enough food to keep my body living."

"Will you ever physically get out of that terrible place?" I sighed.

"Absolutely," Kasho immediately reassured me. "Quite soon, I believe. No tyranny lasts long on my planet."

I felt I owed poor Mossiface everything, because he was keeping my beloved alive, hopefully soon to be released. I visualized this jailer as a stocky, swarthy, bandy-legged man sometimes walking in circles aimlessly, his bloody mouth wide open in silent protest. Of course, his anguish would often have overwhelmed my Kasho, who would care more about his jailer than himself. And, indeed, it appeared that Mossiface actually had less to look forward to than my Kasho! I imagined my beloved, who always had a sense of what a situation needed, singing soothing songs to cheer him.

"Hey, I'm here now," Kasho interrupted my thoughts. "I'd really like to bring your mind back to share my playful mood with me, in Caffe Giacosa. Maybe I can unite with the pregnant woman who interests you, and as a result inspire you to create magical verses. Verses about new birth that could carry you and Daisy further than you've ever dreamed..."

"Thank you very much, Kasho," I said. "But I sense that this is an unsuitable time."

"You're right," he abruptly agreed. "You need to pay attention to your present surroundings now."

Having finished writing my tale, I allowed myself to look around. I noticed that a few men standing in conversation with the loud woman wore Italian-style light shirts that could be pulled over the head, with two buttons only, below the throat, attached to a collar that would open out. "Next time I see that shirt in a shop here," I resolved, "I will buy it and wear it, though it's for men. People in Australia will find it attractive and unusual."

126

Just then Daisy walked in. Without a thought, I rose to my feet. I felt like an eager child; I'd been so looking forward to our meeting. She wore a stark white *broderie anglaise* dress that drew long, blatant stares from every male present.

On a chain around her neck was a yellow flower made from seashells. It recalled a necklace I loved as a child. Such necklaces, I was told, were "cheap jewelry, and you won't want to wear them when you're grown up." I could see that Daisy's fresh, confident air had startled even the women at the bar, who were flashing her surreptitious glances.

We kissed on each cheek, and Daisy put her lips to my ear. "Are both our stomachs rumbling or only mine?" she whispered daringly, I thought. Imagining how my mother might react to such a question made me gasp.

"I don't know," I answered. But then, hearing a sound from mine, I laughed. "Both. That proves we are in sympathy. Stomach rumbling is pretty basic."

Smiling because we couldn't help it, we sat facing each other, Daisy crossing her legs to one side like a mermaid's tail. Or like the tails on both the lucky and unlucky seals in my just-finished story.

When my new friend concluded smoothly, "Our stomachs are digesting their breakfasts," I giggled at the ridiculous contrast between her demure expression and the outrageously unladylike thing she'd just said. And this time Daisy joined in, her giggling soon growing to a peak of laughter. Several women at the bar frowned. Even in Italy, two human beings' joy in each other was perhaps not often as uninhibited as ours.

"That dress suits you so well," I mentioned to Daisy, sincerely expressing what I felt, what I had also seen in the admiring café patrons' eyes. I was painfully aware that my parents would never allow me to wear a modern straight dress like hers.

Daisy beamed. "But you said that clothes don't mean much to you," she reminded me.

"You are converting me," I admitted.

Noticing Daisy glance at my papers spread out over the small table, I began gathering them into a folder. I felt embarrassed to think she might have seen words like 'thrashing body' and 'terror' that expressed the agonized side of me.

"Am I late?" my friend asked anxiously. "You've made so many notes."

"Not at all," I reassured her. "I wrote almost all of them before coming here. I'm absolutely delighted by your timing. You've given me a chance to finish my story. How was your morning?"

"Better than yesterday, not as good as tomorrow." Daisy's hand fanned her face. "It's too hot for a *cappuccino*."

"Generally speaking, Florentines refuse to drink *cappuccino* after nine in the morning," I commented. "Tourists drinking it later often get teased."

Daisy glanced at me; and, as she nodded, I saw what looked like a white butterfly reflected in a bowl on the bar. It was Daisy's white-blonde hair.

"I feel like having a strawberry ice cream." Her soft smile stretched and thinned to a gleeful child's grin, and she clapped her hands lightly. "But rumor has it that everything in this café is genuine. It's too early in spring for fresh strawberries. I might have a vanilla ice, to go with my dress. In case I spill any."

I recalled again the vision I'd once had in a twilight stage of sleep of myself as a child, with wild grass in my hair, shouting freely, and chocolate ice cream smeared around my mouth. I'd been staring at the sun way out in a meadow with other children. And I'd built a grass hut with a tall girl dressed in white like Daisy.

Observing her manner now—truthful, enthusiastic, loving and fearless—I felt a courage grow in me that was more simple

128

and direct than the backhanded kind I'd forced myself to have before. It made me bold enough to ask, "Did something weird happen to you when we first saw each other?"

"No, oh yes," my radiant friend answered. Though her tone was matter-of-fact, she looked right into me. "After I changed into the ball gown, and walked back from the changing room, the air seemed to come together between us, thicken, like a giant column made of wool. I thought I saw some presence. And I heard, but did not hear, children's voices—not with my outer ears. And yet I knew the exact tone of, the exact note, the exact excited words spoken. Do you think I'm crazy?"

"You know that I don't," I replied, meeting her eyes boldly. "I'm not sure exactly what happened, but I heard the children, too. In a way I was one of them, and so were you."

Daisy looked—unseeingly, I thought—at the polished wood table. She said quietly, "Yes, I remember that." I felt an ecstatic burning in my chest.

A pigeon fluttered in and settled on the back of Daisy's chair. It cocked its head, blinked and seemed to eye the food on a table near us. "Oh!" Daisy exclaimed, leaning forward, "Those wings cooling me! I wish I had some birdseed!"

I too leaned, but towards the bird, my nose touching its beak. I longed to stroke its smooth feathers.

A passing waiter immediately stepped closer and flapped a napkin. The pigeon panicked, flying around the whole café. After hitting its head a few times on the curved wood-paneled bar, from which patrons jumped away, the bird found the door and freedom.

Many of us in the café let out a sigh. We smoothed our ruffled clothes, like disturbed pigeons, and tuned into a long moment of calm. Then waiters started bustling again and people began talking.

Daisy had become dreamy during the pause. "I miss my parents," she mentioned surprisingly. "If I can establish a career here, I'll try to go home for a while every three months. Maybe that's unrealistic, but I'll try."

"You love your job, don't you?" I asked.

"Naturally. Don't you love your school?"

"Absolutely!" I exclaimed fervently.

"But surely you also long to see your parents."

"Yes and no," I replied. "They're pretty old-fashioned. In contrast, I have a sense that you feel you belong everywhere. What is the reason? Why are you so happy? Do you come from a big family?"

Daisy seemed taken aback by the desperation in my tone. An obvious appeal for guidance. I was on the brink of realizing that some families were not even remotely like mine, and I needed my friend to give me a glimpse into another life.

"Oh, yes," she agreed. "My family's quite large. Seven sisters and brothers altogether. All of us good buddies most of the time. How about you?"

I just shook my head sadly.

"I guess you'll tell me more when you're ready," Daisy concluded, straightening her necklace. After a brief silence, she went on, as if her information would stimulate me into providing some too. "Cousins and aunts are always coming over. We have visitors from many backgrounds, all kinds of cultures passing through. I learned a lot from them; those years while I was growing up were wonderful! Our guests' roars of laughter with us could be heard outside our house! Yes, really! People passing by sometimes stopped near our window to listen, and my parents would invite them in too.

"Our house guests' jokes often made light of terrible incidents beyond my understanding, but my mother and father knew that hearing about these experiences would help us kids grow," Daisy continued, telling me what I thirsted to know. "And that they themselves would grow through listening, too. Our parents taught us that a sense of self-worth would come naturally

130

if we always acted according to our conscience. They taught us to care for the earth, all living things and remarked that a small child, taught to think universally, can talk with the learned."

I felt so glad I'd met Daisy! So grateful for her solid presence, here, proving that loving upbringings did happen. Having never actually heard one described before, in my soul I couldn't quite believe it. Yet her words sounded like what I expected to be more common in the future, what I wanted to write about and, amazingly, with profound relief, I realized that this beautiful woman saw me as family.

I wondered what the earth was like that she had been taught to care for. For some reason I imagined her surrounded by nasturtiums, with fields of mustard not far away.

"Did you have a garden?" I asked. "What animals did you have?"

"Just my dog and a guinea pig. The guinea pig was so sweet—it would start crying for its breakfast when I went to the fridge each morning. When it died, I sat on our steps and howled through most of the night. My father eventually picked me up and carried me to bed. My father is as special as my mother, and I saw him almost as much."

I so envied Daisy for having been allowed to express her emotions. A wave of bitterness passed over me, and I thought: Obviously, unlike mine, no one has sullied *your* pool. It looks like no one has ever crippled *you* by telling you, as my parents told me, that writing songs is a criminal activity. No one has threatened to destroy you if you make your feelings public. No one has drummed into you that pursuing justice means disloyalty to your class. I bet no one has ever tried to take away *your* future, or told you that modeling—having people stare at you—is beneath your predestined place in society. You don't even seem to be afraid that your writing might turn out to be corny. Children gain courage from the family support that I never had.

Aloud, I demanded, "Daisy, why don't the adults in your life believe they own you?"

"*Own* me?" Daisy looked aghast.

Her shock was like a cold draft inside me on this hot day. I berated myself. How could I expect this wonderfully free girl to understand my life in a totally different world from the one she knew?

Daisy repeated, "What do you mean, *own* me?"

I began rather carefully, "In my country, and in many others, parents own their children by law. That can cause those parents to dominate every aspect of their child's life. To tell her frequently how grateful she should be that two people as important as they were had given birth to her." My words gathered momentum, "A mother might boast to her friends that constant beating for nothing kept her child quiet all day. A daughter might feel suffocated because every little thing triggered rage in her father. And that daughter might also despair, realizing in the end that daily punishment was inevitable, whether she did one thing, the opposite or nothing at all. Her mail might always be opened before she saw it, and everything she wrote creatively might disappear forever before she could finish it."

I paused with my mouth open, shocked at my own lack of control. My being so relaxed around my new friend might not bode well for Daisy's and my future relationship, I assumed. Of course, I'd never been one for small talk. 'Keeping the ball of conversation in play' was what my parents had tried to teach me, but I felt I owed Daisy more depth than that. Since meeting Kasho, I'd enjoyed absorbing the feelings, often communicated through silence, of almost any person in whose presence I was. But what was my new, less inhibited self in danger of doing to Daisy? I'd observed in my short life that people tend to bring out in each other whatever quality they have most in common. But Daisy reached across for my hand.

"Oh, my dear! I'm so sorry!" she said. "I feel I was born whole, into a world with eyes to watch over me and plenty of hearts to love me. I can see that wasn't the case for you."

In one flowing movement she stood, then knelt, putting her arms around me. "Nevertheless, I've often witnessed something wonderful—moments when people with terrible pasts realize they've *become* whole. Never give up hope!" she said. "Never underestimate the power of connection with the invisible realm. Nothing is impossible. If only you could have been my sister!"

My tears flowed freely. Daisy wiped them with her hands. I was aware of no one but her.

It seemed that her warmth towards me reached into a place so cold and hurting that I didn't know what to do.

"You and I are about to enter a world of greater reality," she said. "I sense it. These days, I'm delighted to say, very few parents still try to make their strong children stronger by continually punishing them for nothing. Parents are beginning to understand that *happiness* gives us wings! That at times of *joy* our strength is more vital, our intellect keener, and our understanding less clouded. Please may I tell you more about my big family, the one I wish you'd be part of? Would you perhaps like to see my world through my eyes?"

Profoundly moved by her kindness, I nodded. And Daisy, instead of describing her whole world, instinctively focused on the aspect of her family that I most needed, just now, to hear about.

"Far from owning us," she explained calmly, returning to her seat, "my lovely mother and father see themselves as no more than our guardians, with the job of bringing out the best in us, so that we in turn know how to bring out the best as adults in everyone around us wherever we happen to be.

"They see us kids as beings with greatness in us, whose desire from conception is to live a life of purpose, to develop all the gifts we have inside us. Especially trustworthiness."

Such an upbringing was hard for me to visualize, yet wasn't Daisy saying the things I'd always believed in and stood for? I tried to picture a world in which human beings could all count on each other, where the joy of one was the joy of all, the hurt of one was the hurt of all and the honor of one was the honor of all. My ideas were already being practiced somewhere! Heaven was real! All I needed to do, in order to understand that a good world was out there, was to know Daisy longer.

"Like my parents," Daisy went on, "I believe that forcing my will on someone else would be criminal behavior. Even children have their own truths. When we held discussion circles at home, the youngest of us would be listened to with the same dignity as everyone else.

"We learned that a person with little capacity who uses it fully is ultimately better than one with enormous potential who has never tried to stretch. But, of course, no one can ever feel superior to another, because none of us knows how our end will be.

"Unity, open communication and respect are still important to us as a family, wherever we happen to be. Our house was full of music, art and chaos! And love was what bound it all together."

I fell silent, thinking: Daisy, you are a big wind—a wind that blows the cobwebs out of my brain. Aloud, I felt the need to ask timidly, "Were your parents really like that all the time?"

"Well, naturally in my opinion they're wonderful," she said. "They've always emotionally supported us children. They are Baha'is, you know—and it gives them strength. So am I."

"Wait a second. What was that word?"

"Baha'i."

"What's Baha'i?"

"It's my religion. No, don't make such a face. It means I see everyone I meet as my father, mother, sister or brother so that, in any situation, I know what to do."

And Daisy began singing:

"When the wall says, 'Stay away—you're from a different race,'

Gotta tell them, 'There's just one race—it's the human race. We're building bridges out of the walls that keep us apart.'

When the wall says, 'Stay away—your religion's not the same,'

Gotta tell them, 'We just worship God by different names.'

"The *job* of us Baha'is is to create unity," she clarified. "Wherever we gather, even in a small group, if we've learned our job properly we'll have qualities that bring out the best in anyone entering. Logically, if this happens everywhere, there'll be heaven on earth. Our work is that simple, and that deep. We are the builders, the bricklayers. But if *we* don't do the work, God will raise up others for His purpose."

"And what is His purpose?"

"To bring Heaven to Earth, as I said."

I was curious, but didn't know enough to be able to frame further questions. Instead, I mused to myself: If *I* told my parents about yours, they'd disapprove. They'd think your ways were vulgar, and that your parents are far too relaxed. *You* think they're wonderful, but I'm not sure. All I do know is, they'd suit me.

Daisy added, "My mother had a hard upbringing herself, so her heart is fully in whatever she does for us. And it's not just racial and religious equality that Baha'is stand for. We expect that, in the age to come, the masculine and feminine elements of civilization will be more properly balanced. Because, so long as women are prevented from attaining their highest possibilities, men will be unable to achieve the greatness which might be theirs. One of the potentialities that has long been hidden in the realm of humanity is the capacity of women; but now, we believe, women will be the greatest factor in establishing universal peace." Then my friend lapsed into reverie.

My mind whirled. I did understand that Daisy's parents wanted their kids to bring out the best in whatever company they

135

found themselves. And I realized Daisy had done this—not fully, but to a large extent—when first I met her in the dress shop! She'd done it by *focusing* on the best in us, so that everything else fell away. I tried to picture a whole generation of children inspiring and healing the people around them.

Jerking herself out of her dreamy state, Daisy eventually said, "The world in the past has been ruled by force, and men have dominated over women because of their tendency to have more forceful and aggressive qualities both of body and mind. But the scales are shifting, force is losing its weight, and mental alertness, intuition, and the spiritual qualities of love and service, in which women are strong, are gaining ascendency."

Daisy lifted her garish colored handbag onto the table, and removed a small dark blue book with 'Baha'i Prayers' embossed on it. I inwardly groaned. But, after contemplating the shut book for a few minutes, she returned it to her bag.

I stared at the vulgar picture on her leather bag. It featured some skinny jungle animal, probably a cheetah, below palm trees.

"What is that feline-looking creature?" I asked.

"I don't know," said Daisy, eventually moving her bag to her lap. "But while describing my home, I mustn't forget the mysterious panther. I feel it was part of my life too. The residents of our area said that a man living at the bottom of our hill used to keep a small zoo, and two black panthers escaped. A typical suburban myth! But an afternoon came around when I definitely saw one, sitting on a garbage can. My family believed me when I told them, though a couple of neighbors said I must be crazy. I guess some people just have to experience such things before they can believe them."

I felt tempted to tell Daisy about Kasho. So I tested the possibility, by saying "*I've* had experiences that would make most people think I was crazy."

"We both did, when we met at the dress shop. I have much to learn from you. Your being a little younger has nothing to do with that fact."

Deciding this might not be the right time to mention Kasho, I stated fervently, "I have a lot to learn from *you,* too."

I thought sadly of my parents, and their women friends, whose lives were a round of parties. "I've spent a long time among people who believe that all learning stops once you're an adult," I added. "A couple of centuries ago, that might have been a common belief."

Daisy drew her breath in. "I give thanks every day that I'm living in this Age," she exclaimed. "We are all so much freer...

"Do you feel like saying any more about *your* upbringing?" She leaned back, with the air of one who could listen all day.

I looked down. "Remembering it upsets me. My parents didn't want me to write. My father said, 'There are too many books in the world, and no daughter of mine is going to add to them.' This despite the fact that, at home, my desire to write when I grew up was the only thing keeping me alive!"

Noting Daisy's glance of understanding, I added, between my teeth, "My father and mother still want me to be part of their own 'high society'. They are determined to destroy my mind, my heart, my soul."

"So why are you going home?"

I looked down again, muttering, "I have to test my strength. I have to see if I can keep my integrity in adversity. It's easy for a happy individual to have a beautiful personality. I have to go back to reality. Otherwise I will be a coward. I have to do what I don't want to. And it will shame my parents if I don't go."

"Are you being proud?" Daisy asked gently. "Perhaps no one is as strong as you think you must be."

"But it's selfish to want to be independent!" I protested. My fingers wiped tears from under my eyes. My future life had begun to look like a desert.

"You can't give to others unless you're free," said Daisy. "You can't give unless you are yourself. Maybe your main task in this world is to learn to stand up for yourself. Please may I read what you were writing before I came?" She reached for my folder.

For a moment I wanted to pull it back, but a kind of ecstasy came over Daisy's face when she took out a paper. I watched helplessly. Glancing at the page briefly, she murmured, "I've been looking forward to today ever since I saw you. I wrote to my brothers in Cambridge about you, and my older brother wrote back, 'People always come into your life for a reason, sis. You and Melissa will help each other in some way.'"

"Your brother calls you 'sis!" I exclaimed. "But that's what the brother calls his younger sister in my story!"

Had Daisy noticed already? I could not tell. Head lowered, she had begun reading in earnest, her expression hidden. Now that we were not looking at each other, I put on my sunglasses, which caused me to see rainbow lights in some of the glassware on the bar. This phenomenon reminded me of Kasho's skin, and I asked him inside how he was feeling.

Kasho responded at once. "I don't want to think about me," he said. "This is *your* time. I'm happy to see you with a different kind of friend."

"Can I tell Daisy about you?" I asked him.

Kasho didn't answer directly. "With Daisy," he said, "you can be a self you've never met before. I love her."

Did he mean he loved my different self, or Daisy? Or both of us? I wondered.

Daisy gave me back my story. A few patrons had stopped talking and were watching us. "I want to hear what you wrote, with its beginning, middle and end in the right places," she said. "It's like a legend, I feel. Would *you* read it now?"

I removed my sunglasses. "I wrote my story for *you*," I mentioned calmly. "*I* don't have a brother—living, that is—and you have several..."

"Oh, I *am* sorry," Daisy immediately responded, her eyes growing watery. "How awful for you." She reached out and placed her hand gently but firmly on mine. "I can't imagine anything so sad."

She paused, and I knew she didn't know how to express herself further. I half smiled and said, "It's all right. He was ill, and he's never really left me. I feel his love every day." I thought in passing of telling her how real Kim still was to me. How he was my protector even in death. But this didn't seem to be the time. Squeezing her hand, I said, "Do you, as I imagined, live on the ocean?"

"The Pacific," Daisy confirmed, fingering a clump of her hair into ringlets. "Go on. I couldn't make head or tail of that page of notes."

A number of café patrons were obviously paying attention. How many would follow every English word? Maybe plenty, if they listened with their hearts.

"On a softly-lit day," I read, leaning closer to Daisy, "my big brother and I have rigged rods to the sides of our fishing boat. Off we speed, in holiday mood, to catch a fish or two.

"Suddenly I sight comical, patchy heads bobbing everywhere. I scream out, 'We're sailing into a seal colony!'

"'Don't worry, sis,' my brother reassures me. 'We won't harm them. I've never hooked a seal yet.'

"After a short time, a huge fish thrashes on our sternward line. Instantly, an adult seal engulfs it and swims off with rod, line and—buried deep in its body—dangerous hook.

"Sobs rack my chest, and I am preparing to go to the animal, when a plump smaller seal lurches below me, already entangled hopelessly in our left-hand line. It has split its flipper on our hook, and is trying with its other flipper to push out the point. Its

139

mother arrives, nosing her youngster. My brother and I lift her baby tenderly into our boat.

"The mother circles us, barking unbearably, while I grip her young denizen of the deep's head between my knees and hands. Its flippers are tangled in a praying position, but its body thrashes in terror. I hold its head steady, gazing into its lugubrious eyes, while my brother works to disentangle it. Painstakingly, he slides the fish hook from its flipper. Early on, I tell the distraught mother, soothingly, 'We won't hurt your baby more than we have done,' though my heart is breaking.

"But my thoughts are also way out in the ocean, searching for the injured previous seal that, moments ago, swallowed the great fish we had been hauling. I know my duty is to investigate its fate.

"My spirit slips into the water in the form of a shark. I *must* choose a shark's body because, I suspect, I will have to play dutiful executioner. We monsters of the deep carry out the ocean's law—wherever possible, to give quick deaths. Choosing a shark's body has equipped me, both physically and emotionally, to kill kindly.

"The hunger! The terrible restlessness! For, I believe, in most conditions we sharks cannot live once we stop moving. I join others of my species. I am a menacing shadow among other menacing shadows.

"We smell blood, and begin our frenzied dance.

"At length I come upon my prey—and we all move in for the kill.

"Blood is pooling from this seal's mouth, and it knows its fate. Making the jerky movements of despair, it is actually willing its demise.

"A giant shape glides swiftly towards its tail, but I head this shape off.

"The first rip, the mercy rip, must be from me—at my prey's throat, so that it will lose consciousness as rapidly as possible.

"I barge into the black fur. I delight in my strength and power. My massive jaw closes.

"The seal's body rips in half. My co-workers immediately form two tail-lashing circles around the descending pieces.

"Its job done, my spirit returns to sit in my brother's boat and continue the slow, slow process of actually *saving* a life."

A handful of café patrons clapped. It felt good to be surrounded by empathy and support.

Daisy began singing, very softly, so that probably only I could hear:

"To take a life is to lose two souls:
The one you took, and your own.
To save a life is to reach inside,
And pull out the strength that you find.
Lost in the ocean and you're the prey
Losing motion, all you see is gray –
Do you hope for a swift death from your friend?
Instead of fighting to breathe till the end?
Do you: Give in Give up
'Cause you don't want to swim too far?
Do you: Hold on Look up
Pray for one more piece of good luck?

"You are not the shark that you write about. You are the injured seal in the ocean. You are drowning." Daisy's eyes met mine as she emphasized, "But I won't let you die.

"My sister," she went on, "do you write poetry? Anything I could set to music? We could collaborate. We could do great things! Because I could never write a story like that. I'm too happy. I don't know enough about how other beings suffer."

Now I knew what I could offer Daisy. I *had* a blissful feeling that my way of seeing things would fill a gap in her repertoire. I looked up once more at the pregnant woman leaning against the

141

bar, and what I'd felt earlier at the sight again enveloped me. I asked Kasho to help me express to Daisy what I wished my mother had felt for her own babies—and words that did not seem to be mine burst from me:

"Before you were born, I was just a little girl;
Now I am a woman, a mother.
Before you were born, I was basically alone;
Now we are bound to each other.
We meet only through parting,
And you'll never remember this time.
"Before this labor I thought for myself;
Now I and the universe are one.
The pains that I suffered are shared by humankind;
And the happiness that's only just begun.
We meet only through parting—
And you'll never remember this time…"

"Yes!" Daisy interrupted excitedly. "Yes! You have stated it yourself, exactly. Childbirth and motherhood are about unity, but also about parting. Everyone is happy when a baby is born—but the parting must come again, and adolescence is the right time to decide one's own destiny."

Consciously, I was more impressed by my friend's no-nonsense manner than by what she said.

After a deep silence, during which I increasingly felt scared that Daisy had hated the poem, she replied, "Melissa, that is really beautiful but I must tell you—to me there's an ingredient both your works lack—hope. Both your story and your poem need to end on a more satisfying note. If we collaborate, I'd like to bring hope into your life."

"You're exactly what I need, Daisy!" I exclaimed, much relieved. "A critic to improve my work. We'll make a wonderful

142

team! I look forward to trying to be the best lyric writer in the world!"

Daisy lowered her head sadly, as if I'd failed to grasp exactly what she meant. "We are entering an era where we do nothing alone," she mentioned.

"Remember the baby seal who survived in your story?" she then asked. "Suppose we focus on turning your tale into a song? Suppose I make blissful, ethereal music at the end, and you contribute words focusing on that baby back where its heart grows strong, cavorting in the ocean, or at its mother's breast? Music can uplift. Let's fool around with it!" And she began to sing "I hold the seal's head on my knees—"

"And I sob so when I see," I contributed.

"He split his flipper on our hook," sang Daisy, looking up. "The other flipper tried to set him free."

"Well, we'll have to work on it," I concluded. "I can already hear sobs in the rhythm of your last line."

My friend failed to respond, and I felt guilty for having focused once more on hopelessness. But then I realized Daisy was signaling to me. Glancing sideways, I noticed that a waiter was standing politely at our elbows, ready to take our order.

Embarrassed, I spoke in Italian, pretending he hadn't understood. "I'd like a hot chocolate," I told him.

"Are you *sure?*" asked Daisy. Her strong hand fanned my face. "It's so *hot,* Melissa." She was almost pleading.

The breeze she made was beautiful. But of course I was sure.

"Yes," I replied calmly.

"Are you *sure?*"

"I could turn the tables on you, Daisy," I joked. "Temporarily living in Italy may be heavenly for us, and *you* want heaven to sprout up everywhere in the world. But," I continued, while smiling at the waiter, "your first sip of *Giacosa's* hot chocolate is what *I* would describe as truly heaven. The best solid chocolate you can imagine is melted to create bittersweet syrup flowing all around your insides. You can also ask for a dollop of fresh whipped cream. Nudged a bit by your spoon, say, the cream could perform a slow, sensuous dance in your cup, winding in and out with the hot chocolate. The mixture might even overflow a little."

My friend's eyes widened dreamily as if, I thought, she were remembering the tantalizing party pictures that she really couldn't be remembering, because only I had experienced them before sleep—our carefree time together as children in the swimming pool.

"Then I'll order exactly the same as you," she laughed, "with plenty of whipped cream. And we'll drink a toast: 'Happy Birthday to us!'"

Chapter Nine
An Unwanted Suitor

I heard labored breathing and then Bruna, with her plump cheeks and white eyelashes, peered around the doorway of my tower room.

"You are wanted on the telephone, *signorina,*" she announced.

"I'm sorry you had to climb all this way," I replied. "Thank you very much."

I had been standing in front of the full-length mirror brushing my hair, thinking about how my friendship with Daisy had grown during the last two weeks. Before we met, the idea of having anyone like her in my life was beyond my imagining. Now, every chance we had, we spoke over the telephone, and we often grabbed a few moments to drink hot chocolate together at Giacosa's. And happily today, at last, we'd spend longer together than usual, because we were going on a picnic. Not even the dirty-looking clouds looming outside could spoil my mood.

"Prego, signorina," replied Bruna. Flattening herself against the wall, she stood aside for me to descend.

I knew who wanted me, and was already laughing by the time I reached the telephone downstairs. It stood on a shelf beside the kitchen. "Are you chickening out?" I asked.

"Not at all!" Daisy's happy-sounding voice came through. "I've been humming all morning, really to you, 'Singing "I will if you will, so will I'" above the storm. But I just need to know your plans. We do have to be a little braver in this weather."

"Daisy, nothing's going to spoil our day," I promised recklessly. "I'll meet you in the Boboli Gardens at eleven. Bruna and Giovanna have prepared a picnic."

Daisy, in response to *la Contessa's* invitation to play and sing at our school, had let her know she was free today. But our Countess would be out, at a committee meeting arranging the Ball. She'd said she wanted to be present—on another day—when Daisy came.

Upon putting down the telephone receiver, I wondered if I'd been selfish. Should I have asked my friend if she'd prefer to meet indoors? The majestic Boboli Gardens, designed in the 1550s for the ruling Medici family by their 'green architect', Tribolo, cut into the hillside below our school, which stood across the Arno from the main city. The gardens happened to be within easy walking distance for me, but less so for Daisy. I didn't like to fuss, however; so I decided to leave things as they were.

Just as I started to head upstairs again, the telephone shrilled. Obviously, my duty was to answer it, and then—I expected—to search the building for whichever of my friends was wanted by the new caller.

"*Pronto?*"

"Melissa! I'd know your voice anywhere. Is that really you?"

"Yes, I suppose it is!" I squeaked, surprised.

"Melissa! It's Christopher. Remember me? Try to laugh. I want to hear you laugh! How I've missed you! We only have three minutes—even that costs a fortune—and then you'll be snatched away from me into darkness. Not forever, I hope. It's night time in Australia."

The voice sounded urgent, even passionate. But it made me uneasy. Remembering who Christopher was took a while. Since the age of five, I'd been trained to hand savories around at the

146

cocktail parties at home. Just before I left Australia, my parents' friends' sons had been scattered among the guests—I realized what a deliberate move that was—and one of those young fellows had come to our house a few times since. I mostly witnessed him deeply discussing matters with my parents, so I'd assumed they wanted privacy. After a few short conversation exchanges, I always left the room.

"Did you read my letter, Melissa? Melissa? The one your mother enclosed a couple of months ago. Your parents are quite sure we'll be brilliant together. They've been incredibly encouraging."

My uneasiness grew. Of course, I'd been writing to my parents every week—they taught me that people who didn't write letters were selfish—but tears from remembering their lack of love, which took me right out of my free mood in Italy, often dropped on the pages. Both my parents had written regularly to me—my father's letters absurdly claiming he knew what I did each day, my mother's describing the high society people who attended her cocktail parties. But if I read their notes' enclosures—which were my own letters returned, 'corrected' into archaic language with all liveliness removed—finding the strength to write again was too hard for me.

Had an envelope from my mother a couple of months ago felt fatter than usual? Had my intuition told me not to throw it away? Had I disobeyed that feeling? Recently, my mother's letters sounded even less sincere than previously. But none mentioned Christopher.

I did, however, recall the cocktail party where he and I had met—I'd brought a plate of delicacies to him and his friend while they were bickering about the exact wording a hanging judge was supposed to use, in Australia, when sentencing a man to death: "Have you anything to say before I pronounce sentence?... You shall be hanged by the neck until you be dead... and may the Lord have mercy on your soul." Christopher's friend had

147

mentioned he regretted the fact that no legal hangings had occurred in Australia since 1952. And both young men had agreed that, if a hanging did not occur soon, the present government might lose power. "A good hanging has never harmed an election!" Christopher's friend said, adding that he knew the wording of the order customarily given to the hangman: "Do your duty."

Raising a glass of sherry to his lips, but only pretending to sip it—I noted—Christopher had thrown in that he rather envied the 'state of mind of a fellow awaiting hanging'. To me, he added quietly, "I myself dream every night that I am hung. At first I saw what I was experiencing as nightmares, but now I've come around to enjoying them."

I replied politely, as if responding to his first statement, "Yes, I don't want to miss the drama of my own death. I'd rather not die in my sleep. But I also want to *do* something for the world." I lowered my voice a bit as I said this, not wanting my parents or their friends to hear. After all, I'd been taught that a well-brought up young lady didn't *do* anything apart from being an ornament to the home.

"Whatever makes you think the world is worth it?" Christopher's friend had asked, blowing—I now remembered—cigarette smoke in my face.

Lowering his glass, Christopher chided him for his bad manners.

"It *won't* be, unless we do something for it," I'd daringly replied and excused myself for a minute.

Hoping to point Christopher in the direction of life, I returned with a really terrible song I'd tried to write some years ago, when I'd been immersed for a while in old traditions and felt abnormal despair:

"Sentenced to Life! God calls in Heaven's high court,
'I'll pronounce sentence now; do you wish to say aught?'

'No – but hurry, please hurry!' was the wee soul's thought,
For now the Great Adventure was to be.
And the child knew nothing of the cruel world of night,
Of the tunnels of darkness, and pin-points of light;
The world it expected was sunnily bright,
So it danced in excitement and glee.
And God condemned the child's soul—suddenly forlorn—
While angels all stood quivering and tense:
'You shall dream in the darkness until you be born;
'And, World, have mercy on its innocence!'

"I really don't want to show this to anyone but you," I whispered sincerely but flirtatiously, maybe, from Christopher's point of view. However, when I handed him the paper, my parents had turned away from their guests to stare at me. They'd seen my poem before, and had corrected it. My mother walked past her friend's son—Christopher—as he perused my work. "Wicked, ungrateful hussy I've brought up all these years without knowing!" she muttered.

Children are not allowed to have feelings, I confirmed to myself bitterly. Kim's death had taught me this long ago.

"The angels will certainly weep for you." With an ironic, feeble smile confined to his lips, Christopher had paraphrased Bernard Shaw.

"Melissa!" exclaimed the voice through the telephone. "My little wife, oh, my own little wife!"

From its assumption of future lovemaking between a near-stranger and myself, this outburst made me squirm but I also felt, behind it, my father's heavy hand on my neck, as if he were showing a dog who was master. And there was room in my heart for distress on Christopher's behalf—or on behalf of anyone who might love me without my returning his intensity of feeling.

Christopher went on, "Do you remember what I said to you, in visits to your house? I've never been able to confide in anyone,

149

even as a young boy. But I'll surely be able to confide in someone like *you.* You are to me the living proof that beauty, goodness and intelligence exist—that life is not a horrible farce. We'll have rather short children, that's the only thing. But, with you as their mother, they'll certainly have opinions of their own. You are very intelligent for a girl."

In shock, I recalled how much my parents had disapproved of 'opinionated women'. This stranger apparently loving me, despite the fact that I actually dared to think, made me feel as if my own parents were accepting me at last. I felt their outlook pouring into my brain like a fog.

"Did you get my flowers?" Christopher sounded desperate to hear me.

Silence.

"I gather not. You'll smile when you do. I love you for your independence, and for remaining silent when silence is better than words. I love you for a thousand things, and I can't say all of them."

Suddenly I remembered a promise I made to myself as a very small girl, "I will give my life to the first fellow brave enough to fall in love with me because I know, deep in my bones, what an agony it is to love and not be loved back."

A noise of disgust entered my head, followed by Kasho's rasping voice, "*Think,* Melissa! It's not my place to go so far as to tell you what to do, but this is too much. I know you expected a life of suffering. However, if *I* have a say, you're not going to get it. Do what you can without denying what your innermost being needs. Your behavior *must* come from that."

I felt confused and amazed at the same time. Through my Kasho's words, I glimpsed a world still more foreign to me than his barren planet—my own soul.

For the first time since our opening conversation, I found my voice, "You don't *know* me, Christopher." My words came out with more strength than I'd intended.

"It is not necessary to know someone in order to love, Melissa. I know you are good and beautiful. And that you will make a ladylike wife. That's all that counts—really!

"Two days ago I was invited to tea with a friend in the city. I spent the whole evening thinking that none of the girls there had beautiful hands, beautiful eyes and a beautiful mouth like yours. At last I went out. It was raining, and I was so desperate, I tried to find pleasure in getting drenched. I made myself ill, and still have some fever.

"If I were on a mountaintop, I would shout out, 'I love Melissa! I love Melissa!' But, over the telephone, unfortunately, I can't shout like that. You would think I am crazy. We will have such fun in our life together. We will do everything that I want and you will make it fun."

"You can be his doorway to fun without *giving* away your entire life!" I heard Kasho urge. "You are not someone's doll."

I answered Christopher, "I can't express enough my gratitude to you for loving me. But it's easy to love. I don't see why you'd find falling in love with another girl difficult."

The telephone connection went dead. Whatever Christopher might have wanted to answer was silenced as surely as a hangman's noose might cut off a criminal's cry.

I sensed Kasho laughing heartily. "*Brava,* Melissa!" he eventually exclaimed.

"But I was cruel to Christopher!" I protested in confusion. Profoundly distressed, I felt desperate to consult Daisy, and hoped she'd show me a way out of my dilemma.

"Your response came from your innermost being. I'm proud of you, and hope one day to make you proud of me."

Anything further Kasho and I had to say to each other was interrupted by the kitchen door opening, and a powerful scent taking me to another beautiful world as Bruna and Giovanna passed in front of me, bearing armfuls of deep yellow and red roses. Some instinct for drama and romance—a desire to show

151

me the blooms in their profusion—must have stopped the women from bringing this love-offering out already prepared, in vases.

"These flowers are for you, *signorina,*" Bruna said solemnly in passing. "You have a lover who doesn't trust you. He sends you yellow for jealousy, red for love but no white for purity." She turned, and held my gaze for a long moment. I felt a flash of foreboding, but let it pass.

I followed the women, feeling as if they were the police summoning me to identify my own body. They went up the three steps to the dining room, where they strewed the flowers over the table as if over a coffin.

"We'll go to find some vases now," said Bruna unhurriedly and the women soon left me alone. I'd been too ashamed to speak to them. Italy, after the War, was suffering such heartrending poverty, and here I was the recipient of almost priceless hothouse flowers, probably flown in from another country.

Abandoned, I was too startled to do anything other than stare. The body lying among those luxurious blooms was Melissa's, all right. That's how I felt. On the sideboard beyond the table, which now resembled a flower-strewn bier, a many-branched silver candelabra cast a funereal glow from its white candles. The Countess had been placing slow-burning candlesticks throughout our *palazzo,* as a step towards deciding whether to use them at our forthcoming ball.

Each rose looked caught at its perfect moment, before beginning to die. But I could bear the scene no longer. Descending the steps, I opened the kitchen door and asked Giovanna to see to it that the flowers were distributed among all her friends.

"You are an *angelina di paradiso,*" she replied, giving me a gentle hug.

Beside the sink squatted a cloth-covered picnic basket. Giovanna now picked up this cane basket, shoving it into my arms. The mild elusive smell from its hidden contents tantalized me. "Here! Here!" the servant woman exclaimed. "You'll be late for your friend."

Chapter Ten
I Lose My Resolve

The weather was tempestuous, white mist moving like a slow ocean along the cobbles of our steeply zigzagging road, as I climbed with difficulty down our hill towards the Boboli Gardens. Over the stone wall at the sloping road's right hand, lower side, the olive trees looked like old people ashamed of their gnarled feet, which were being covered with warm fluffy slippers of fog.

Further down, the earth's low mouth puffed upwards great swathes of mist. They blinded me, enveloping me in mystery. But I was grateful to have to concentrate on every step I took, rather than dwelling on Christopher and the roses.

So I stumbled on, towards my rendezvous with Daisy. Eventually, after being dripped on by many trees, I neared the place where we planned to meet. It was at a wild part of the gardens—not an official entrance.

Bundled gray-brown twigs, caught in moss beneath my feet, and enormous overgrown hedges reassured me I had arrived.

Shifting the picnic basket to my left arm, and reaching up to nearby color, I felt the moist, bulbous pressure of pink blossoms inside my curled fingers.

I heard my name called, without the long "ee" that Italians always say. Daisy was at my shoulder, dressed in gray like the landscape and smelling of lavender.

"Did you have trouble getting here?" I asked her anxiously. I'd never seen Daisy so solemn before. "Is everything all right?" I persisted.

"I must admit, I *am* preoccupied," said Daisy. "But I'd rather not talk about why, at the moment."

A chill crept between us. As far as I knew, Daisy had never previously deliberately hidden her thoughts from me.

I noticed her hair was held in a swirl by multicolored plastic clips shaped like butterflies. It suggested a frosty meadow with flower buds scattered here and there. She shook droplets out of it, some falling on my face. "Those distant trees rising out of mist look like rolling hills," she remarked, adding, "This place would take more than a day to really see."

"A hundred and one acres," I agreed, relaxing into my old love for my friend and into my familiar sense of recklessness at knowing her. My parents would have objected to her grammar—splitting an infinitive—and the cheap clips in her hair. Of course, I did not agree with my mother and father on either count.

Movement in the huge white clouds covering the sky made me look up. Kasho appeared there, raising an object like a flute to his lips. "I'll make music to help you penetrate the Boboli Garden in a dignified manner," he said, with an ironic smile.

Kasho's head vanished but then a whirly wind blew up, which I understood to be my beloved's over-boisterous way of making music for us both. Two branches crashed to the ground not far ahead.

Daisy, going first, picked her way between the branches. She and I followed a barely visible path, on whose stones our feet sounded like spattering rain. Everything gray, trees as if covered in snow; beautiful, all the same. The mist spreading its arms for me to fall in. Furry, dove-soft outlines. Occasional stars on the ground. Dim rocks—or distant sculptures.

I could not resist shoving my hand under a handful of stones and exclaiming, "Look at me! I can catch bubbles! They feel like

155

eggs." Then, dropping all but one, aware of how angrily most people would react, I risked reaching up and pressing it against the back of Daisy's head, "The yolk's on you!"

Daisy gave a little shriek and swung around. Then, giggling, she bent and gave my arms tiny pinches. She pulled forward, from bushes each side of our path, some stalks with long leaves, and tickled my cheeks with them. The stroking leaves felt like Kim's newly-washed hands when he used to soothe me to sleep. I had forgotten the sensation till now.

"That was a good way to start our day together," Daisy murmured.

After she turned to face again the direction in which we were going, I saw a thin shaft of sun—golden-brown like Kim's hair—light up the overflowing shell of a nearby fountain. Wrinkled brown leaves had blown into this shell, making way for more spring buds on their trees. They wriggled like tadpoles so the water looked brimming with life.

I thought I could see, below the fountain, the rest of Kim's face emerge out of white gloom. His head looked radiant, glistening with drops in the sun's rays that penetrated occasionally. The mist wrapped him up like a present for me. Though moving shadows soon made him become part of the textured air and ground, I felt bathed in his closeness. His eyes looked trusting and filled with love. He appeared so young and brave.

"As are you, my beloved sister," he seemed to respond to my thoughts. "You know, we will never stop loving each other. My heart is your heart. We did have joy when you were a child. Our joy together. You knew love then, too. You made me strong."

Something about his tone—a hesitancy and hint of sadness—caused me to protest, "Why are you talking this way, Kimmie? It sounds as if you're saying goodbye."

"So wise and intuitive you are." Kim's focus on me made me feel truly loved. But he continued, "You don't need me as you

156

did. You have made such good friends here. And you have Kasho. Yes, I must go and you must grow up. But take heart. You will live brilliantly. I know it."

I felt him pulling away until all I saw were his trusting eyes. Then they faded into trees and mist. His words resonated through the fog, blowing around me, covering my face—and he was gone.

Feeling as if I might fall off the edge of the world, I shifted the picnic basket, holding it now across my chest by its edges, as if defending myself from the unknown. And then I felt Kasho near. "Help me," I silently pleaded. "I don't know what's happening. Kimmie!" I began, but could say nothing more.

"I know, I know, my Little Mystery. All is as it should be. It is time for you and Kim to let go."

Let go? But Kimmie had been my connection to life for so long. Why would I have to do this?

Kasho didn't answer. Only silence. And I realized he had left me. To what? To Daisy? My inner being was wailing from mountaintops. Kim's and my world twice lost. First, with Kim's dying alone, away from my family. And if he were truly gone from me now, how would I live with my parents when I returned to Australia? Without my brother? Without our world of imagination and warmth? I couldn't do it. I wouldn't. How could Kim not know that?

Suddenly, I knew the reason for Christopher's call. Alone, I would never be able to slip away from my parents' power. No one ever escaped them. But if I married Christopher and we lived on his family's property, I'd be close to my mother and father. And that was far, far better than living *with* them. I'd be their dutiful daughter, strong as the soldier they'd trained me to be, with my emotions forever under control. Yes, I would corral myself, follow the rules that had been laid out for me. I would do it for Kimmie.

A pigeon, cooing, brought me out of my meditation. I watched as it swayed back and forth on its branch. Another bird echoed the call, harshly and slightly discordantly. I laughed bitterly to myself. Harsh and discordant. Yes, that was my destiny. Well, so be it. Kim was gone. Most likely he had never been with me all these years. Rather, he was a figment of my imagination. For all I knew, perhaps Kasho was, too. They'd both left together, which must indicate something. Snapping out of my self-indulgence, I moved one hand off the basket's edge to wipe tears from my cheeks.

At this point Daisy turned back from walking ahead and, facing me, exclaimed, "Sorry for being so preoccupied. You look overburdened. Here, let *me* take the picnic basket now. It's time I did a bit of work!"

When she reached out her hands, I saw 'long grass' scrawled across one palm, just like the marks when I first met her. I was so good at hiding my emotions, it was hardly pretense to point to the words as she unburdened me, and casually ask, "When did you write that?"

"This morning. I was making a note to talk with you about a waking dream I had of you," Daisy replied. "You were dancing barefoot in grass, with red shoes tied around your neck. As a result, I've already begun to compose music that sounds like wild grass waving in the wind but I want *you* to write the lyrics."

Staring at the words on Daisy's hand, I remembered what I had till now forgotten, "When you and I first met at the dress shop, you had some black marks on your hand. Do you remember what they were?"

"Oh, yes, my beautiful blind Scotch terrier back in the States. His name, Charlie," Daisy explained. "I miss him. I was reminding myself to finish writing a song about him."

"I miss my dog too," I whispered. "But, please, I'd like to know about yours."

Daisy sighed. "When I used to take Charlie for walks at home, we'd race among the dry hills. He'd charge at high speed in one direction, and I'd hurry in front to catch him. He used to wriggle like crazy in my arms. It meant so much to him that he believed he'd found me again by himself, despite his blindness. However," she brightened and continued, "the song I'm writing has us playing in a field of giant yellow dandelions. My parents are looking after him now. They *have* to love Charlie, whatever he and I do—we're family. Though I had a happy childhood, I wanted to see the world. Enough about my dog. Tell me about your own."

I nodded, at last accepting that I had to take my turn graciously. I had to talk about Black Dog. I was impressed by how much Daisy's family loved Charlie, especially in her absence. Describing Black Dog to Daisy took me back to Australia, reliving that day I came home from school to find my father waiting by the gate.

"Little Misery, I have something to tell you," he said.

"Is it Black Dog?" I immediately asked.

My father had looked taken aback at my thinking so immediately of my dog. A wave of rage passed over his face and then was gone.

"What?" he demanded.

"Is it one of the animals?"

"Yes, it's your idiotic Black Dog. He was lying in the sun, of course, in my truck's path as usual. I was fed up, so I ran over him. Your mother took him off to the vet, and he's back now looking a little sick. But he's quite all right really. Just like you, your dog is always getting in my way—"

I dumped my school bag in the laundry part of the house and went to Black Dog. I found him in his big basket in the garage, curled tightly like a thin ball, a vacant expression in his soft dark luminous eyes. He didn't seem to recognize me, only to be reliving a nightmare.

I overheard my father demanding of my mother, "She wasn't crying, was she?"

"It's quite natural," replied my mother's voice. "It was the shock."

"She ought to get out of my sight forever. I'm quite disgusted."

My mother came in and explained, "The vet said his liver and kidney are ruptured. We are to keep him quiet and he might recover."

I loved my mother for that. She didn't like people, but relaxed and could be more her true self around animals. I thanked her from the bottom of my heart.

All that night, I lay beside Black Dog. I could feel immense tension in him, and feel him fighting to bear the pain inside. Every time I looked at him his eyes, wide open, contained blank fear, confirming that he was living only within himself.

From time to time I fed him glucose and water in a teaspoon, for he wouldn't eat or drink.

Next day being Saturday—no school—I managed to carry his whole basket outside for a while, and the transformation was wonderful! He sniffed the air, crawled onto grass, wagged his tail and panted with a smiling look in the sun's heat.

But his tongue was brownish purple as he hung it out, and his eyes like opaque lanterns retained their look of fear.

He drank a little milk by himself.

By evening he'd gained enough strength to go around his favorite haunts, lifting his leg at every tree—but nothing happened. At last he lay flat and howled wolf-like long into the air. I knelt by him in the gathering darkness, stroking him and sobbing quietly. Eventually he was able to urinate a little, without seeming to move a muscle. I took my blouse off and used it to gently wipe his hind legs, which were a little messy. Then I carried his body back to his basket. He lay perfectly still, his eyes hidden by a blanket. And died.

Telling Daisy the gist of the incident had meant exposing my soul to her, but she said nothing. After throwing me a shocked glance, she simply kept her eyes fixed on our way forward. Through fine mist then denser cloud, which thinned again, the end of a low stone wall showed itself. It turned out to be snaking along the inner, path side of a hedge's slim base. I expected that this wall would soon become a good place to sit down. Sure enough, in keeping with the rest of the Boboli Gardens' sculptured hedges, the hedge behind the wall grew taller, and stuck forward at the top—the way the upper story of an Elizabethan half-timbered house juts over a road—sheltering us.

I climbed onto the wall then but, through my dress, the wide stonework felt cold and damp under me. Devastated by the severity of my friend's silence, I curled my ankles back and sat on them, pondering. It occurred to me that I had murdered my dog by hesitating to train him better. I failed to add to his chastisement because my parents had thrashed him for going near so many things he had not intended to touch. Now, however, I couldn't cope with what I saw as Daisy's condemnation, which echoed my own. Oh, what a wretched creature I was. Probably not even Christopher would want me when he found out the truth of my failures.

Daisy dumped the basket, a smaller version of my dog's but with a handle, beside me on the wide wall, and quietly indicated a painted wooden sign thrown onto a heap of leaves: "Lost—green and red parrot! Reward 20,000 lire." I wondered if the harsher coo I heard earlier, in answer to a pigeon's, had been this parrot's. My thoughts explored whether or not the accidentally freed bird *wanted* to be found. Despite its owner obviously valuing its company, wouldn't this bird's senses expand in the presence of tall trees, sunshine and other birds? The answer became very important.

"You know," Daisy bent to remove her shoes, "when you and I met at the gardens' edge today, it felt like ages since I'd last seen you."

That had been my own reaction, but I didn't feel like answering. Instead, I distracted my friend by lifting the cloth off our picnic in the basket. Watching, Daisy sat easily on the basket's other side. She reacted with "Yum!" as mingled aromas strongly arose, dominated by sweetness. With obvious pleasure, she wriggled her whole body, even her stocking toes in the squelchy mud. "Please give Giovanna and Bruna my thanks for making such a wonderful picnic," she said. "I can hardly wait to get to that fresh apple tart!" She began slicing rolls to make *panini.* I eyed the delicious looking Italian flag colors Bruna and Giovanna had provided for each *panino's* filling—green basil, white *mozzarella di bufala,* and red tomatoes.

Then, not distracted for long, Daisy dreamily chose to continue her earlier thought, "I don't know what it is." Seated on the wall, she went on, "Perhaps that my hours with you are longer than anything else I do. Before and after them, I tend to rush."

I hesitated for many minutes before answering. However, eventually, I managed to switch into a new compartment of my brain as I'd done earlier today, as my parents had brought me up to do in crises, so that I could cope with the social situation that Daisy was foisting on me. I even tuned into her point of view. "There's calmness in our being together," I said.

"That's it!" Daisy agreed.

"Two different worlds combining," I suggested, warming to the subject as I uncovered a jam jar of olive oil. I spread the oil with the back of a spoon into Daisy's sliced rolls. "And yet, with most people I meet, it's also two different worlds. So *that* can't be the explanation."

"Yes, I've noticed you respond to strangers from all walks of life like family, as I do too. Sometimes you need to be careful, though."

I heard a slight stomach noise, and felt angry with my body for betraying me. Immediately, I murmured, "I'm sorry."

Daisy replied, "It's me."

162

"Oh, well." I laughed uneasily. But the freedom of talking about the body with Daisy was still so new and wonderful that I felt myself relaxing. "You and I speak on many levels," I contributed.

I freed my legs and swung them while we continued to converse. "How are your parents?" I asked.

"Funny you should mention them just now," Daisy replied, "because the only other person I always felt I hadn't seen for ages was my mother, when I came home after working all day. You hold a similar quality for me. Time outside time. I'll think about things over the next few days, try to gain insight into what's going on."

"It's a spiritual thing," I prompted, relaxing totally into sincerity at last. "It has to be."

"But *always* when human beings meet," objected Daisy, "it's a spiritual thing."

Like a chill wind from the past, Christopher's telephone call had made me think about more ancient values than Daisy's, and surely that was best for me now. Those values would surround me when I returned to Australia. I might as well get used to the cruelty of them, because I planned to be cruel to myself by returning. So I pointed out, "Try telling *that* to monks and nuns in the middle ages. They used to shut themselves *away* from everyday people so as to give their spiritual lives a chance."

Daisy rolled her eyes in my direction and produced a secret-looking smile. "But such customs are turning upside-down now, my friend," she stated in the tone of one expressing an acknowledged fact. Having finished preparing, with tomato, cheese and basil, a *panino* I'd given back to her after oiling it, she nestled it into my hand. "More and more, we're realizing that we're all one. If a baby hears another baby cry, it feels the crying as having come from itself. The baby is right. When friends, strangers or even people from different races or religions— including former enemies—come together these days, we most

163

often bring out the best in each other. At least, we do in *my* world. It's wonderful to experience."

I drew my breath in. Once again, Daisy had confirmed that she already lived and moved in the world I had only envisioned as the future. Leaving her and returning to Australia to live with Christopher meant I would never know it. I would always be an outsider, watching others achieve my best hopes and dreams. Why had I even thought I could go against my parents' wishes and achieve them anyway?

"I must say, if you and I work together, I won't see the results as coming solely from us," Daisy added, confirming my thought. "I think spirits from other dimensions are guiding whichever hands happen to be available at the time. Because it is all God's plan. We are like little children building sandcastles, with grownups helping us."

My ears pricked up. Daisy sounded just like Kasho talking. How had she come upon such an idea? Needing to escape my own narrowing thoughts of the future, I asked, as she took a swig of *acqua spumante*, "How has your week been? How are things at the dress shop?"

"Oh, the usual. I love my work. Yesterday evening I shopped for groceries. But you are making shallow conversation with me, and I know why."

Oh no, she didn't, not fully. I ignored Daisy's reproach, and continued both to probe and to make polite conversation. "Did you do anything this morning other than compose music, and call me?" Unintentionally, I'd let an angry edge creep into my voice.

"Yes, something happened this morning. I'm really sorry. It's made me too preoccupied to be good company today." Daisy gulped down a mouthful of roll, then shocked me by changing the subject. "It's not only me, though. What about you? *You* are different today. What has changed *you*?"

I felt that Daisy had begun opening up to me, at last freeing me to express what was really upsetting me. "When first I saw you," I explained, "I wanted very, very much to tell you about a certain telephone call. And now I can't." In my mind, I smelled Christopher's humiliating roses, but wasn't sure I'd tell Daisy anything now. I pulled back, forgetting about her having echoed Kasho. I knew Daisy wouldn't like my news.

Daisy spread her arms out wide, palms uppermost. "Of course, you can tell me," she encouraged. "I'm very sorry. Now I'm listening. And I want to apologize for being too shocked to respond about your dog. Can you forgive me? Probably not. I sense that my failure to answer then is making you angry now. You *are* angry, aren't you?" Tears flooded her eyes. "I just couldn't bear thinking about what happened to you. Oh, poor Black Dog! Poor, poor Melissa! My God! Nothing like that occurs in a normal family." She held her arms out to me. I did not react.

My indignation was too difficult to express. I'd known no other family than mine, which I thought of as only a bit abnormal. How dare Daisy attack it just now? Much to my surprise, I found myself blurting out, "I've decided to please my mother and father, so I'm marrying the man of their choice." With these words out of my mouth, I felt amazingly relieved. It felt more and more that returning to Australia and marrying Christopher represented a need of my innermost being. The relief I felt was so wonderful that I concluded this was the case. I half remembered Kasho's words, "Your behavior *must* come from that." No more fighting myself, or running from my parents.

"What?" Daisy demanded, recoiling. Then, after a pause, "Tell me about this guy."

"There's nothing to say," I admitted. "I know hardly anything about him, except that he loves me to distraction. You should have heard the things he said on the telephone today! I can't—I really can't—bear to think of someone loving that much and not being requited. If I am strong enough, and manage to see things clearly and keep my feet on the ground, I might even be

165

able to save him from having his character twisted by the worst excesses of the society I've come from."

"You *are* joking, aren't you?" Daisy asked earnestly. "You don't mean it?"

I reiterated firmly, "Yes, I do."

Daisy's voice took on a tone more solemn than I'd ever heard from her, uttering words strange to me, "I believe in reciprocity, where both people love each other equally." Her words made me think of Kasho's and my love, but I knew that dealing as best I could with my life on Earth did not mean betraying his and my long-term future. And as for Kim—well, all that was fantasy anyway. I was too old to need some pretend brother, just as, according to my parents, I had always been too old for toys.

"Safety means a lot to me," I stressed. In that moment I felt virtuous, stating my family's point of view. After explaining all about the telephone call, I asked, "Daisy, can't you see that I've been handed on a plate a magical solution that will make everybody happy—my parents, Christopher and me—and fulfill all our desires?"

"Not unless you desire to die. Do you *want* to lose your soul? Your father and mother tried to make you become mindless and heartless, I think. But you resisted. Your spirit has survived till now. So why are you deciding to jump into a grave that others have dug for you? It seems to me that your parents' huge efforts to keep you away from reality have all been unnecessary. *You* have grown skilled at keeping *yourself* away."

I pulled my feet onto the wall again and stood up, feeling as if I were perched on a diving board. I waved my arms around for balance, and fixed my eyes on Daisy's. For an instant, sunlight blazed behind her, blinding me. "I'll *never* be worthy of your world," I wailed. "Never, ever. I've been too well trained. I'm not sociable enough, not relaxed enough. I want to serve, but don't know how. I don't know how to *do* anything! Feeling strong and secure is foreign to me. I have no idea of how to

166

behave in your culture. I can't cope with all the love. It's too strange for me. All I know is to sacrifice."

"But *not* to the past! If your sacrifice is a gift to God, yes," exclaimed Daisy. Attempting to touch my shoulder, she instead knocked our wonderful picnic basket to the ground. But we were both oblivious to the sight of food falling out. "Tell me, what does a piece of iron in a blacksmith's fire sacrifice to be made into a horseshoe?"

"I can't think," I said.

"Exactly."

"I suppose the iron gives up hardness for malleability, coldness for heat, darkness for light and uselessness for usefulness."

"Are you doing that? Or possibly the reverse?"

I couldn't think at all.

Once, long ago in Australia, my horse made a big pile of manure, then turned around and bucked me head first into it. I felt as if a hillock of manure were below us now, beckoning me irresistibly to plunge into its filth. And plunge I did, though I remained on the wall.

Daisy moved closer, as I went on, "I just want to be *safe.* I can't face going back to live with my parents. My marrying the man they recommend is a solution that would make them happy at last. If I remain in Italy, my parents will cut off my allowance and there's no way I'd accept money from them in that situation, anyway. Married to Christopher, I'd probably have enough money to help the world. And if life with him gets too much for me, I believe—though I admit I could be wrong—he'd understand if I shut myself away to write.

"But if I stay here in Italy, I'll be leaping into the Unknown, with nothing—no support, almost with no clothing."

Holding out her arm to steady me, Daisy locked pitying, tear-filled eyes on mine. "I don't know what your parents did to you, to make you lose courage today. I'm aware that I hardly know anything of what your folk did. But it is *not* a sin to have a positive impact on the world. And a loving being always used to whisper in my brothers' and sisters' and my ears at night to tell us that lack of love is insanity."

"You know about Kasho?" I exclaimed, incredulous at Daisy's calm demeanor.

"Did he come to you, too, when you were young?" Daisy asked, transformed, her wet eyes shining. "That's wonderful! That we have something so primal in common. Yes, when all of us children were little, we got used to him talking with us every night. He was so kind! He maintained a special relationship with each one of us which deepened towards his time of saying goodbye, when he left us well equipped to grow on our own. I know he whispers to a lot of children at night. It can't be easy. I bet it's very hard work. But his heart is in his work while he is doing it."

"How do *you* feel about him?" I asked, a bit jealous.

"When he first turned up, of course, I was scared but then he told me such exhilarating things! He told us all stories of his childhood. Such a happy upbringing, full of laughter, love and life, in an enchanting forest! I feel immense love for the man and his generosity of spirit. And I believe I have you, my dear friend, to thank for his coming to me today."

"*Today?*"

"Yes. Just after phoning you," Daisy explained breathlessly, "I opened my door to the street, to get rid of kitchen smells from having cooked myself an American breakfast. I went back to my bedroom and sat alone with that door open, too, for a while, thinking about meeting you at the Boboli Gardens. And how we'd be picnicking *inside* a sculpture—the Boboli Gardens—thoroughly carved out of the hillside.

"Suddenly, a strong atmosphere of Kasho was beside me. I got the unmistakable feeling he was giving me his presence to comfort me, because something would go wrong when you and I met today. I almost called you to cancel our day. But the love, love, love and relaxation that came through from Kasho to me made me feel that whatever happened would strengthen my bond with you in the end."

All I could do was stare at Daisy. I was terribly afraid. She sighed and went on, "Absorbing the intense beauty here will help us, whatever comes. I feel as if I've been holding my breath for hours."

I dug my nails into my arm, to punish myself for my fury at knowing Kasho had been so recently with Daisy, and said, "These days, Kasho actually has *conversations* with me. He is willing to help me write lyrics."

"Does that sound as if he expects you to marry Christopher?" Daisy demanded with heavy irony.

"Don't you realize that my father has real power?" I hissed, wobbling on the wall. "He has business networks in every country. He can grab me like an octopus, so I might as well make the best of things."

Daisy kept her arm protectively in front of me. "What business could that be?"

I fell silent, not wanting to voice my suspicion that my father might be selling armaments.

Daisy glided off the wall and stood in the mud for a while, her posture impatient. But she then crouched to rescue the delicious-looking apple tart. Slowly and calmly, she looked up at me.

"I don't believe in arguments where one person tries to crush another," she sorrowfully stated. "I believe in us both having open minds, so that we end our discussion by reaching a wisdom of which neither of us was fully aware before. It's my fault that hasn't happened. I should have conceded that Christopher is probably a fine man, that he might even be right for you. But you've never even *dated* him. Don't you each *want* to find out what makes the other laugh or cry? Only then, you might

169

consider spending your lives together. *Please look at reality, Melissa!* Because it seems to me you're at the edge of change, and it's so terrifying you're leaping *back* into the past. That you are addicted to obedience. That you can't think straight."

"In the Christian marriage ceremony, a wife vows to obey her husband. And my mother sees obedience as a valid excuse for *everything* she does!" I stammered.

Daisy pointed out, "It would be much simpler and more sensible if a couple's wedding vows were made directly to God. Then the husband and wife would be equal partners."

I stared fiercely down into her eyes. "Well, now that we're talking about God—long ago, I promised God that I'd accept the very first man who loved me."

"Did God *ask* you for such a promise?"

"My parents *want* me to marry. They don't want me to do anything else. They pity and despise women who work."

"Work, where you do your best, is an offering to God. I want you to see with your own eyes, not through the eyes of others."

"But if I give my parents a present this big, surely they'll change towards me?"

"Oh, my God!" Daisy dropped the apple tart she'd been cradling and stood again, slipping on her shoes. "Are you *really* a child? I know you love your parents, and want to please them. So does everyone, and harmony in the family is a beautiful thing. But it's crazy to count on other people changing. You have to grow up; you *must* cut the umbilical cord. It's strangling you."

"If I asked Providence for more freedom than Christopher can give me," I whispered, "I would really be greedy. I've heard him talk like my parents in some ways, but more leniently. He is kind. He once scolded his friend for blowing cigarette smoke in my face! I won't forget that."

A spider web, jeweled with raindrops, stretched between two great trees, blocking an alternative route out of the gardens. At my eye level, the web held a trembling red-and-yellow leaf left

170

over from last autumn. Daisy now backed through, tearing the web.

"I can't talk with you when you're like this," she said. "I thought you were on the threshold of life, and might eventually meet a man who inspired you. But you seem to be twisting your creativity around to fit in with Christopher's ways, as far as you understand them—which is not much. I have one thing to say: an unhappy marriage has terribly destructive ramifications. Your parents had one, and I can't believe you're planning the same. Do you really think you would be happy? Do you think your children would be happy? Do you think you could make your mate happy in the long run? Could you help each other grow?"

My resentments of the day were building up—Daisy not responding about my dog, saying my parents were abnormal and her getting on too well with Kasho. So I fought as dirtily as I dared. "You're not understanding!" I flung as she backed further away. "You are so badly brought up, you have no idea how selfish and rude it is not to marry who your parents want! Do you realize what my parents would say if they knew of your friendship with me? They'd never let me see you again! They'd tell me 'Oh, she's nice enough—but not the kind of friend you'll have when you take your correct place in society.' They'd sneer at everything about you: your job, your clothes, your outlook, your mannerisms… They'd see them all as 'common', and a terrible influence on their daughter."

Daisy had begun striding away, but she glanced over her shoulder—then turned, stepping forward and looking me in the face, "You'll die fully conscious," she pronounced bitterly. "It will be a slow death. From your tiny jail, you'll hear of my doings, *Signora la Contessa*'s doings, the doings of my home country, the United States, where life is booming now, where opportunity abounds. You'll likely hear of songs I've written that I hope are played all over the world. You might even write me gracious letters but it won't feel the same as having you by my

171

side. You'll give up a big life for a little life, and your archaic idea of duty will *cost* you your life."

My intuition, had I faced it, was also telling me I'd be unhappy. As a result of my perpetual stress, and their environment, it told me, my children would become heartless, and snigger about me among themselves. When they grew up, they'd continue living in my house off my loving hospitality. They'd worm my dreams out of me and prevent me from realizing them. I would be afraid to do anything I believed in for fear of offending my children.

Everyone around me would ignore my soul, having covered their own souls with layers of dust. My children would fight over my Will among themselves in front of my living body until I felt dead already. And it would all happen because I died today in spirit.

"Turn your back on the past, Melissa," I heard Kasho encourage in my head. "It's dangerous for you. I want to save you. Just hold my hand."

But I could not, of course—either physically or spiritually. Nor could I return to calm thoughts. "What's between you and Daisy?" I shouted unreasonably, jumping off the wall onto the already muddy apple tart that Daisy had dropped. I watched it vanish into filth. "You promised me that you and I would be together through all the worlds of God. Are you building yourself a harem now?"

I gathered that Daisy couldn't feel Kasho in these gardens. But she knew, all right, at whom I was shouting.

"I don't have to take this," she muttered. "Call me if you need me, Melissa, because I'll always care. We have been like sisters, but now you have sunk into denial." Her gray form melted, silently, into greater gray as if into a dimension, filled with expressionless snowy shapes, which I could not enter.

"It's all right, my girl," Kasho comforted me after she'd gone. "Imagine you're a child, and I'm kissing your skinned knee

172

better. Don't worry, my girl, I understand how you're feeling. You are bringing tears to my eyes but, also, what you just said about my harem was very funny!" And he began to laugh, hugely and long. His laughter did not stop before I desolately left the gardens.

Chapter Eleven
A Night Visit

The *palazzo*'s wrought iron gates stood wide open as, panting after climbing the steep hill, I eventually trudged through. I spied, below the arched *palazzo* doorway far beyond the gates, a mist-distorted blurry figure whose shape slimmed as I drew near. Swishing past me, a black taxi made me jump. By the time I reached it, the car's driver had stepped out. Our feet crunched on the gravel alternately as he walked around to open a passenger door for what turned out to be the waiting Nicole.

She called, "Are you all *right*, Melissina? You're *crazy* to be wandering around in this weather. They're crazy in there too!" She jerked her head towards the *palazzo* doorway.

I stumbled to her, almost breathless. "What are they doing?"

"Playing a stupid game but I might have put a stop to it now. You know our *Contessa* placed candelabras everywhere this morning, trying them out for our coming ball? Robin, Roland, Karen and Julie have been taking the candles out and bringing them closer and closer to each other's necks, saying 'Let's see whether you are brave or not.'"

Though I drew a deep breath of concern for my friends as I visualized the drama, it challenged something old—reminding me of the hour, soon after we arrived in Australia, when my father used a poisonous spider like a yoyo. It had repeatedly climbed up its spun thread to his hand, only to be repeatedly jerked slightly down. Watching my face intently for any sign of fear, he had given the thread to me, aged six, and ordered me to play with the spider in the same fashion.

Most mornings, my father tested my courage. I soon learned what was expected of me in situations like the one Nicole described.

"Well? Could anyone stand the flame?" I asked hopefully.

"Don't be ridiculous. Julie taunted Roland, saying, 'Show us how brave you are.' But he sensibly answered, 'Don't. I'm *not* brave.' I spoke more calmly when Robin tried to do it on me. I let everybody know I could go on, but there was no point. I advised them to stop, Melissina. But I warn you, just in case! I'm off now for a fitting of my Ferragamo shoes!"

She slid her body, waist first, into the taxi, the driver shut the door and they noisily drove away.

"Hi, Melissa!" Roland grabbed my arm when I burst into the small sitting room. "Do you know what we've been doing?"

"Putting candles beside each other's necks," I muttered.

"Ah! Nicole told you. Would you like me to try on you? Go on—a girl must suffer for her boy."

I removed his hand from my arm. The candlelight spread an atmosphere of holy preparation.

"Don't involve her!" exclaimed Karen. "She looks awful! What happened, Melissa?"

"I'd *like* to play your game," I asserted, desiring to repeat the only kind of situation in which, as a child, I'd occasionally been praised. No soldier would have said to his commanding officer during the War, "I can't do what you have ordered, because it will hurt." And no child of my father's would say that either! Both my parents had taught me, "Never disgrace us by being merely human."

Human is exactly what, according to Nicole, my friends in the little sitting room had been! However, as a child I'd heard adults constantly praise British soldiers who, under torture, had not betrayed their comrades. My parents had expected similar self-control from me.

Roland pushed back my hair; and, dislodging a candle, held it to my cheek. He looked questioningly into my eyes.

"The flame didn't touch me," I told him.

"Oh," he said. He moved, and I felt pain.

Once he'd returned the candle to its holder, I remarked, "Yes, you certainly *did* touch me that time."

Roland shook my hand ceremoniously. "You're *brave*," he stated.

But what, I wondered, had been brave about enduring a burn? In my own view, I'd cheated, because the flame had not hurt nearly as much as everyone present appeared, from their admiring faces, to assume. My courage had not really been tested, and I was far from worthy of going home to face either Christopher or my parents.

Disgusted at my own imposed cowardice, wanting to prove myself to myself, I pushed behind Roland and shoved my wrist out over a candelabra on the small table there.

The middle fire parted itself in a semicircle around my wrist. I waited to hear sizzling and smell flesh melting, to have the satisfaction of mortifying my body like the heroic saints of old.

Open mouths, like dark holes, floated around me. From them, many different voices called, "You're insane!"

Strong hands pulled me back, and Karen or Robin yelled in my ear, "Promise us you'll never do that again!"

Pain and balm, day and night. Night and day, balm and pain. Anguish and soothing confusion, soothing confusion and anguish. Daisy and my other friends. My other friends and Daisy. Dark and light, light and dark. What have I done to her? What have I done to myself? What has she done for me? I admit my cheek hurts and my wrist throbs, but my greater anguish is how

I've treated Daisy. My deep confusion is how my friends are treating me.

Yesterday I was the luckiest person in the world. I had Daisy, I had wise, tender, sincere Kasho, I had my beloved Countess. Beautiful people had been my family, my bodyguard. In a new beautiful country. And I threw it all away, because my old-fashioned past returned to haunt me.

Amidst an assortment of pillows and blankets that they'd carried in, Julie and Nicole were sprawled over my tower room floor. Karen filled my four-poster bed—on her back, snoring with her arms spread wide, one of them squashing me.

In a mock male voice, raising the edge of her blanket, Julie invited Nicole, "Come and keep me warm!"

Without stirring, Nicole made the concession of returning her banter with, "Darling, this is so sudden!"

I sported a cooling magic balm on my burned wrist. I'd heard of sleepovers, but of course my parents had never permitted one. Fun seemed to be in the air, and I didn't know what to do with it. Surely what I deserved was not care, but severe punishment— doubly so, as my injury had been self-inflicted. I'd always been punished for stupidity if I accidentally hurt myself, and had learned long ago not to admit to either emotional or physical pain, which was why even my peers—who, I assumed, wished me well—could so often hurt me unknowingly. But that was far from happening now.

What *was* this lightness in the air? All my life, I'd wanted to find a different kind of humor from that of my parents, who used laughter for only one purpose: to put people down. Members of the society in which I'd grown up pretended too much—had been proud of their insincerity when they flattered those whom they joked about in private. My situation now felt too good to be true. Here I lay, surrounded by a sense of humor apparently innocent of racist or class hostility. A sense of humor which, like Kasho's,

I at last knew suited me. Utterly confused, I ended by curling like an animal into a ball on my empty pillow.

"Why are you doing that?" Karen asked. As I thought, she was only pretending to snore.

"To give you room to sleep comfortably," I said.

"You don't need to," she said, but without moving.

In shadowy form, Kasho now surprised me by appearing through my open bedroom door. I understood all too easily why I hadn't been aware of him in my time of crisis—I'd gone mentally, emotionally, physically and spiritually back so far into my parents' world that nothing positive could have gotten through. But now he leaped across my broad room, over my friends' heads. He landed on the wooden staircase that led to the water tank above my ceiling, opened his arms wide and declaimed like a tenor opera singer:

"When I stand up on these stairs and see your friends all round me,
Melissa sweet, my heart is full, and I'm so glad you found me—
Every time I stand up here and see the faces round me.
Children of Mother Earth, we belong to each other!
I feel for you, and you feel for me.
Denizens of Mother Earth, we belong to each other!
I feel in this lovely room how your world shall be."

Swept up in the moment, despite my worries, I began to giggle. But Karen asked, "Melissa, is the radio on downstairs?"

"Can you hear it too?" Julie burst out.

"A faint but definite tune," Karen replied.

I stuffed the pillow corner into my mouth, to stifle my mirth.

In a tone of horror, Nicole exclaimed "Oh, *merde*!" Having thus resorted to her native language, she scrambled to her feet. "Shi-it!" she translated with emotion, mispronouncing the swearword—"*Je crois que* I felt the ghost! *Un homme ancien* who bent over me!"

Kasho protested, with a big grin, "I didn't! I'm nowhere near her! And I'm not *that* old!"

"He's leaned over me twice now!"

"No one in town ever said the ghost was an old man," objected Karen.

"Whatever it is!" Nicole allowed for a possible change of sex and age. "Why did I ever come here?"

"To make sure Melissa is okay through the night," Julie said.

"You two can do that," complained Nicole.

"To show Melissa we truly love her," Karen threw in.

Trying in vain to absorb what this might mean, I shut my eyes.

"Just as *I'm* here out of love," I heard Kasho murmur close. "We all love each other! Hooray!" I tried hard to feel his breath tickle my ear—recalling his bear hug from when *both* our spirits left our bodies.

"But Melissa *attracts* ghosts!" Nicole answered Karen tensely. "I'm absolutely rigid! *Mon Dieu!* How will I ever get to sleep?"

I opened my eyes in surprise when Julie volunteered, "Maybe what we thought might be singing was a mosquito."

I saw Kasho make a playfully indignant face, then leap onto a small cupboard. My spontaneous chuckling at such a vision must have jarred the others.

"It will all seem so silly in the morning," sighed Nicole.

"Morning!" I thought with a shock. Morning would come without Daisy. *Night and day, balm and pain. Daisy and my other friends...*

When I burned myself, Roland took my hand by the fingertips and said, "I do not consider myself a coward, but I'd never do that. You've spoiled something beautiful. Tomorrow your wrist will have an ugly suppurating lump, at the very least.

And I'd never mark my cheek." Now I thought about Daisy, and how I'd spoiled something beautiful there, something far more important than my wrist. I wondered to which lucky human beings her life would be of service now. I knew that if I saw her I'd only break her heart again. I didn't trust myself with her. I was too full of anger and hurt and a drive to repeat only what I had known.

Giving up trying to understand myself, or why my companions were around me—but consoled by their presence anyway, despite my deep sorrow—I lapsed into a sleep of exhaustion.

The days following moved slowly. I willed intensely for Daisy to telephone me. The girls continued to fuss over me, which I found as confusing as ever.

One night, my own screaming awakened me. I'd been dreaming I was chained instead of Kasho in his dungeon, where the stone pillars were also trees. Our dungeon, of course, was almost level with water. I could hear it close by, whooshing up through the pockmarked floor from the blowhole. My compassionate jailor, Mossiface, was about to pass me as, limping heavily, he dragged and kicked something like a dead sheep towards the hole.

Once in front of me, he glanced up with wounded, terrified eyes. For some reason, I nodded.

He shoved little, kangaroo-like arms under the body he'd been dragging, and held it straight out. Realizing that it was Christopher, I nodded again.

After he'd laid the body across my knees, Mossiface's expression changed to my father's menacing one, and he grabbed my chained leg.

My eyes shot open, and I realized Robin was stroking my bare leg. "Oh, you scream now when an unknown hand grabs you," she said, "but you should be pleased. I would be. I should have tried massaging your stomach instead. If I stroked your stomach, as the man who grabbed my arm when I ran away from home did to me, you'd be giggling and squealing in delight, doubled up—yeah, you'd be heaving and squirming, kicking out with all your might."

"No—" Recently, I'd toyed with the idea that marrying someone of my parents' choice would suit my temperament. Knowing I was married would stop men from misunderstanding my friendliness. However, after my horrific dream tonight, I had to face the fact that in such a situation my private life with my husband might keep me forever screaming inside. I hadn't thought at all about how it would be. Certainly I would not be getting away from my father.

"Why are you here?"

"Oh, the hospital rang. The other girls and I were coming in from a film—*A Farewell to Arms*. It's not bad. Your Chris Collins is in the men's psychiatric ward of Santa Maria Nuova."

I sat up and shook my tousled head. "What's going on?" I asked in disbelief, as if she had not spoken.

"It's true. Would I come all the way up here at this hour for nothing? His wallet contained your name, and our *palazzo's* address and telephone number. Apparently he went crazy on the train from Rome, then passed out for a bit. When the train reached Florence, the police took him off."

"The poor man. But why's he here? I don't want him here." I hadn't known this till now. And I was not awake enough to choose my words.

"Are you aware of what they say in Italy about people from our country? 'A mad Australian!' And you *are* insane. Do you want to be a bachelor girl all your life or something? I like anyone in trousers, and I think most girls feel the same."

"I give you Christopher, then." Robin's hurtful comments had told me that, in her view, I'd never stopped being a freak.

"He's yours. Half your luck! Well, I've done my job—you know where he is. Do what you like about it. I'm going to bed."

"Wait! Tell me what made him go crazy."

"A fellow passenger said it happened after he drank a bottle of local red wine. It was in one of the picnics that get sold through the window when trains pull into stations. Chris must have fooled himself into believing he was on holiday from his usual problems."

"What problems?" My curiosity surprised me.

"He's allergic to alcohol. Didn't you know? Everyone in our parents' social circle knows that. Where've you been all your life? Locked away like a precious jewel?"

"I know nothing about Christopher."

"All I can say to that is, 'You'd better learn fast.' Bye now. I'm off to lie in the arms of Morpheus—god of sleep."

And she charged off like a train. Half stunned, I moved to the edge of the bed and sat there for a while, engulfed by something like despair. My legs felt paralyzed.

"Forgive me—I only want to help—but I believe you need to take action," Kasho commented in my head.

"Oh, Kasho, I'm so glad you're here at last! Why did Robin *do* this to me?" I demanded. "Surely she's realized by now that I can never fall asleep after I'm awakened. Am I supposed to sit or lie here doing nothing till morning? Worrying about that man? Getting more stressed? Unable to have a bath downstairs without waking the others, unable to have breakfast? Maybe the train arrived late, as usual, and maybe the hospital staff only just got around to going through Christopher's things. But why couldn't Robin have left telling me till morning?"

Kasho said calmly, "Little Mystery, you can count on me whenever things get too much. It's hard for Robin to imagine how anyone feels except herself. Your Countess has been counseling her, but it takes a long time for someone to change fundamentally. Tell me, what do you want to do now?"

"I've never been out alone at night," I confessed, "but I *want* to see Christopher."

"You will be far from alone. All your life, the spiritual realm will guide and protect you. And so will I."

"I've never flouted our Countess' unwritten rules before. I love her."

"It's totally your decision. If you'd prefer not to go now, morning will do fine. But I have the feeling you won't wait."

"It must be nearly midnight," I quibbled. "And I don't know what room he's in at the hospital."

"Be like us!" Kasho encouraged. "Nobody ever gives an indigenous person on my planet directions where to go. When beginning a journey, we just relax, say 'I'm in your hands' and let our ancestors of the spirit world guide us—let our intuition lead us to our destination. 'Turn here, turn there, go straight ahead' our intuition will say, and, 'This is the place!' Though I am no ancestor, I'm asking you to put your confidence in me. I will guide you."

Slowly I lowered myself to the floor, and walked to my wardrobe, opening its door. Clearly, I had made up my mind, without consciously doing so, that now was a reasonable time to visit Christopher. "What will I wear?" I asked, dazed.

"You'll be telephoning for a taxi," said Kasho. "And, when the driver arrives, you must impress him that you're in control of what you're doing. After that, and especially, you'll need to let the hospital officials know you mean business."

"Yes," I agreed, "I am no longer a naïve waif of a girl. I'll wear the tailor-made suit I've hardly ever put on since arriving in Florence. And I'll stick that graceful gold-and-diamond brooch I never wear in its lapel."

"Of course, I'll look the other way while you dress," promised Kasho.

First, I had a good wash at the goose-necked basin. Something happened to me there in my room, beneath the stairs that led to the water tank. I lifted my head to the small mirror above the basin, and saw my eyes radiating light. I felt as if my naked arms had grown to giant size, containing all the strength in the world. Through my tower wall, I saw clouds in the night sky vibrating.

All my life I had been impractical, but not now. The sensation filled me that, from this moment on, every word my body spoke would be tremendously fluent, significant and right.

"Ah! *Amore!*" exclaimed the affable taxi driver, after I'd explained that I was traveling to see an *amico* at present in the men's psychiatric ward of Santa Maria Nuova *ospedale.* "Young love can work miracles," he said, as he took off with a terrific jolt. "Its power has brought a beautiful young girl out alone to face the dangers of night! The best poem in the world cannot describe the power of new love. It can conquer easily the greatest evils that terrify humankind—pain and death. Even if a man in love had to witness the world ending, he would merely squeeze his lover's hand a little more and contemplate with indifference the burning universe."

"I notice his reckless driving is not scaring you," remarked Kasho, with amusement, in my head.

"You said you'd look after me. What more could anyone want?" I sincerely replied.

"What a romantic and mysterious night it is tonight," my driver went on, but added, "You have an overwhelming shyness about you and that is tremendously attractive."

Something about me is overwhelming you, I thought, but I know it's not shyness.

"You'll find Santa Maria Nuova so beautiful, though seeing it in daylight is better," my driver continued, despite my having stopped paying much attention. "Our hospital is the oldest in Italy. It was established in the *trecento* by the father of Dante Alighieri's love, Beatrice. Its instructions to staff have always been that they shelter and tend the sick poor as they would Christ Himself. That they console them, and cater for their individual needs. Hoping for God's mercy after death, the saintly staff has a tradition of great kindness—huge numbers died during the plague years from nursing the sick poor in their homes."

Speeding down our zigzagging road, our car's headlights flushed out loving couples who had been leaning against the wall on our road's lower side. The embarrassed pairs reminded me, with a sad pang, of rabbits in Australia being spot-lit at night by shooters.

In a few minutes Christopher and I would meet. And the question performing a bright dangerous dance at the forefront of my mind was: what could he and I possibly say to each other? And what would be its implications?

"The new main entrance is still under construction," Kasho pointed out. "So get your driver to drop you off at the corner of Via Buffalini and Via dei Servi. That will suit us fine."

After paying the driver, I gave myself totally over to the spiritual realm—knowing that Kasho, too, would help me. I trusted the unseen world so implicitly that I never questioned, or felt the slightest fear, while climbing out of the cab. I moved under dimly-lit porticoes, and penetrated a hospital side entrance. The immense stillness within hit me as soundly as the morning heat at home did when I drew the curtains back. The arid, sterile hospital air hurt my nostrils. We ascended in an elevator and seemed to float through a silent passage or two much like those in any hospital.

A broad, uniformed night watchman with an alert but friendly face approached us from around a passage corner. He asked, with grave concern, "*Bella signorina,* why are you wandering these dark corridors at this deathly hour?"

I stated with dignity, "I've come to visit the Australian patient."

The watchman changed direction to walk beside me, and it felt wonderful having both Kasho and him helping me cope.

"How did you *do* that?" I asked Kasho. "This watchman appeared at exactly the right time!"

"Whatever time he appeared, I believe, you would think was right," Kasho replied. "And your whole world is on the brink of knowing how! You have total bodily existence, but are in an altered state. You are in tune with the entities in the spiritual realm. They *want* everything to happen smoothly, want you to witness Christopher tonight without interacting. My job is simply to facilitate this. My job's easy!"

"Kasho, are you telling me that *you* didn't organize the watchman turning up—*I* did?"

"Exactly, child of the future. Never, never underestimate the power of thought. One thought from a pure-hearted person can change your entire world overnight."

"Surely not one from me?" I objected.

"Always be aware of the invisible world helping you," Kasho replied. "You know already, as well as I do, that is the solution. And it's time I told you how impressed I was when I turned around in your tower room, finding you dressed and ready to go. You had the air of a strong mother. No one would have contemplated taking advantage of you then, as you sailed forth into the unknown. I saw the future you."

"I did feel I was having a powerful moment," I agreed. And sensed Kasho wink at me.

But, as we continued walking, the night watchman by my side warned companionably, "You know the patient's violent, don't you?"

I raised an eyebrow in surprise.

"Yes, yes!" The watchman underlined his statement. "It took four men to hold him!"

I almost burst out laughing. From my hazy memory of seeing Christopher, I'd thought he couldn't hurt a flea. But that was the impression many society men gave at my parents' parties. Bruna, her arms full of red and yellow roses, appeared in my mind, warning again, "*Signorina,* you have a lover who doesn't trust you." That recollection curbed my mirth. It even awakened suspicion that the behavior of some well brought-up men, behind closed doors, might be the kind of which no one dared speak.

Without replying to the night guard—but happy because, after all, I liked having my courage tested—I kept pace with him, pausing eventually when he did outside a tiny office at a corridor's end. My companion knocked, and stated my business to the gray-haired woman who opened the door. He took his leave when she led me into her office. She welcomed me with enthusiasm. "Please sit down – *s'accommodi*. We are already discussing Signor Collins's case." She introduced me to a man and a much younger woman, already there, seated. She herself, she said, was named Francesca Innocenti. All three looked worried.

Francesca Innocenti explained, "We believe Signor Collins has a psychiatric illness that will worsen with age, if it is not medically controlled."

I asked innocently, "Mightn't he just be allergic to alcohol?"

"His symptoms may abate if he keeps off it," Francesca Innocenti mused politely. "But I wouldn't count on that." Sitting among clutter, the three medical people subsequently carefully included me throughout their intensive discussion in Italian. I listened, answering at the right times. The man finally told me that, as Christopher had been uncontrollable, they'd been forced to give him an injection, and he would certainly not wake up until the next day.

The younger woman, whose name I'd forgotten, then led me to Christopher's bedside. "When you are ready," she assured me, "we'll call you a taxi. And our watchman will accompany you out."

Left alone, I contemplated the scene before me. My sleeping suitor was covered with a tight flat sheet, stark white from neck to toe. His pushed-out cheek and ash-blond, ethereal-looking hair were the only color I could see. Rebelliously, I tugged the sheet over him back, looking for a straitjacket—and felt relieved to see

187

none. In that moment, to me, the hospital staff's humanity was confirmed. I could hardly bear thinking of a living thing being confined. I hoped that, in Christopher's world of sleep, colorful unbroken horses were galloping through beautiful landscapes and waterfalls and spray-filled cloudy sky.

I glanced around. White ceiling, white walls, white beds, white floor. All other beds in the dazzling white room vacant. A white table and chair at the back. The white walls reminded me of the prison cell in the play about a rapist and a murderer that Kasho had helped me write so long ago. A thought struck me: Did Christopher, like the protagonist of Kasho's and my play, imagine he was the only person in the world with feelings? He certainly seemed to have strong enough feelings for us both. Words from the play entered my head: "I just keep on doin' whatever I'm doin'." Poor Christopher! How unreasonable of me to remember those words! But I recalled that our play had featured alcohol.

"So innocent-looking," I thought, watching Christopher's even breathing. "Yet, just by being here, he must be destructive. Poor Daisy whom I treated abominably and you, Kasho, and our Countess have tried to help me not look back but Christopher is making me look back. He destroys my heart, my mind and my soul in the name of love. Because I know now that it is my duty to spend my life with him. If his illness will worsen with time, it is my duty to care for and nurse him. Kasho!" I called in anguish.

He answered instantly. "Your decision must be respected. I have found out, if I didn't know before, that you, my Little Mystery, can be fully spiritually equipped and aware of souls helping you during your everyday life. You don't need my assistance. But I can't resist warning you. Don't let the straitjacket be around *you.* Don't let these walls cover *your* spirit with white from top to toe. Don't be the painted young girl in our play over whose head a thick knotted rope net was thrown. Like that girl, you would look upon your tormentor with a gentle smile and defiant eyes full of pain. Within, you are oceans, wild waterfalls, clouds and human beings comforting one another."

Because Kasho was only telling me what I partly needed to hear, I felt grateful for his consoling words but couldn't quite believe them. Anyhow, my attention had drifted away. The more I stared at my sleeping suitor, the more his jawline reminded me of Kim's. The sight was moving me profoundly.

"Yes," Kasho confirmed, picking up this later thought, "you are right. Christopher used to be a dear little boy. I would whisper in his ears at night. But, as he grew older, pressure from his parents and others proved too much."

I prompted Kasho, "He must have been terribly hurt."

"Oh, yes! He saw a calf's head in a bucket, and decided 'It must have been a very bad calf.' Sometimes, as a boy, he would cry all night, but now he doesn't feel pain—his own or anybody else's."

"You *did* put something in our play about him!" I acknowledged at last. And added, "I have seen the slow destruction of spirits too often among my parents' friends' children. I can't bear to think of it anymore. So many of us have become machines, and lost our humanity. We learned not to show our feelings—not to *have* feelings anymore. We lie and lie and lie."

After lessons next day, I was swimming vigorously in our *palazzo* pool, which overlooked Florence city, when Julie came to the side. "There's someone here to see you," she told me. "He's waiting in the hall."

I climbed out, shook my wet head, wrapped a rainbow-striped towel thoroughly around myself and slipped on gold sandals.

Disapprovingly, Julie looked me up and down. "You'll need to sneak in through the lower level side door and dress," she said.

"Climbing to my tower room takes forever," I replied. "You know I can't keep anyone waiting that long."

But I took a few steps backwards when I saw through the front door that my visitor was indeed Christopher.

His angular form rose from a bench in the hall's shadowed recesses, and his fair complexion turned more scarlet as he moved towards me. His clothes hung meticulously upon him, his fine hair looked newly-washed but his eyes were bloodshot. Redness wafted around, oppressed and captured me when he kissed me twice on the cheek. Appearances never worried me much—I reacted with pleasure to the individuality in each person's look—but at this moment the thought crossed my mind that I preferred Kasho's golden skin.

"At last!" my suitor exclaimed. "Melissa! You'll remember our meeting here all your life, won't you?"

I half smiled.

"I am your boy. Pretend we are the only two people in the world—male and female, thank God. I am your protector."

"Don't worry too much," Kasho, in my head, sounded both amused and serious. "If you need to, you can rely on me to protect you from your protector."

"How well do you love me?" my suitor now asked, with a confident smirk.

I shook my head.

"What! You don't love me?"

"No" I said coldly.

"You're playing games, after I've come all this way."

"Sorry," I whispered. I didn't know what to do.

"Your father told me you were madly in love with me."

I sighed. Would I ever escape my father?

Christopher struggled to clasp my hands, but I was using them to hold my towel around me. In order to avoid his touching me further, I relaxed my hand's grip on one side.

"The hospital staff told me you watched over my sleeping body last night," he went on, with a wry smile. "You came all that way in the night. I find such spontaneity endearing. I believe no one will ever understand you as I do."

I recoiled at the coldness in Christopher's touch. Holding his loose-skinned, bony hands had forced my towel to part, revealing too much, I felt, of my bathing-suited body.

"Yes." Christopher's eyes assessed my near-naked appearance. "You are beautiful."

"I'm not." I stepped back, pulling my hand from his.

"Why do you say that?"

"I don't feel it," I snapped, once more fully covering myself with the towel. I needed to change the subject. "Did you check out of the hospital today?"

"Of course. *And* I want you to have dinner with me tonight in the Grand Hotel, where I am staying."

"Have you spoken with the Countess?"

"Not yet."

"You should, because we always eat with her in the evening. I definitely can't join you."

"If you're not with me, I'll be lonely."

"I have homework to do anyway. I don't have time."

"My Melissa, we haven't seen each other for so long. Won't you eat with your boy?"

"I'll show you around Florence tomorrow. We can get to know each other—as friends."

"Tomorrow is Saturday, followed by Sunday. You can easily do your homework then, and come out with me tonight."

"No. Call for me tomorrow."

"We could go dancing after dinner, my Melissa."

"I'll have to ask *la Contessa's* permission tomorrow. And now, please excuse me. I'm really embarrassed. It's high time I changed out of my bathing suit. But I'll show you where the telephone is first, so you can call a taxi."

Flames appeared in my suitor's eyes. Curling his fingers and lifting his shaking fists towards my neck, the way my father used to do, he hissed, "I didn't travel all this way and suffer last night for nothing! Don't abandon me like cast-off clothing! Don't kick me out like a mangy dog!"

Heavy footsteps sounded. Christopher hastily gave in, through his teeth, "All right—show me where the telephone is, then."

Bruna flung a small door open and padded into the hall. "*Signorina*—" she began.

"Oh, Bruna. This is my friend Christopher from Australia. He needs to call a taxi. Would you please show him where to do it?"

Next morning during breakfast, Bruna leaned out of the dining room window and hailed the postman.

"Ciao, postino!" she called. "My name's Bruna! What is yours? Do you like me? It's a lovely day! Shall I come down?"

The postman shouted back, and Bruna left us in a hurry.

I barely had time to help myself to a smooth, freshly-baked roll and a glass of milk before she returned to hand me a telegram.

Full of apprehension, suspecting the message was from my parents, I tore open the special envelope, and read:

YESTERDAY WONT HAPPEN AGAIN – STOP – I COULDNT SLEEP TREATED YOU BADLY – STOP – AM IN FOREIGN LAND AWAY FROM FAMILY FRIENDS MY OWN PROPERTY OWN COUNTRY SEEING ONE I LOVE BEEN WITHOUT NEARLY YEAR – STOP – HARD TO KNOW WHAT TO DO OR SAY IN SUCH CIRCUMSTANCES – STOP – YOU ARE IN DIFFICULT POSITION TOO BEHAVED AS LADY SHOULD WHEN I INFLICTED INDIGNITY – STOP – HAVE GENEROSITY ACCEPT APOLOGY HEAL BAD FEELING = CHRISTOPHER

I guessed that my insensitive suitor, profiting from the reaction he expected his missive to stimulate, would be arriving at our school within an hour. He would expect me to introduce him to our Countess and request permission for us to go out together. And I knew that, for a while, I would have to play his game. Otherwise, news of my abominable manners would get back to my parents.

Christopher and I left the school together, having enacted the drama I'd predicted. I said, within myself, "See, Kasho? I can tell the future a bit, too!" and heard him chuckle.

Just outside our finishing school gate, a large seated tomcat was suckling furry outstretched Ombretta—who, I assumed, had secluded her most recent litter in the shrubbery behind. Ombretta's eyes were turned up in bliss, and the tom's paws went back and forth on her stomach. As my suitor and I walked down the *palazzo* hill in golden early morning light, I stopped to stare happily at the tableau.

"Don't look!" Christopher urged. "Those cats are disgusting! I'd like to kick that thing away with my shoe."

"Sukey is her fully-grown son. I thought the sight was rather nice," I remarked as we continued downhill.

Christopher contributed sourly, "It was unnatural."

Feeling a surge of tenderness, I asked, "You were never a 'mama's boy', Christopher, were you?"

"Boarding school at the age of six and proud of it. Best thing that happened to me. It made me a man."

"Well, *I'm* a teenager, and even at my age I still long for my mother to show love."

"The older boys used to torture the new children at night," Christopher continued his own train of thought. "A second pair of best friends would take over when the first lot stopped. Eventually, I found that I could do it too."

193

I gazed at him with sympathy. "Physical torture can't happen without mental torture," I observed. "Suppose I am punished regularly at seven p.m. I spend all day dreading that hour."

I bit my lip then, afraid of having hinted too much about my own childhood. Luckily, however, the hint seemed not to have penetrated Christopher's brain. Despite feeling sorry for him, I could not understand why this self-confessed bully had later failed to take new boys under his wing.

"I assume you got your homework done last night?" Christopher inquired with a sly grin.

"Enough," I admitted. "I'll finish it tomorrow."

"Does that mean I won't see you?"

A moment's pause. At last, here was my chance to tell Christopher I didn't need his company. But how? I couldn't. I felt trapped. My behavior would be reported to my powerful parents.

"I can spare an hour or two," I said.

"You didn't really want to come out with me today," he whined, seeking reassurance, I felt. "But I'm not so bad. You never asked me how my flight was, or if I'm comfortable in my hotel. Don't you *care?*"

That last jibe went straight to my heart, shaming me. I'd been too worried about how to handle this man to treat him like a human being.

But, just then, terrible wailing echoing around the thin terraced houses on our road's upper side, and the stone wall below gave me goose bumps, touched my soul and obviated any necessity to answer Christopher. "Oh!" he exclaimed immediately. "I've never heard anyone cry *like that* before! As if the world is rent in two, and everything noble has died horribly."

My own reaction was to leave him and run towards the violent, convulsive sobbing. Turning the next corner, I saw a hulk of a woman, with one eyelid sewn shut, the other eye bulging and a distorted mouth that a boot might have kicked in. Seated on a wide doorstep, she was rocking her huge body back and forth. A

194

crowd of little boys had gathered around the woman. Some stared and giggled, but most were throwing pebbles.

During the few seconds it took me to take in the scene, the tallest boy picked up a larger stone and said, "Let's throw harder and see what she does. At her face."

I hurled myself at the urchins, kicking in the direction of their shins, yelling *"Va via! Go away! Va via!"* But my actions were soon blocked by Christopher leaping in front of me with fists moving back and forth. "Don't come near my wife!" he shouted. "If you hurt her, you'll be sorry!" The children were already running away in all directions.

Aware of sweating profusely, I approached the woman, knelt by her and put my arm around her hell-racked body. I shoved a handful of thousand-lira notes into her pocket, stroked her hair and kissed her half-deformed blind-looking eyes. "Would you let me be your friend?" I asked timidly. "May I come to see you often?"

The woman clutched my stroking arm, and exclaimed, "Please don't leave me! Oh, please don't leave me! You don't understand. You are a true soul in this barren world, like me—and I am so alone! Though hundreds of so-called characters are around me every day, I'm still alone!"

Her words gained momentum. After a while, she was screaming and choking in such a rapid dialect—not Florentine—which I had to concentrate hard on. "Everyone's against me!" she groaned, slowing again. "They think it's such a joke, they don't mind! Everyone's against me. I am sick at heart, oh, I am sick at heart! Mountains have fallen upon me, and my enemies cry against me!" Her voice sounded Gypsy-like.

Everyone is alone, I mused, noticing out of the corner of my eye that Christopher was standing in profile throwing me worried looks. It is magnificent to watch, alone, I thought, the beating of spray on a rock or anything that brings awareness of God's wonders. But having dead, insincerely smiling faces all around—

195

that is the real, heart-rending loneliness. I knew that everything Kasho and Daisy had said was true—how, in Christopher's social circle, even if the faces were talking to me, I would be alone and always trying to fit in.

While I was kneeling, another realization visited me: "I come alive in the street." I whispered to the woman, "I suspect you are a widow who traveled far, possibly overcoming village prejudice, to marry a good man. That you have been loyal to your own heart."

Someone was pulling me back by the shoulders, almost lifting me up. Christopher hissed in my ear, "For God's sake, you've done enough! Stop! Stop now! Come away! Do you hear? You're insane! You're as crazy as this harpy!"

Outraged by Christopher's outlook, I stared at him with indignation. I'd been too long among people with enormous compassion not to feel shocked to the core of my being. I burst out, "If that's true, it's still no reason not to help! Don't you realize how cruelly you are hurting this poor woman? Don't make her more ashamed—she has no reason to be."

The woman's big, warm hand grew gentler on my arm. But, in my head, I heard Kasho say, "Are you planning to become a crazy old lady?"

The woman let go of my arm, moved her hand to her pocket and gave me a crooked smile. "You must get on with your *own* life," she said. "I feel better now. I'll meet you on another day, *non è vero?*"

I turned around and noticed that, the way I'd seen my father do countless times when he wanted to control a situation, Christopher was composing himself. I moved hesitantly to his side, once again predicting exactly what he was about to say. He cleared his throat, as my father used to, pursed his lips and chided me, "My poor dear baby, you should learn to turn away from drama in the streets. It will only distress you later. You're too naïve to know what you're getting yourself into! The police might have come and taken your name! You could have been carted off to jail! You'd be hurt physically more than you imagine, and what reputation you have would be ruined. Do you think, had *you* been in trouble, that woman would have helped *you?* Not likely, not possible. These poor creatures are nothing to you, and have nothing to do with you. You can't expect the lower classes to observe our standards. Don't get involved! The children will only throw stones again tomorrow. Why bother with her? She's clearly insane. Let's put all this behind us, and enjoy the nice day we planned."

"I'll come by tomorrow to make sure no one has attacked her," I said defiantly, to which Christopher gnashed his teeth. I had longed all my life to give social outcasts a voice, but realized there was nothing more I could do today. My soul began calling for Daisy, who I knew would understand.

Once our weary feet had reached the city, I thought I ought to show Christopher first the Piazza della Signoria, the center of political life since the fourteenth century. We took a circuitous route so that we arrived, as I had planned, facing the majestic Palazzo Vecchio. Christopher headed straight for the graceful Loggia dei Lanzi on its right, full of such violent statues as Cellini's bronze Perseus standing on Medusa's body, blood gushing from its remaining portion of neck. Perseus held aloft her head, from which blood also gushed. Grand Duke Cosimo dei Medici the Elder, who had commissioned the sculpture and ruled Florence from behind the scenes, was in the mood at the time to let her citizens know symbolically that he would not tolerate opposition.

"Hmm," said Christopher, contemplating the sculpture. "I understand Tuscany was the first civil state in the world to do away with torture and capital punishment. But I would like to be hanged. I would almost commit murder for the sake of the dramatic experience of being hanged. Death is the supreme excitement. Everything else that we do is exciting only because

197

there is risk of death in it. I will never satisfy my longing until I can think something like:

"The rope is biting into my neck deeper and deeper, so that I feel my veins swelling and my eyes bulging and my head throbbing. This is the biggest thing that ever happened to me—far bigger than being born. I can only gasp—I can't breathe. In three seconds I shall be dead. I am going into darkness and the unknown, or perhaps into the light. It makes me feel giddy, falling into the darkness and moon and stars, or perhaps no moon and stars falling, falling, choking. I shall die when I hit the bottom, or is there no bottom?"

"I can't take any more," I objected, remembering that this was exactly what he talked of at my parents' cocktail party. "You've been punished so often, you're in love with the moment of death. I'm going through to the *cortile* of the Uffizi, where it's light and airy. 'Judith and Holofernes', over there by the Palazzo Vecchio, might fulfill your appetite for violence when you've finished in the *Loggia*. And, after you've sated your lust for blood enough," I smiled apologetically, "you can join me to look at some beautiful paintings in the Uffizi Gallery."

Chapter Twelve
A Russian Count and Another Out of Body Experience

Heading towards the Uffizi, I felt overwhelmed by relief. Once more the wonderful flavor of ancient Florence flooded my senses. The gratitude that I usually had for living here again became part of me. Just a few moments ago, Christopher's mere presence had reminded me that my family thought people who loved anyone or anything were stupid. While I was with him, the beautiful statue in the *Loggia* of tragic Polyxena being carried off had ceased to bring the lump to my throat I'd always previously experienced.

But not till I entered the Uffizi's internal courtyard, the *cortile,* did the exquisite beauty of Florence fully push out all my negative feelings. What I first noticed there were human beings painted white and posing to resemble statues, and then many artists, sitting and standing, sketching the portraits of passersby.

And there, in the courtyard, I saw *him*, a tall, white-clad man, seeming like an apparition in his loose, flowing, Russian-looking white silk top. Everyone, myself included, appeared to want to speak with him. By the way he bent, smiled and chatted, it was clear he enjoyed people's company. Having obviously entered the courtyard at the river Arno end, he was still far away but the vision of him filled me with wonder, above all at myself. It was as if all pleasant emotions returned at once. What made me react so intensely to someone I didn't know? Could he be a film star? A child near me on his father's shoulders gave words to my unspoken question. "*Babbo,* who is that man who belongs to everybody?"

The seeming apparition continued to spiral here and there into the darker knots of people that hampered his happy progress. Men patted my moving apparition's back, or tried to put an awkward arm around his tall shoulders. Women moved close to jostle him, or to blow him kisses. Great laughter exploded around him when he chatted with a couple of idle artists, one of whom, wearing a jaunty fedora hat, was as tall as himself. The people he greeted looked transformed. Their body movements loosened, dipped, went all over the place and, I felt, exuded joy.

As the vision approached me, I noticed that the loose, white silk top he wore was richly embroidered at the sleeves and collar, and tucked with Italian neatness into long white trousers. Unbelievably, this apparition paused in front of me. His whole body seemed to open into a smile and, instinctively, I curtseyed.

Then I smiled back, trying to lift my eyes to his face. I saw a full-lipped wide mouth, with high cheekbones above. Mysterious eyes, so bright that pain shot through my own eyes, and I had to look down.

I felt wobbly, and embarrassed about feelings I couldn't believe I had. So this was what it meant to be an adolescent girl, almost a woman. Now, more than ever, I felt scared to be human.

Soon he was gone, moving on to others. Everyone and everything else was a blur. As I watched his progress, my arms moved sinuously at my sides while my breath came fast. Never had I felt such warmth in my body till now. My feet performed a neat dance on the spot, pretending my apparition was spinning me around.

Aghast at my shamelessness, yet delighting in it, I approached the taller of the artists with whom my vision had spoken. He raised his fedora hat to me, and seemed to look right into me with conspiratorial friendliness. I guessed he must have noticed my recent antics in the crowd. His shoulders were bowed, giving him an air of humble sympathy. Chewing the cigarette dangling from his mouth, he said, "I could paint you, beautiful *signorina,* if that is your desire, but I don't think it is."

"I'd prefer you to sketch the person you've just been talking with," I said breathlessly. "Do you know him well enough to do so from memory?"

"You've chosen the right craftsman," he replied, waving his hat-holding arm in spirals and humorously bowing. "Daniello, at your service. Tourists call me Big Dan, and say I'm nice. All of us here know your Russian Count well, but I am the perfectionist. Are you American, by any chance? Forgive me, *signorina*—I notice your slight accent. English?"

So my apparition was a Russian Count. I fervently hoped his family was safe. While at my finishing school, I'd met a number of Counts but this one, coming from Russia, was likely to be more vulnerable. We all knew that Stalin had slaughtered most of the aristocrats left over from the bloodbath of 1917.

"My parents are far away in Australia."

"I admire the Australian taste in men, then. I hear a couple of young Australians are staying up at the *palazzo* that is also a school. Are you from there?"

I nodded, but had already lost Daniello's attention. He had stepped sideways to obtain a better view of his white-clad idol, who was disappearing past the Palazzo Vecchio corner.

I took the opportunity to imagine my Russian Count's beautiful head filling the large blank square of paper on Big Dan's extra tall easel. Sighing, Daniello returned to make a couple of presumably inspired pencil strokes across this paper. Frowning as if the result displeased him, he glanced at me at last, his cigarette stuck to his open lower jaw, and observed, "If you *are* from the school, you're the luckiest person living! How lucky can anyone be? You'll see your *Romeo* at the ball. Would you invite me? I'd love to be in your pretty little shoes!"

"At the ball?"

"Absolutely. But the man's going on to a less formal party afterwards. I myself will be at that one! Ready with others to give him a truly big welcome. Lovely looking, isn't he? His eyes are to die for. And don't you think that's a beautiful skew-collar shirt he's wearing? White embroidery on white. *Accidente!* Just like the great snowy expanses of Russia, not that I've been there. Ice-embroidery over snow-decked trees and windows. I'd surely like to see the handsome chest hidden under that shirt. I know he's proud of being Russian, and it's brave of him to wear that outfit here now. I don't believe the Russian aristocracy generally wore Russian clothes, but the military might have used a peasant-style shirt for underwear. Your Count's no snob. I think he's just been wearing his grandfather's old uniform without its jacket."

"How do you know so much about him?" I asked.

"He's a popular man, rumors abound. And I pay attention to each one, because I'm infatuated with him. Do you think he'd like me with a beard?" The artist stroked the stubble under his lifted chin thoughtfully. Not understanding the question, I didn't answer. He went on, "Your Count's so romantic in himself, he stimulates my imagination, as he does yours," Daniello looked right into me again. "He might have just stepped out of the most majestic painting you'll see in the Uffizi. Like I say, though, he's no snob. In my experience, he's happy to get his hands dirty. Let me show you."

With a couple of gestures more graceful than I—or, I felt, any females I knew—could ever make, Daniello removed the big paper together with its plywood backing, and upended his easel. "See here?" he said, tapping its leg. "Your *Romeo* came upon me rubbing my neck one day because I'd been bending over too much, and engaged me in conversation about the pain. He mentioned that if only my easel were taller, I'd have no problem.

All of us artists here will tell you, he's chatty and affable. And will help anyone. Some of us sit to paint portraits, but I prefer standing. And I like to look up a bit, which does my back good. The Russian Count took away my easel and returned it, improved, next day. Look—brackets screwed to its legs, and extensions screwed to the brackets. A simple solution but it made a huge difference to me!"

Big Dan flexed his muscles and twirled his easel, then steadied it on the ground. He replaced its plywood backing and thick paper. Then he sketched a round head with hair parted on the right. "Your man's Stateless," he commented. "His grandparents escaped from Russia just before the Bolshevik Revolution. His grandfather was sent to a diplomatic job here in Italy—good timing—and the whole family got out. In their own country, they used to live at Court. People say his grandfather was responsible for the Czar's personal white-uniformed regiment..."

Big Dan sketched the Count's mysterious black eyes, shaping them like bowed swans' necks at their inner corners. I observed a trance overtake him. For what seemed ages, I watched, careful not to disturb his mood. Then, "Look how well my drawing's turned out!" he teased. "I think I'll keep it."

"Oh no, it's mine!" I cried, laughing as I held out a fistful of money.

Daniello, laughing with me, uncurled my hand and counted the notes. He rolled his sketch, tied it loosely with a ribbon attached to the paper's back, and handed it to me. He removed his cigarette, and said, through slightly clenched teeth, "I hope you enjoy the ball!"

I could have flung my arms around the man, I was so happy. But Daniello gave me a courtly bow, and said, "I'll look forward to seeing your Count at the party afterwards. I don't like my chances with him, though."

"He's your friend, Big Dan! And you'd get on well with anyone!" I exclaimed, confused, but instinctively reassuring the artist without knowing what he meant.

Now I moved away, joining the people queuing to enter the Uffizi Galleries. As no one yet stood behind me, I stepped back a little to untie Big Dan's sketch and stretch it out. Studying it, I felt I was gazing at the head of one who would always try to understand others' points of view. In my imagination, I attempted to enter his world. I thought that the character who sprang lifelike from the square paper had a temperament that would be equally tender and receptive to a hard-faced old woman with dyed hair or to a high-born adolescent who looked like a wistful child. I could see him bowing to a malnourished beggar, her clothes full of holes, with reverence for the greatness of her spirit. He might catch her in his arms and dance round and round in moonlight. And, with no effort at all, I saw him eventually whirling his own children around, he and all three or four laughing.

That moment, however, I glimpsed, from the corner of my eye, lost-looking Christopher approaching out of a crowd. I rolled up the big sketch, and tied the ribbon attached to its back. I resolved never to unroll the drawing in front of Christopher, however often he might ask, not even if his whole body were to quiver with rage.

"You've acquired a print already!" he exclaimed, taking my elbow when he caught up with me.

"Sort of," I muttered.

"May I see?"

"I'd rather not unroll it."

"I'm very suspicious," he said.

I said nothing, and we entered the Gallery.

He brought up the topic of the 'print' every so often, as we toured the Uffizi. But my sincere reactions to the works at which we were looking enabled me to change the subject every time. And in our taxi home, I continued to laugh the situation off.

I was overwhelmed with relief when, on our reaching the school, Christopher failed to get out and hold the taxi door for me. Clearly, he was miffed and saw no future in hanging around, which would eventually have involved his ordering a second taxi to take him to his hotel.

Half an hour later, I was walking down our hill taking shortcuts through farms wherever I could. I handed in the following, hopefully not infuriating, note for Christopher to the concierge at the Grand Hotel desk:

Dear Christopher,

I can't marry you, partly because I'm not yet ready. I don't want to lose my freedom, my youth or my virginity. All these, I know, would mean nothing if I loved you the way a woman is meant to love a man. But I don't. I have never loved you that way.

It is possible I am cruelly wrecking your life. I beg all the powers that be I am not. I thank you from the bottom of my heart and soul for the honor you have done me in coming to Italy.

I don't know how to apologize enough. I only know I can't marry you—or go out with you again. My decision is final.

Because I see love everywhere, I send you much—my kind— from Melissa.

Robin usually arrived late for dinner. Tonight, however, when reprimanded, she simply said, "I've been performing a good deed—one that was long overdue."

Ritually questioned by Signorina Cecchi, she added, "You wouldn't understand." And threw me a hard look.

What's going on? I worried. But we all left the subject alone. I began daydreaming about the Count again.

After our meal, when I reached the top of the tower stairs to my bedroom, I heard a sudden noise and sensed someone was there.

Before I could do anything, I heard Christopher's cheerful voice. "Come in—I won't eat you. You like men a lot."

What could he possibly mean?

"And," he continued, "you owe me."

All light went out of my life. The sun dropped dead. Turning to flee, I stumbled and instantly, out of darkness, Christopher's bony hand emerged and dragged me into the room. Then his upper arm, stronger than mine despite his appearance of frailty, pressed across my throat, and pushed me backwards. Helped by his other arm, he tossed me easily onto my bed, halfway across the huge room, where I landed too terrified to cry out.

Next, humming loudly—rubbing in that no one could possibly hear us—my oppressor pulled my door shut behind him. When I struggled to sit up, I caught sight through the gloom of a triumphant expression, as he barred my door with a body that now appeared immense. With obvious delight, he waggled a long finger at me in a way that said, "Naughty—naughty."

From where, I wondered, did Christopher's Herculean strength arise? How could that frail boy now look like a Colossus, standing astride the closed doorway as if he owned my room?

Christopher was barring the door to my life. I would not let him do this to me.

Remembering the self-sufficient friends I'd made here gave me a fierceness I'd never known before. Sitting up fully, I puffed out my chest with dignity. "You are actually intruding on my world, and that's aggressive," I said. "Throughout the whole universe, you are in the most inappropriate place you could be. Please get out of my room! I didn't ask you to come in. Your world is no longer mine."

"Oh, yes it is, baby," Christopher sniggered. "You are rightfully mine, and no one else is going to love or hurt you ever again. And you'll do no more favors for anyone else. I need the pleasure of capturing something wild. It's not going to be easy to save you. Looks like I'm getting the leavings of every Tom, Dick and Harry." Then his voice softened. "But you do bring color into my world. You make me come alive, make me think."

What madness was this? Both the situation I found myself in and Christopher had to be insane. I echoed his words. "What in the world are you talking about?" I whispered. "I like men a lot? Every Tom, Dick and Harry?"

Christopher's maniacal laughter, in response, chilled me to the marrow.

"Who let you in?" I demanded. "Who told you where my room was?"

"Oh, you poor innocent!" Christopher sneered. "What Robin does for me, she does for you. She told me on the telephone she thought you ought to learn what life was about. She's sick of you running around through the streets unscathed. You imagine you can walk in mud without getting splashed. But when people lie down with dogs, they get up with fleas."

"*Robin* said that?"

"What do you think? Robin tells her parents everything you do—and they tell I don't know who else. Your goings-on have kept everyone except your mother and father entertained for months, back in Australia. However, don't worry. I promise not to eat you. But I want you to listen to me. And don't fool yourself, it is never appropriate for a girl to be in control."

"So Robin let you in." Of course, I should have known.

"Yes, for your own good. You wander the streets like a bitch in heat. You say you don't want to lose your virginity, but the way you behave is far from conducive to keeping it. If, indeed, you've done so. You invited a man to your bedroom on your very first night in Italy, Robin said. And hold dangerous conversations with street youths. And now I've seen for myself how you wander the city, speaking to both women and men. Oh yes, I peeped around the corner for a minute while you were talking to that artist. A lady doesn't speak with strangers, or make an exhibition of herself. She just doesn't *do* that. I'd like to drag you by the hair around this room and kiss you with force until you beg for mercy, or beat you to death slowly. But it is stupid to imagine only. Now it is I, not you, who am begging for mercy. Do not treat your first love like this! You have made an ugly joke of me." Christopher's voice betrayed a sob.

My whole body was trembling. *You invited a man to your bedroom on your very first night in Italy. You have made an ugly joke of me.* The words reverberated around my walls. How could I have failed to understand the ways of the world when everyone else did?

Kasho had suggested that I should handle real life situations by myself these days, and I wanted to honor that. I was determined to draw on my own strength, no matter how feeble I felt. I summoned all my courage. "Have you been drinking?" I demanded.

"Not a drop. But you are planning to go back to that crazy woman without me. You told me so! You are planning to wander the streets alone again, without me, just like Robin said you were doing!"

"I refuse to be phony all my life," I returned imperiously, feeling like stamping my foot.

Giving an affronted snort, Christopher briefly turned his head away. "Your father would have heard the rumors about you. He told me, 'Our daughter's behavior will be getting out of hand, and she'll need disciplining, need reining in before it's too late. And you're the man to do it. So go ahead and be a man.' One word from you in a letter, he said, could spoil his week. It's about time you showed your parents a little gratitude. They had hoped this finishing school would rub the corners off you, but your father says you seem to be getting worse. Poor fellow, I know what he means now."

"So I can spoil my father's week. I regret that. But one word from my father to you has ruined my life," I said daringly.

Christopher turned back and glared at me. "You *made* me come all this way. Your only reason for refusing me is to be nasty to your parents."

After a long silence, during which I realized I could never make a dint in Christopher's outlook, I asked quietly, "Did my parents pay your passage here?"

"They are angels. I suppose you know that your father has recently changed his Will, settling all the money due to you on me? So the only way you'll gain access to your inheritance is by marrying me! Did you think you could thumb your nose at your dad so easily? I wasn't going to tell you, but he says you're too scatterbrained to be trusted with finances. I'd never have come, or stayed in the Grand Hotel, if your father hadn't paid for it."

I suddenly realized that, for some stupid reason, I'd had the sneaky feeling that I'd earned my parents' money through suffering. But, of course, I had not. Disinheriting me made sense; I'd always known my father wanted power beyond the grave. "It looks like I've just joined the impoverished class, so you had better despise me as you do the crazy woman we saw today," I joked to Christopher, recognizing only too well that my immediate danger was from him. What good would humoring him, agreeing to matrimony, do now? At this moment, I felt Christopher had the upper hand. He'd grab any excuse to shorten the physical distance between us and a good reason, in his eyes, could be impending marriage.

"It's not funny," Christopher objected. "You should learn to know your motives without hiding them under noble appearances. Just face the fact that your father is doing his duty out of love for you. What would a silly woman do with all that money anyway?"

Peace and calm flowed into my bone marrow, as if Kasho had sent it. I remembered what Daisy had said about feminine qualities being more important in the future. That instant, I totally forgave my father. In ways I didn't yet understand, his giving my inheritance to another liberated me. I felt encased in total protection, looking out through a window at my greater room. I was retreating into a space beyond panic. Is this where animals go, I wondered, when they're terrified? Where mother kangaroos go when their pouches grow limp, not allowing their babies back inside?

My intruder took a step forward, annoyed by my second profound silence, I thought. "Come on, you can trust me," he said. "You might let me hug you and kiss you. I'm not heavy."

"I've never been hugged or kissed in my whole life!" I protested. "Please keep away!"

"What do you have against *me?* How many blokes have you stayed with?"

"I never have in my life, and never intend to, outside marriage. And I'm certainly not ready for *that!*"

"No girl has ever said 'No' to me. I won't hurt you. Just don't try to leave this room. *Never* try to leave me. Robin said what we both needed was to be shut in together, to sort ourselves out, so that I could show you who was boss. I'd be ashamed in front of Robin if I didn't force a part of your body where I *know* no man has been before."

Christopher's eyes had glazed over, and he looked like a hunting animal, so focused on its prey that no thought of mercy could disturb its concentration. "You'll never get away from me," he muttered. "I'll take what's mine."

And his mountainous weight was upon me, pushing me over. Sliding his hand up my leg, he said, "She is all made of nylon," lightly, playfully, now that I assumed he felt he had won. He added, "Is this nylon too?" His hands were on my half-slip, and I could feel something hard pressing me. I shoved my own hands against his with all my might, while a wordless high animal scream that went on and on emerged from my body. It was the biggest protest I had ever made against injustice, but I had plenty of room for more! I drew my foot back to kick as hard as I could, and heard Kasho's voice join with mine in shouting "You are trying to destroy my heart, mind and spirit, but I won't let you!" A dizzying buzz in my ear gave me the feeling Kasho added, hissing, "Little Mystery, yes. I know you can look after yourself, now, but I can't deny my bursting heart. You are tiny and physically fragile like a child. I am a man, and can't help feeling protective. I vowed to help you always. You need to let me deal with Christopher. You have gentleness and compassion, but also my fierceness within you. Try to become part of me."

Kasho and I were swapping bodies! Physically, at last, he was aiding and abetting me in expressing my defiance of the negative world from which I had come. And, while he was in charge of my body, I had faith that he would not allow it to be violated.

One moment of tearing away, of focusing more deeply in my heart than ever before on Kasho's wise words, which I'd heard throughout our relationship, was all it took. Then I found myself transported across galaxies onto another planet… where, I had no idea.

As I whooshed rapidly through the air of this strange place, I experienced the human beings here as mere presences with feelings. I was moving too fast to see them. I could feel the indignation of the innocent at the devastation of their land, at the cutting down of their forests. And I tuned in to the savagery of soldiers, without even *self*-control, who mercilessly oppressed the conquered.

But other soldiers, too, encircled the territory my spirit was swishing through so dramatically—hostile, well-armed presences, stationed on high ground above every pass. I sensed a rival ruler behind them planning an invasion, during the terrible chaos of which I hoped my beloved would be freed.

Across a great lake, where a bat-like bird hovered and hunted, I noticed what I assumed to be my Kasho's ruler's gloomy castle—quite sweet-looking from outside, spanning a big semi-underground cavern. It looked as if the smaller lake I glimpsed in the crags above had tides. Its water, therefore, would periodically rush underground, leaping up through the blowhole I knew—because I'd been here before—beside Kasho in the castle dungeon's slippery floor. Gurgles and sounds like groans from this blowhole intimated to me, the way dreams do, that every so often a human being, weighted, would be thrust alive into its swirling, sucking depths.

I entered the dungeon to find Kasho's pillar empty, with slack chains around it. Kasho had obviously been led to that other part where he previously hadn't wanted me to know what went on. And I burst through walls into that other part now.

Hammering noises here almost drowned the roaring and crashing and groaning of waves. I tried to lean against, but fell through, a pillar as big as the most ancient hollow trees of Australia, inside which one can park cars. I felt a heavy smelly drip, from some cavernous roof, fall through my head and achingly through my feet to land below me. I dimly saw men broad in the beam, like rugby players in a scrum, leaning over a table. I heard their subconscious minds calling out, "Help me *feel, Kasho! You* can feel. Oh, help me! Help me!"

Occasionally, the hammering stopped, and the men, pulling on ropes, lifted the squirming, living object they were hammering up high. I constantly heard them mockingly call whatever they were holding 'Kasho'. "We'll turn you into a pile of dust, and rake you into the corner over there," they jeered. "You, who see yourself as an ambassador for everything indigenous. You, who lament our cutting down trees. You sissy. Then you'll return to your mother the earth, your mother the soil, your mother your tribal land that you are constantly standing up for, and accusing us of raping."

Though I could not bear to see what these square-shaped men were doing, I desperately wanted to share my Kasho's bodily suffering.

And soften his pain, if I could. Also, I wanted to know whether a ghost, whether I, in this case, could experience physical agony.

With just this thought, as easily as I transported myself to Kasho's planet, I feel his flesh on the table enfold me. From inside his body on his normally distant continent, for a moment I know the extreme desperation of a wild animal over which a net has been thrown. Then, his flesh and my spirit become one creature and that creature is magnificent. This man is—I am— all heart.

They have me chained to a table on all fours by my wrists and ankles. They have a good view up, but the table can be lowered too. My body is in agony. So what? I think. Torturers are causing the agony on purpose, and I long for death. All I can hear now is the rasping thunderous breath of my desire to escape. But I have the sense and detachment to know that the unbearable agony will not last long.

It ceases abruptly. The first seven blows have been painful, but now I cannot feel them. I long to clasp both my hands over my mouth to try to stop myself from laughing out loud. I somehow know that Kasho has done this every day too.

Five men are hammering me but I sense a sweetness in my strong heavy limbs, relaxed by the never-failing love, loyalty and responsibility my spirit sends up towards my tormentors. The relaxation of my timeless limbs which expect suffering, and do not know tension, can never be violated because, beneath the hairy chests looming over me, with the power of bestowing life or death, more fulfilling life, or theoretically more agonized death, I feel a strange exhilaration at being united with all that suffers. Death-dealing, painless blows descending now link me with all women in labor; with an Australian Aboriginal man in the past, being dragged through dust by a chain around his neck attached to the back of a motor car; and with an animal being

213

experimented on, who jumps off the laboratory table, jumps out of a window and runs up a tree. I even remember again, in a time before time, my Kasho and myself pressing our foreheads together. How big and bony I felt his to be. Now, I want him to impart to me his strength and wisdom. Also, his innocence—wild and wise, thoroughly different from mine. I can feel his whole character coming into me, and myself changed by it.

"You're so real!" bursts from my phantom lips, and my ghostly tears flow. Kasho's body is like mine only more so, and I am ready to be more so from now on.

I came back into myself on my knees in the middle of my bed, grimacing fiercely, hands open. I felt exhilarated and confused by the strength of my chest, shoulders and upper arms, and wondered if I could hang on forever to the physical power I had now. Despite this, the surrounding atmosphere of my tower room gave me an ominous feeling—something was wrong—but I couldn't remember what had happened here. I knew it had been terrible, and during that moment of realization I wanted to climb back into Kasho's body. But then I understood it was Kasho's strength I felt within me—his strength was mine now—and I could deal with whatever might be wrong. I would always be able to do so.

It was probably this realization that made me aware of pitiful sobbing coming from the semi-darkness. Completely alert at last, I could make out a crumpled, wretched shapeless lump on the floor to the other side of my wooden staircase. I leaned over my bed's edge and extended an arm towards it in compassion.

"Don't come near me! Don't touch me again! I want nothing to do with you," the horrible thing shrieked, jacket over its head, scrabbling on the floor. "You're inhuman. You're an animal! You've pulled me apart, and want to eat my heart. Oh God, I'll never touch a woman again. I have to get out of here. This room is full of danger. Mummy, mummy, help me! Where are you?"

The lump was Christopher. I panicked as I watched him back towards the door, knees bent, his hands between his legs, moaning "Oh, pweeth don't hurt wittew Cwithy! I'th a *good* boy! I wuv my toyth! They don't thcare me. But I don't wuv *you* anymore."

Opening the door, he was gone.

"Oh, Kasho, what have we done?" I exclaimed in anguish. "That baby talk, coming out of darkness—"

"It was necessary, for me, in your body, to defend myself," I heard immediately. "I feel very, very sorry for young Christopher. But the most important thing of all is that you're safe. Don't worry—I'll still help that poor, poor fellow if I can. He has given gut-wrenching displays of regression before, ever since he was first abused."

"Was no one ever kind to him?" I whispered, my arms wrapped tightly around myself.

"No, not till he became an adult, and was seen as worthy of attention. I've witnessed that custom too often among your people." My beloved's tone was stronger than it had ever been. "But tell me," his voice became gentler, "how do *you* feel in *yourself,* after having occupied my body?"

I shook my head, as if shaking the worst of recent memories out of my hair. I felt happy to be with Kasho, knowing both of us were safe at present, but realized I'd never forget his extreme suffering, or hearing Christopher talk like a baby. Kasho was waiting for my answer. "Stronger and wiser," I said. "I know now that you see yourself as an ambassador for all the indigenous people in the universe. Through your eyes, I have seen the land-grabbers in my own world murdering your people to get at forests and destroy them. I see indigenous people upon my Earth, my world, refusing to abandon their ways and move to the cities, even when their women are murdered by swords thrust up their private parts, and although their children are being taken away by terrifying blue-eyed men on horseback. Over and over, your

215

people in my world are making the ultimate sacrifice in order to preserve their beliefs like a treasure that they will give to the rest of us when we are ready. And, somehow, your torture symbolized this for me, and your torture symbolized our recent torture of Mother Earth."

"Yes," my Kasho lamented, "I hear Mother Earth crying, and feel pieces of my own flesh torn out when trees are felled unnecessarily. When the trees stop breathing because they are dead, there is climate change, and oceans start rising. Everything is going wrong because my people's oppressors, and many of the conquerors in *your* world, don't love nature. For centuries, men have raped and tortured your Mother Earth, and raped and tortured her indigenous children too.

"In many ways, Melissa, my planet is like yours during your Middle Ages. Because during your Middle Ages, anywhere a person looked, at least throughout Europe, torture was taken for granted.

"But it is almost time for the descendants of the conquering nations and the descendants of the conquered of your Earth—the descendants of the torturers and the descendants of the tortured— to wipe their slates clean, and meet as if it were the first occasion, expecting to be friends for life. Your Australian Aboriginal people traditionally do not bear grudges, and the rest of your world needs to listen to them."

"But I'm wondering how do *you* feel, Kasho, having been me? That would be so enlightening!"

"Very hopeful for your future," Kasho replied, a grin in his voice. "Will you let me show you why?" I almost sensed him put his arm around me.

"Yes, please!" I exclaimed like a child eager for a lesson.

"Well," he said moving away to face me, "you may be *thinking*, 'what bad thing have I done to my parents, to make them disinherit me—'?"

"Not really," I broke in far too soon, "I'm even grateful to them." Then I caught myself. "Sorry, I didn't mean to interrupt!"

Kasho laughed. "I wanted you to," he said. "But I was about to finish by saying, 'On your deepest level, I sense that their action has made you feel free!'"

His observation was true, I acknowledged, but *why* did I feel that? The facts were stacked against me; and now, suddenly, they seemed to be crowding in on me. I stared into space, at horrors. The anticipated ball being a mere two days away, after it my future stretched out monotonous and lonely, like a long flat barren moor.

"Why make such big eyes?" Kasho demanded, but of course I knew he knew the reason.

"My father used to tell me, over and over," I explained, "that I am his absolute possession, to do what he likes with, until I am twenty-one, because by law I am a child. So I cannot escape. If I manage to get a job in Florence, he is likely to turn up with thunder in his face and take me home."

"Something has changed, though, hasn't it?" Kasho asked gently.

I pondered his question, and realized he was right. "Yes, my father's disinheriting me makes me *feel* free, have hope there is a loophole."

"And indeed you should!" Kasho encouraged. "I believe a good thing is about to happen."

"How can it?" I exclaimed. "If you are tortured, again, as badly as you were when I was in you, you will die."

"My spirit has always escaped," Kasho pointed out gently, I suspect putting his arm around me again, "and my physical release is imminent."

But, facing other facts, a wave of despair spread over me. "How can any truly good thing happen in my life now?" I cried. "I've lost Daisy! Possibly inspired by you, she was going to write great melodies, and I the lyrics. That future has been destroyed, through my saying I preferred Christopher, by my telling her my parents would find her common..."

Without comment, Kasho allowed me to wallow silently a long time in both *my* pain—emotional—and my horror at *his*—physical. Eventually, he asked, "Please, can we speak a little more?"

I nodded dumbly.

"Tell me how you feel about Christopher," he said.

I realized that Christopher's behavior had released me from him forever. Kasho must have picked up my intense relief on that subject, and been satisfied, because he went on, "And Robin's betrayal?"

"It cannot be excused. But, in fact, she has done me the biggest favor of all, provided a reason for me to occupy your body."

"Yes, I have allowed you into my body. So say what you *think*."

At this intimate moment I looked down, fiddling with my continental quilt. "You are the bravest, and most loving man I've met!" I admitted. "It shook me profoundly to find out that you are so badly tortured. Yes, I know that your spirit goes wandering at the worst times, letting those henchmen do what they like without you feeling it much, but this is my experience.

"When the henchmen working on you-me lifted me up high, I looked with *your* unbounded love down upon those so-called human creatures, behaving so cruelly, who were being extra businesslike about the creases of your-my body, extra systematic and *sensitive* about where to inflict pain."

"My ruler's henchmen are like immature children. To them, becoming an adult means squashing their more tender emotions, while to my tribal people bringing up children means expanding their hearts to embrace everything, slowly bringing their emotions in line with those of the compassionate spiritual world

218

around us. But now those henchmen have united you with me and made us strong," Kasho prompted.

"That's right!" I confirmed excitedly, filled with more hope now. "And my whole being is praying and hoping that your ruler's reign and your suffering end tomorrow." Jumping out of bed, running to the fat supportive column in the very center of my room, flinging my arms around it and laying my cheek against it as if it were Kasho, I burst out, "Meanwhile, I've been inside your very sinews. I've had the shock of feeling your character and wisdom circulate through my blood, and I *know* now that I have obligations to the whole human family, not just those who are affected by my parents. And it thrills me to know that. I've no idea how, but I feel that I and many others can do something really important!"

The thrill of freedom was shooting through me. Although Daisy had gone, I would find a way to escape my father. I would really *do* something with my life.

"Yes, you have thoroughly absorbed my nature. Tell me more," Kasho murmured, and I really did feel him stroking my hair.

I nestled closer into the column, weeping tears of joy from having been truly alive, from the depth of my connection with Kasho. I felt happy and sad at once on a profound level. From today on, I believed, everything in my room would remind me of my near-rape, but also of its wonderful but terrible outcome: living for a while inside Kasho's body. "Because of having been you," I reported like a good pupil, "I have learned, first of all," I said as I held my index finger, "that our great unity will from now on be more so, and does have the potential to create wonderful works. Two—" now gripping my middle finger I continued, "that saving lives has always been your calling, and it's time to expand this. Three—that you have a deep understanding of human nature, far beyond most of us, and that pain can release us to our better parts, very often. Four—when all peoples of my world

219

walk with the same spiritual feet, according to your outlook we will have come of age—"

"Yes, growing up means caring outside your own body. But you knew that before." Kasho laughed. "It's time for you to start on your other hand, I think!"

I sensed an enticing flutter around the first finger of my other hand, and even humorous impatience in Kasho's voice. Yet I didn't want to stop. I persevered, holding the finger. "Lastly, inhabiting your body has let me know that we are very lucky on Earth in the places where tribal people have kept their old ways, despite all odds. They can advise us by showing us their ways, by action. Of course, I've discovered much more besides this within you; but above all, to my surprise, that you find me easy to understand, though others don't."

"Enough is enough. I like hearing you so passionate, my love!" Kasho exclaimed, with a smile in his voice. "But it's Sunday morning already, and your body needs food. You must go down to breakfast now. Glowing all over from having been part of me, you can make a tired but triumphant entrance to your dining room. And even join in the conversation there. Your friends are talking about the ball. You and I can continue our marvelous discussion another time."

"As I've mentioned, I've never been interested in balls," I said. "And certainly not now!"

"But won't a certain Russian Count be there?" Kasho teased.

This was bad. I hadn't wanted him to know. I burst out, "Oh, you must think me an idiot, falling for him—"

"Not really," Kasho softly replied. "I must admit to feeling jealous, but I couldn't deny you a flesh-and-blood man. I've had to give myself a talking-to. And I suspect an even better surprise than dancing with your Count is coming your way."

"Oh please, what will it be?"

"You'll find out soon enough!"

Before I could press further, he had left my side.

I was just beginning to change my clothes when Robin burst through my tower room door and stormed up to me, apparently angry. "What the hell happened?" she demanded. "I was peacefully sitting on a step when Christopher himself hurtled down your stairs and shoved me away. He nearly knocked me over. I accompanied him to the lower level and let him out quietly, but we didn't speak, and he looked in a bad way." She eyed me as if she had no knowledge of the recent drama in my room.

My silhouette, with morning light blazing around it, stared at me from my dim bandy-legged mirror, giving me strength. I drew myself up, feeling even taller than my closet, sensing the depths of Robin call out, like Kasho's torturers' spirits, "Oh, help me! Help me!"

I asked calmly, almost pityingly, "What were you doing, sitting on my step in the middle of the night? Christopher left three hours ago." Then I accused, "You knew he was here! You sent him to rape me!"

Robin's face reddened, and I spotted a glint of fear in her eyes. She shrieked, "Liar! You're inventing it all! You're making it up! Why would I do such a thing?"

With my eyes never leaving hers, I said, "I wondered that myself."

In the silence that followed, I felt surprise at my own detachment from the machinations of mind that were clearly tormenting Robin. Eventually, she concluded with bravado, "This tower room is so remote and soundproof, no one will ever believe you."

"They don't have to," I said firmly.

"What do you mean? Aren't you going to complain about me, at least to your precious Countess?"

"Not to anyone. I'll leave all communication with you to your own conscience. But *why*?" I demanded. "What harm have

I ever done to you? You knew exactly what you were doing. You set me up as a target, believing all my resistance would be futile!"

I saw a flash of the old Robin when she said, "And how come it wasn't? How *did* you defend yourself against him? Did that silly old ghost help you?"

Naturally, I laughed. "Well, as a matter of fact, he did."

"Oh, I really don't want to know. But I bet your parents will!" Robin turned on her heel. "I'm going down now to enjoy my breakfast."

As my fellow Australian slouched down my stone steps, I put her words from my mind.

Chapter Thirteen
First Kiss, June 1958

The amber afternoon sun was slanting through my tower room windows, awakening the hundreds of lights that twinkled back from my dress. The day of the ball had arrived.

I had laid the blue gown's top, cummerbund and cascading skirt on my bed, beside silver nylon gloves that reached above my elbows. Silver jeweled high heeled shoes sat together underneath, on the floor.

My Russian Count's sketched head, taped inside my now open wardrobe door, dominated the whole scene for me. However, the ache in my heart was not of that Count's doing.

All I could think of was how Daisy had looked, modeling the dress. For me, the gown symbolized all goodness—the selfless love about which Kasho had sung to me among sand dunes in a magical place I knew not where. I recalled with agony the enchanted unity of spirit between me and Daisy at the dress shop. Daisy had talked me into buying this gown, which I had promised to give her after the ball. But what to do now?

I had never in my life broken a promise, but what alternative did I have? If I sent the dress back to Daisy, she would take it as an insult, a symbol of my betrayal of our friendship. She would hate it. So I needed to keep it. Nevertheless, probably I would not be able to bear wearing the dress again. Instead, I'd pack the lovely garment away reverently. But I wouldn't be able to resist, every so often, taking it out and gazing at it, remembering a special friendship, and wondering what Daisy was doing.

Then sudden terror swept over me at the thought of going home. How had Robin depicted me to her parents, who, according to Christopher, had gossiped about me with everyone they knew? How would my parents react when Christopher told them I had refused his offer of marriage? I sensed a sword hanging over my head. I shuddered violently and felt icy cold. An early veiled threat of Robin's began to make sense. "You know, Melissa, what we can get away with in Italy we can't at home."

Outside my door, which once again always stood open, a discreet knock sounded. I came back to everyday reality. Who could my visitor be? Karen? Robin? But Robin was seldom discreet.

A voice, unusually timid, asked, "May I come in?" The one I'd not seen for weeks, the person I'd missed so dreadfully, was here!

As if afraid to break a spell, I tiptoed towards the doorway without replying. My heart beat fast. We stood silently staring at each other. Daisy's presence felt like an honor that would never again be followed by shame.

Her eyes steadily on mine, my good friend began singing softly the words she'd made up when I'd read her, so happily, my seal story in the café, at our relationship's beginning:

> *"To take a life is to lose two souls:*
> *The one you took, and your own.*
> *To save a life is to reach inside,*
> *And pull out the strength that you find"*
> Now I tried to hold the tune with her:
> *"Lost in the ocean, and you're the prey*
> *Losing motion, all you see is gray— "*

224

But I couldn't go on. I broke down. Singing together touched something deep inside me. "I'm so *sorry*," I sobbed.

"Hush!" Daisy responded, a gracious finger to her lips. She stretched her arms out like an airplane and I fell into them, laughing and crying. We held each other forever, it seemed. I felt safe in her arms. If only she could return to Australia with me, and there impart her strength!

"My dearest friend," she murmured, "you've nothing to be sorry for. The only thing you're guilty of is being human. We all lose our tempers and get confused at times. And it is our job to forgive one another."

"Am I really human at last?" I sighed, breaking away.

Daisy laughed delightedly, and glanced at my teary face. "You're so human, I've come to see if you'd like me to make you up for the ball."

How natural it felt for us to be together! Daisy looked radiant. Everything was just as it had always been, healed between us, as if nothing had ever been wrong. I determined not to let thoughts of Christopher and going home ruin this wonderful moment.

Breaking my train of thought, my friend added, "I am a model, after all."

"I *hate* makeup," I protested. "In my opinion, my friends always look more beautiful without it."

"Did they ever lend you any?"

"They've tried to."

Daisy pulled a big bottle from her handbag, and held it high. "This perfume," she said, "is called 'Miss Dior.' It confuses men when worn by a teenage girl, because it suggests a sultry woman."

Caught up in Daisy's world, I performed a couple of dance steps towards her and extended my wrist. Taking my fingers gently, she remarked, "You have the hand of a child." She dripped the perfume.

I breathed it in. Heady, seductive and richly hypnotic, it turned my tower room into heaven and helped me trust that, if I allowed Daisy to use her artistry, I wouldn't end wearing a clown's mask.

"Who is that?" Daisy asked, indicating my picture of the Russian Count. "Is he a real person? Did your Countess invite him to the school?"

I stopped dancing, fluttering my eyelashes at the portrait on my open wardrobe door. "He's the loveliest creature I've ever seen," I replied. "But I've never spoken with him, only saw him in the street. Would you believe it, the painter who drew that Russian Count told me he's coming to our ball! But he's going on to another party afterwards, so he might not be here long."

"I can see he's special to you. And you'll want to look special for him, even though your Countess told me you're all leaving Florence in a few days. Just a little lipstick."

"When did you see our Countess?" I asked, but Daisy was searching through her purse. She unscrewed a gold cylinder, and held it up. For the first time, I noticed her clothes.

"You're wearing everyday things!" I pointed out accusingly. "But, now you are here, won't you come to our ball?"

Grimacing, Daisy shook her head. "On my way to your room, I apologized to your Countess in her office. Had her invitation to your ball been formal, I'd have felt duty bound to attend. But remember, she asked me casually, leaving me free. I have access to all kinds of dresses. That's not my problem. But propping myself against your ballroom wall, all dolled up, hoping some guy will cross that immense floor and ask me to dance, is not my idea of fun. You, on the other hand, have a purpose—" she added knowingly.

I looked down, embarrassed, murmuring, "He won't even notice me."

"I never thought I'd see you *blush.* I suspect he's noticed you already." Daisy moved closer to the portrait. "Wow! He does look nice. Dancing with him would be a fabulous experience, I imagine. But, you know, although he's obviously far more confident, something about his expression reminds me of you."

I couldn't imagine she'd see anything of me in that beatific face. "Really?" I demanded excitedly. "What?"

"Oh, I don't know. Certain things can't be put into words." She turned to hug me, then closed my wardrobe door. "He'll notice you at the ball, I assure you. Especially if you let me help bring out your natural charm. May I pluck your eyebrows, just a fraction?"

I allowed Daisy to work on me, and she made soothing conversation all the while. However, I was too focused on what she might be doing to my face to listen. Then a thought came into my head, and I knew I needed to clear something up. I said, "You were right about Christopher. That's all I want to say on the subject."

"You are like a Baha'i," Daisy answered, beginning to rub my cheeks. "We won't ever say anything bad behind someone's back, unless it's totally necessary."

When she lifted a brown pencil to my eyebrows, I instinctively put my hands up. "Oh, come *on!*" she exclaimed. "We can always take it off again."

Opening my attitude to my friend's gentle strokes on my brows, and to smoothness on my lids, fingers through my hair and perfume in the air, I resigned myself to becoming a well-sculpted work of art.

Entering the ballroom in my beautiful dress, I felt it had a personality of its own. Wearing it and smelling so desirable, I knew myself to be a woman. Here I was—but before leaving my bedroom, I had checked myself in my old dim mirror, and seen that the satin's soft-hard sheen, its cold blue, brought out the warmth of flesh next to it. There, in my bedroom, I smiled at my reflection whereupon an unfamiliarly luxurious mouth smiled widely back. During the rest of this evening, nothing—no catty

227

remark, no dread of the future—could wipe that smile off my face. Daisy had returned!

Standing at the ballroom's entrance, searching for my friends, I felt overwhelmed by light. There was so much of it, pale mellow orange on some walls, dazzling lemony on others, from imported chandeliers, wide and lovely enough to have a natural air. Below the chandeliers' multitudinous slim mock-candles hung seeming glistening dewdrops. However, the light did not reach many alcoves.

Lining the ballroom walls below the chandeliers, behind rows of massive columns, sat over a hundred people—men on my left, women on my right—and, judging by the number of empty benches and chairs, this great room was about to fill with about a hundred and fifty souls each side. I was glad, and grudgingly grateful to Daisy, that the bright lights would not drain color from my newly bronzed skin. In contrast to the other ladies reflected in the great ornately framed mirrors, I had not allowed Daisy to pin up my hair.

Observing my reflection, Daisy had remarked dreamily, "Your dress contains night itself. Or, when twilight gives way to dusk, no one can see things clearly; a haze, a blue-gray mist, quivers between a person and even close objects. In the same way, it always looks as if your dress has taken on its mysterious color because of dim lighting."

Obviously, Daisy still felt love for my Dior gown. I had laughed with pleasure inside, thinking of her enjoyment when it would be hers.

Though my mirror had shown me in the foreground, it was Daisy's larger overshadowing shape behind that fulfilled me. Daisy being here, and our renewed happiness, made me feel I had everything a girl could want. How could I bear leaving her? How could I return to the darkness that Australia held for me?

Tonight, I would not think about it. Tonight, I would be brave, living and laughing. So I looked for my friends. At last I caught sight of Nicole, Karen, Julie and Robin far in the distance to my right, across the huge floor that was soon likely to be entirely filled by closely paired dancers. My friends sat next to a stage that supported a grand piano and a darkly dressed man arranging music sheets on it. The wall behind boasted a magnificent blue, gold and red painting from floor to ceiling—of earth, ocean and Apollo in his chariot.

Somehow, Daisy coming back and the knowledge that it was time to join my good friends made me stand straighter than ever I'd stood, except when confronting Robin in my tower room. The Countess bustled up to me, exuding elegance in a straight black gown with strings of pearls. She had been standing talking with others at the ballroom's entrance. Her eyes shone as she smiled and nodded at me, making everything feel right. "You look wonderful," was all she said. Seated nearby, an empty chair between them, Signorina Cecchi and Professor Brunelleschi's sweet-faced wife nodded and smiled too, though I'd expected the *signorina* to chide me for making my entrance alone. For a few seconds, I thought I saw into her soul, and heard the depths of her speak to me, saying, "When I was a young girl, brought up in the Tuscan countryside, I was beautiful but wild. I could leap on horses without saddle or bridle. I loved the freedom, I love good horses." I realized I had something in common with the *signorina* after all!

Professor Brunelleschi, on his wife's left side, grinned broadly. Delighting in all my teachers' apparent approval, I was hardly aware of other eyes upon me as I readied myself to walk the empty area's length.

I moved slowly, surreptitiously glancing to my left, hoping to find my Russian Count among the openly staring men. In my mind I saw him still wearing white, so that he would stand out beautifully against his dark-suited comrades.

Nearing the stage, I began to look at the girls and young women on my right. The majority seemed to be tense, but pretending to relax and enjoy themselves because they would not attract partners if they looked sour. My own friends, on the other hand, appeared truly relaxed, and happy to be with each other. As I approached her, Robin remarked, "And why are *you* so dolled up? Makeup and all?"

I replied quietly, "You've done me no harm, and I wish you well."

Though I intended no one else to hear, Robin snorted, turning away to face Julie. Her chair angled and pulled in front of us, Julie was, I saw, demonstrating what she called the 'language of the fan'.

Wearing a dress with white birds' breast feathers all over it—not only on its pre-shaped bust—Julie looked swan-like as she waved a fan beautifully decorated with a painted garden full of playful lords and ladies. "This means 'Leave me alone,'" she said, holding the fan to her left ear. "And this means 'You have changed,'" sliding it across her forehead. Moving the fan slightly, still with her left hand, she informed us "And this means 'The adults are watching us.'"

I chose a chair next to Karen who had on a beige gown with a design of pink roses. The moment I sat down, she nudged my hip and slid a page with a golden letterhead out of her jeweled purse. "Tomorrow I'll be busy packing," my friend softly said. "I'm due to fly home tomorrow night—rather, at the next crack of dawn. But I wanted to let you know I've been watching you and Daisy. I don't want to make a big issue out of it, because I know you like to achieve by your own merits, but I couldn't leave without saying this: if you ever need a real friend, here's my address. Whether you club together with Daisy or not, please send me some of the songs you write. If I like them, I'll show my father."

Prickly tears crawled down the sides of my nose, doubtless making grooves in my so recently resented makeup. I knew this would be the first of many goodbyes. Smiling weakly through

230

my weeping, taking the paper with my outer hand, I grasped Karen's with my closer one, saying, "You seem much surer of my future than I am myself."

By focusing on what my other friends were wearing, I managed to check my tears. Nicole, her arm draped gracefully across the back of the seat beside her, had on a brown, flimsy, layered, almost transparent gown. Robin was obviously wearing the corset-like garment that she loathed underneath her red and orange dress, and her large clear eyes drooped more than usual at their corners.

Julie continued talking to us, with exaggerated animation. "Towards the end of the nineteenth century," she explained, "young girls of our class were chaperoned, and so a silent language developed for the benefit of their suitors."

She opened, then shut her fan several times, telling us, "This means 'You are cruel.' And this means 'Do you love me?'"— keeping her fan closed.

A saxophone, waving about, caught my eye. The orchestra members were finally all on stage, unpacking around the grand piano. Opening her fan, Julie held it in front of my face, touching the edge with her fingers. "This means 'I want to talk to you,'" she began, and smiled at me. "Pretend you're a boy."

But the *Contessa* was standing before us. "I'm proud of all you girls!" she told us warmly. "You're truly looking beautiful. Julie, try to seem less aloof. Karen, you have a bad habit of putting your head down and gazing at men with big eyes. Keep your chin up. Robin, I can tell from your drooping eyelids and breath you've been drinking alcohol. Be careful not to overdo it. Melissa, when I look at you I have to blink and look away. Your gown's embroidery never twinkles in the same place twice, and I keep thinking my eyes are deceiving me. Wearing such a dress and such a smile may carry you through. But still, please remember to flirt. With your nature, you can never overdo it."

Leaving us with this advice, our Countess next hurried across the immense floor to talk with a few smartly jacketed male strangers who awkwardly stood, nibbling savories and sipping from long-stemmed glasses, near an improvised bar.

"She's probably about to lecture those guys on how to behave with us," observed Julie.

Brief vigorous rolls of drums, from the waists of two uniformed youngsters we had all passed on the landing, announced repeatedly that couple after couple were descending the stately marble far-away stairs—as I had done alone, recently—to reach the lower level.

Between drum rolls, and orchestra members tuning their instruments, I could still hear from some open windows in our ballroom the crunch of cars on gravel outside, as couples arrived at our *palazzo's* upper level entrance. Of course, we couldn't actually *see* anyone until they entered the great room where we were now posing elegantly, impatient for everything to begin.

Whispering, "You may kiss me," Julie touched her fan handle to her lips. She then opened her fan slowly, the words 'Wait for me' accompanying her gesture. Apparently taking to heart our Countess's advice not to be lofty, she next abruptly threw her fan to the floor, yelling "I hate you!"

The orchestra drowned her words, striking up the noisy popular song, *'Ma Perche Vuoi Saper' la Mia Storia?'*—loosely translatable as 'But Why Do You Want to Know about My Past?' A tall handsome young man from across the room approached, raised the fan to his lips, returned it to Julie and invited her to dance. She accepted graciously, and moved with him towards the center of the floor.

"Well, that fan gesture had the opposite effect to the one traditionally intended," Karen pointed out, amusement in her voice.

Not to the one *Julie* intended, I thought.

The dance floor was already filling. In the middle, a man cavorted with two giggling bleached blonde society women at once, an arm around each.

Soon I became aware of Roland bowing before me. "Melissa, may I have the honor?"

The orchestra began playing 'Who Wants to be a Millionaire?' and, as we danced, Roland answered "I do" to all the song's questions.

"Are you enjoying yourself?" I inquired, moving in rhythm with him as I'd never moved before.

"Oh!" Roland exclaimed. "I feel so sad at these parties that Florence society holds in your *palazzo*. Not only because they usually mark the end of your school year, but also because you are all insincere to me. That I start it, by being insincere to you, only makes things worse. I tire of insincerity. I know none of you will care about me when you leave. No one at all. You will be lost in a whirl of fun with your other boyfriends, and forget about me. Years later, when you are old, you will suddenly say 'Roland? Oh yes, I seem to remember that name. Wasn't he the vain one, the big show-off?' And you won't care a scrap.

"It is like a great wheel," he went on, "that turns and turns unrelentingly, always in the same direction. And it never turns back. The year before last, a group of girls was here; they left soon enough. Then, last year a group came, and the previous year's group left—just when I got to know and like them. And now I shall never see any of you lot again. Another group will take your place. By the way, are *you* a millionaire?"

The question, inspired by the dance tune, startled me, but I realized, "Roland cannot help being Roland."

"No," I asserted, recovering and thinking of what Christopher had said. "And I'm glad I'm not. I don't see how *anyone* with enormous wealth can rest easy knowing that someone, somewhere, is starving. Sometimes I want to ask God why He allows injustice when He could do something about it,

233

but I'm afraid He might ask me the same question. If all our necessities were covered when we work, or were temporarily unable to work, we could appreciate the wonders of life and all our minds could be free. As for me, I will never again allow my parents' wealth to be relevant to me."

"I hope that isn't really so," Roland said sadly, "Because you look delicious. What a waste! You've improved in yourself since you first came here. You used to be *so* childish it was unbelievable. Now you are a woman. I want the next dance with you and the next and the next."

Things changed, however, when the dance ended and Roland escorted me to my seat. There, Robin asked him, "Are your feet killing you?"

"No." He sounded bewildered. "They're holding me up pretty well."

"Could they stand sitting down?"

Roland understood, brightening. "Yes, they could."

Flashing me a triumphant look, Robin led him through the ballroom's hidden exit presumably, I thought, to the sofa where we used to receive Professor Brunelleschi's lessons. Neither appeared again.

"Robin has been a lot quieter than usual recently," Karen confessed to me, as she watched them leave. "What have you done to her? She used to say bad things about you all the time, but none of us believed her. She's such a bitch, constantly jealous of you. We all knew who Robin was."

I was shocked. "Why would Robin be jealous?" I asked.

"For a start, you're good-looking and she is not."

"But that gap between Robin's front teeth is really alluring. I think she has a beautiful face."

"Personally, I don't like the gap. Her face is okay, I guess. But her body, no. Tell me," Karen sounded most amused, "do you find anyone or anything not beautiful?"

A clean-cut fellow appeared in front of us, inviting Karen to dance. I had fallen silent, realizing that Karen had hinted at something true about me. I wondered fleetingly what my conversation with Robin would be like in a few days' time, when we were scheduled to travel side by side on a plane back to Australia. Karen kissed my cheek, lifted her arms to her new partner, he held her waist, and they were gone.

"You should try to get Roland back," Nicole urged, craning her neck to dodge a column so she could watch Karen on the dance floor. "He's as much yours as Robin's."

But I was glad that Robin had taken Roland over. She might have been afraid of never being asked to dance. I was working out how to reply to Nicole when Ludovico suddenly loomed large, perching breathlessly on a chair arm beside me.

"This is the first ball I've attended since a motorbike accident partly paralyzed my face," he informed me. "I don't really want to dance. You know, I'm a bit like our famous poet Leopardi. At least at one stage, he saw life as a man racing through brambles until he falls into a deep pit, a terrible abyss. Leopardi's old-fashioned parents made him profoundly unhappy."

I boldly asked, "Do *your* parents make you unhappy?"

Ludovico pursed his lips, but failed to answer.

The orchestra struck up *'Nel Blu Dipinto di Blu'*, the successor on the streets of Florence to *'Piccolissima Serenata'*. I felt like dancing again.

"How is it," I asked, mildly changing the subject, "that, when a song gets popular, every Italian man working outside is whistling it? Then, another tune comes to the streets and totally wipes out the previous song?"

"You noticed that? You *are* intelligent—for a girl."

"Was the adult world always so terrible for women?" I retorted, remembering Christopher's similar remark. "Did all the great playwrights, scientists and artists talk to their women as if they had less understanding of life than a baby?"

"Wait till you are kissed," Ludovico replied. "Your brain will soften. A kiss on the mouth will take you to where only great works of art took you before."

From the corner of my eye, I noticed a short, heavy-set man of about thirty approaching, and thought, "Oh, please don't ask me to dance! You are probably married, and where is your wife?"

But on reaching me, he did ask, describing me as *'bella'* a few times. In brotherly fashion, Ludovico touched my arm and whispered, "Do you want me to get rid of him?"

Before I could answer, the man had grabbed my gloved hand and dragged me to the dance floor. He pushed his spiky cheek against mine. I angled my head away.

For a while we stepped from one foot to the other, our bodies pressed together. My partner pulled at my neck, trying to close the space between his head and mine, the only bit of me that felt under my control.

Finally, in a frustrated tone, he inquired why I constantly faced the left-hand corner.

"Oh, if I watch long enough, I might see some poor bewildered-looking ant walking in circles on the stonework," I replied.

"You *are* silly. Why stare at empty walls, when you could be paying attention to *me?*" He wrenched my head around, forcing my cheek against his.

When the man walked me back towards my seat, I found all my friends were dancing. An elderly lady with yellow teeth happened to be occupying my seat. She grinned, explaining in slurred words, "I'm planning to get a good view of the Russian Count when he arrives. If I stay here, I can easily stand on the orchestra's stage, or you might help me to my feet on this chair."

I sat in Karen's former seat beside the woman, and she held her glass in front of me. I reacted with, "Thank you very much, but no."

236

"I've seen the Russian around town," the woman went on, taking a sip from the glass. "Have you?"

I nodded, meeting her eyes.

"Ah, yes," she murmured, in a taking-note tone that made me feel I'd exposed my soul. "He's affable, charming and tall enough, isn't he? I bet three quarters of the people in this huge room will be disappointed if he doesn't show. Everyone seated will probably rise to their feet when he comes, but," with a giggle that ended in a hiccup, "I'll be looking over their heads. I've heard folk say his grandfather held his country's Order of the Sword of St. George," she hiccupped again, "for bravery during World War One."

"And when I saw the Count in the Uffizi *cortile,* he was brave enough to wear his grandfather's uniform—" I began.

"That's a pretty bold thing to do these days," the woman agreed. At this point I had to excuse myself, as I was invited onto the floor again.

Breathing heavily, my latest partner kept his salivating mouth pressed against my shoulder, like a wet mollusk.

To avoid being aware of the unpleasant sensation, I put myself into a trance, thinking of the Russian Count who would surely come. But my dancing partner, glancing up, caught my loving expression. He pressed my elbow meaningfully, blew down my neck and muttered, *"Andiamo."*

I failed to answer, so he said more loudly, *"Andiamo via—* let's go away."

"No!" I stared at him in horror.

"Let's go. I know of a place you'll like. Let's go, because you're the most beautiful girl I've ever seen. I want you. Why should I, when you belong to the class that holds the world back? But, do you hear? I want you."

Looking beyond the man, spying lanky Ludovico leaning against the wall and talking with the elderly woman I had just left, my eyes pleaded, "Free me!"

In two strides, Ludovico had crossed the dance floor. He wrested me from the human shellfish and hoisted me high. Belatedly, he tapped the shoulder of my former mollusk-like partner for permission.

Ludovico danced alone for a while, with me on his shoulder. I felt dreadfully embarrassed, but coped with everyone's eyes on me by straightening and gazing through windows. When we passed an opened casement in a corner darker than the rest of the ballroom, I noticed a flickering light among moonlit trees, and what looked like a man beneath. Could that man be my Russian Count? I resolved to investigate as soon as possible.

Eventually, my rescuer carried me back to where my friends once had been. He gently lowered me to the ground, quickly kissed my cheek and said, "Goodbye, and good luck in all you do."

"You're leaving!" I exclaimed.

Ludovico nodded.

"That means I won't see you again," I lamented.

"Nooo."

I wanted to reach up and hug him but, instead, I said, "Thank you from the bottom of my heart for being my friend."

Ludovico stepped backwards, and we exchanged a soulful look. He finally broke it by saying, "I'm going home now." He turned and walked away, the crowd engulfing him.

Nicole, Julie and Karen were nowhere to be seen. Nostalgia swept over me. Soon all my friends here would be gone from my life, even my adored *Contessa.* I also realized that this moment was my last chance to find my Russian Count.

I looked around, planning to slip out unseen. My escape route lay nearby, through the same exit Robin and Roland had taken.

To my surprise, the almost invisible exit, beyond heavy black curtains similar to stage wings, and a small corner door, led, not through a side passage to the vast marble area where we'd had so many lessons but through trees and undergrowth, directly to open air. Out here, I could investigate immediately the man under moonlight I'd glimpsed when Ludovico took me around on his shoulder.

But first, being beyond the moon's reach, I had to be careful where I trod. Tiny leaves and flowers flared like lit candles at the ends of dark invisible branches and stems. Lively giggles and whispers emerged from thickly shadowed bushes behind them. From every corner, the spirit of this night seemed to express the desire of lovers for time to stand still.

I headed towards a whitewashed gravel path. The distant sounds of dogs, motor bikes and cars provided percussion to wonderful soft human singing that guided me near the terrace alongside our swimming pool. Never in my life had I heard such tenderness in a voice, or such yearning.

Tiny lanterns glowed on the railing that led down to our pool and above them, wearing exactly the same clothes as when I'd first seen him, I noticed my Count fixing a very large lantern up high into a huge old tree as he sang. His braided jacket lay draped on the waterfall wall.

My first instinct was to run away—I don't know why—and that's exactly what I did. I'd noticed many female birds hop away from potential mates, stop, go back, and move away again. Did they feel the real fear I felt? Of the future, and of a male who would not behave like a brother, and of, above all, myself? Of entering a whole new country, exciting far beyond the boundaries set by perfection, full of dramatic beginnings?

Still singing, my Count leapt down and was standing with outstretched arms on the path from which I'd come. Wherever I turned, he stood, smiling at me. His face, awash with the moonlight, looked beautiful.

I smiled too, and waited, wondering what would happen.

"I want to thank you for the vision you gave me," he said. "The sight of you in the Uffizi *cortile* has kept me happy on many days. And now you have made my night wonderful too. Are you cold in that flimsy dress? Would you like us to go inside?"

"No, thank you," I said politely. "But you go in if you need to."

"I'd rather be where you are."

We shared a silence.

"Will you teach me all the bad words in Russian?" I asked cheekily.

He laughed. "I can tell you the words, but not the meanings."

"Oh—won't you tell me any?"

"Why are you teasing me? I am afraid of growing too fond of you, when your school year is ending. Do you understand? No, you can't—you are only a child." His eyes smiled. Now I could meet them, softer in the moonlight than when first I saw him.

I asked, "Am I really still a child?"

"Well, tonight perhaps you're not."

My Russian laughed, and I joined in.

But suddenly he turned and grasped me by the waist. I felt myself fall into him as he whirled me up, up, up against his chest until the moon, stars and trees spun around us and all I could see were thin ribbons circling us of black, white and pale yellow. He slowed for a moment, singing incomprehensible words, allowing my feet to touch the ground—then spun me fast again up into the heavens, his magnificent soulful voice roaring what I took to be a Gypsy tune. I felt my long skirt billowing all around me.

Slowing and then stopping, he laid his head on my embroidered breast. His soft curly hair pressed against the curve of my neck and chin. I was in a glorious dream that I hoped would never end.

Faintly, the orchestra began playing. My Russian straightened and lowered me to the ground. From my gladdened heart I burst into fairly tuneful song along with the band's lead singer:

"Come prima, più di prima, t'amerò
La mia vita per la vita ti darò
Sembra un sogno rivederti, accarezzarti

As before, more than before, I will love you
My life for your lifetime I will give you

It seems a dream to see you once more, to caress you..."

I danced away from my Russian for a little while, and sensed him watching me as if enchanted. I returned, to leap towards him with total trust. He caught me and I lifted my arms around his neck.

Carrying me, my Stateless Count moved to the waterfall wall, and, with one hand, wrapped his braided white jacket around me. The air crackled. "I wonder whether you'll write to me when you leave, my small one?" he whispered. "Because your Countess knows where I live. Once a month?"

"If you wish."

"Once a month is very little, but I suppose I'll have to be satisfied with that."

"But what could I say to you in a letter? I am ignorant of the world, and I feel you know so much."

"I want to watch you grow. Tell me, has anyone ever kissed you?"

For a moment I struggled, recalling bad experiences but he soothed me by tenderly stroking the back of my hair. He murmured, "Let me explain to you, my darling: a kiss on the mouth can be a meeting of spirits. It can be an expression of bonding that goes beyond the depths of the earth and plumbs the unity of God. If it does not feel like this, it is not a kiss..."

Gently, my Russian raised his hands to my cheeks, and gazed into my face. He carefully brought my mouth to his.

This—this was heaven. Sweet—sweet—*unbearably* sweet. My Count was all mouth, and I was all mouth. I thought I'd never

241

want to eat or drink again, and that I must keep something of this forever.

Our kiss showed me mystery. I understood with my mouth what Kasho had told me—that a husband and wife who are both physically and spiritually united will be husband and wife through all the worlds of God.

My Count's arms were my arms. His now massive head became my head, and our bodies radiated light. Nothing bad could happen to us. I believe we saw inside each other's souls.

My Count filled my mouth with his own experience and strength. But did he take nourishment from me too? Did he feel my pain, my inexperience, my coldness or my desire?

Never could I be lonely again, for surely kissing is receiving full knowledge of the other. Never again could the past bind me, for sharing—*sharing* a kiss with my Count drew me away from family, from my frightened self into a kindred spirit. I understood the possibility of flesh-and-blood love with a man. Where there is oneness, there is infinity, I realized. And infinity has no small details.

But a small detail did happen before I ran away, overwhelmed, into the night. My Count drew a handkerchief from his clothing, wiped my eyes with it and pressed it into my hand.

Chapter Fourteen
The United States of America

Daisy lay sprawled across my four poster bed, eyes closed blissfully, making me think of her basking in sunshine on a river boat. Sleep was so precious to me but tonight I boldly approached, and kissed her on the forehead. She stirred, waved her arms as if paddling, I thought, and asked confusedly "Mom?"

Suddenly her eyes shot open and she stared for a full minute, then smiled at my doubtless radiant face. "Well, look who rose from the grave! Your Russian Count kissed you, didn't he?"

I felt myself blush; but, after hesitating, admitted, "We kissed *each other,*" and began to dance around the room. "I had the best time! Being loved that way makes me *so* happy!"

Daisy caught my exhilaration. "You're more beautiful now than when you left here," she exclaimed, sitting up.

I stopped dead, confused. Had the Count kissed me only because of my miraculous dress and makeup? "My Russian wasn't insincere, was he?" I asked, expecting worldly wisdom, or at least wisdom from Daisy.

"What I gathered from his portrait was that he's a man in love with life," Daisy answered, "who delights in women. But he'd know he'd taken you as far as you could go."

"Most of the evening, he spoke in English," I told her. "But when we parted he switched to Italian, saying 'You are a very warm person. Many girls are not.' I'm *warm*!" I began dancing again. "And then, when I started climbing the stairs, he added, 'Never forget me.'"

Remembering the handkerchief I was clutching, I stopped dancing to unfold it. Made of fine linen, it boasted a discreet white coat-of-arms embroidered in one corner.

"What's that?" Daisy naturally inquired.

"Something to help me remember," I replied. But then I added, bitterly, "He's going on to another party now. I won't be his last girl this evening."

"I doubt if he'll be giving them handkerchiefs," Daisy chided with mock solemnity. "He's unlikely to forget that he's given you such a family memento, and he's showing that he values you highly."

I stared at the handkerchief with its crest. "Do you know what this evening means?" I whispered. "It's taught me that, if I wish for something, it can happen. But without you, Kasho and the Countess, I'd never have reached such a point." I smiled, thinking I might just be strong enough to face whatever comes up in Australia.

"Speaking of which, I've been planning something for days," Daisy began.

"Yes, I can tell you have," I threw in.

Daisy stretched her elegant arms out to reach my shoulders, and gazed into my face. "I want so much for you to come and live with me in California," she said. "Please let your new-found exuberance take you across the ocean to me, my mom and dad. My family has nothing to do with party politics, but I sense that, socially and politically, the time my country is entering will be of turmoil. However, God has created out of chaos before. Which means that so can you and I. Our songs, honest and naked as wind and sky, could take the real tragedies that are certainly to hand and weave them into heart-binding dramas. All prejudice—racial, religious, national or economic—is destructive, so we must overcome it, and stimulate action. I want to be part of the

244

restlessness, and help transform the world. And what better way than by writing passionate songs that beg for justice, and inviting listeners to explore their own understanding, in a State that is likely soon to be bursting with political movements?"

Daisy paused, waiting excitedly for my answer. What could I tell her? *I want nothing better than never going back to Australia and coming to America with you. I want to create a new culture with you, because I agree that the ways the world has learned to feel, think and act are no longer functional. The thought makes me so happy. I want others to be made happy by us! I want to give birth to a new world! It's as if we're becoming real sisters.* But all I could muster was a stupidly polite, "Thank you so much. I'd love to come, but—"

"If I desire to give you something from my heart, why make both of us unhappy by refusing? I hope you agree."

"But—"

"We can fill the air of America with anthems sung by people rebelling against inequality. Just a few years ago a black woman named Rosa Parks refused to move to the back of a bus, which was terribly brave of her. In the South, in America, black people always sit in the back of the bus. Oh, by the way, people usually say 'negro', but I like saying 'black'. I've always thought black a most beautiful color for skin. Rosa Parks could have been killed on the spot, lynched, hung—that's what they do to blacks in the South. Instead, it has started a whole civil rights movement that's taking off like crazy. Marches and things."

I listened to Daisy without any idea of what she was talking about. But her excitement was infectious. I would have loved nothing better than to write songs in support of black people's rights and have Daisy sing them. But it was a fantasy. I had to go home...but did I really have to?

The idea of not going home made me giddy. For the first time since Kim had left me in the Boboli Gardens, I found myself talking to him: "Is it just a fantasy that I could go to America,

245

Kimmie?" I waited for his reply, but nothing came. Confusion drew me deeper and deeper into silence.

Daisy pressed on excitedly, disregarding my wordlessness. "I believe that my home city will be the best place for you, Melissa. Your lyrics will be very important. You already have the sensitivity to suffering that could become the rallying call of a generation. God knows, that sensitivity *has* to become general. All over America there's a kind of revolution among white kids, Rock 'n' Roll. Oh, it's all about love and lost love and such, silly lyrics, but there's a fantastic energy to it. I predict that it will soon be used for songs of deliverance from oppression. I don't know exactly, but exciting things are going on at home. If I make music with a strong beat, people of every race may begin dancing with each other. You must be part of it all. We must do it together."

Overwhelmed, I couldn't say anything. I could scarcely breathe. I waited for Kim to answer me. After further silence, Daisy went on, "So, Melissa, you see I really can't let you go back to Australia."

She grabbed my gloved hands, one of which still held the handkerchief, and spoke with yet more intensity, "My friend, you don't *have* to be with people who dislike you. You've served your parents long enough. Rather frequently, my mom and dad and I talk briefly together, despite the enormous cost of transatlantic calls. It's our only luxury. And, I must confess, I made an arrangement with them to call me here. As a result, while you were dancing, I've been having a wonderful time speaking with all the members of my family." She looked at her watch. "Oh, my goodness! I can't believe I slept so long. They'll call again in twenty minutes, hoping you agree to come and stay with us. I had a feeling you'd be back by that time. It will be five in the afternoon where they live, just outside of Los Angeles."

Los Angeles, the City of Angels. The name reverberated in my mind like a promise. My heart fiercely pounded. Me in the United States! A daunting and irresistible thought. America had always been forbidden territory for me, open only if I became a spoiled brat, who failed to care about my family's official viewpoint. I exclaimed, "You didn't tell me you were going home, Daisy!"

She gave a small, secret smile. "I didn't want to upset you before the ball. You needed to enjoy yourself, without complicated thoughts. However, the truth is I'm homesick. I'd really like you to seriously consider coming back with me, now that your school year is over. My mother and father were both overjoyed when I suggested it to them earlier this evening. They'd give you the warmest welcome! You'd love California, and you'd fit in well where we live. I'm not the only one in our neighborhood who had such a happy childhood. Many families around us are idealistic, like mine—like you. And there's music! Black and white people play bongo drums in our local park, and strangers make friendly eye contact on the streets. We trust our president, and we trust our country to help rebuild Europe. Our buildings and cars give off a sense of solidity. Not everyone shares in this optimism, of course. We have terrible poverty and injustice—and you and I would be writing songs that aim to stir compassion in the complacent and greedy."

"There's never any music in my house, or on the streets of Australia," I lamented. "But maybe that will come, when my country is more aware of the outside world." *Nonsense,* I heard a voice in my head. For just a moment, I thought the voice belonged to Kimmie. But it didn't. There was none of the familiarity of his presence. *Nonsense, there will never be music in my parents' house!* This time the words burst forth as if from my own heart—my own knowing.

Daisy put a hand on my arm, pressing her point home. "My religion," she said, "though always emphasizing unity, also stresses how important it is that human beings bring out the best in each other. You know very well yourself that, if they don't—like you and your parents—something must be done. I may be

247

wrong, but I have a feeling that from now on it would take only a small thing to trigger their accidentally beating you to death."

Which they would truly do, if they had even a hint of what had passed between Christopher and myself, I knew.

"Oh my God, Melissa, your arm has turned icy. I didn't mean to upset you... You don't have to answer now," Daisy went on, more gently. "It's a huge thing, I know. But please don't refuse till after you've spoken with my parents...

"Oh, you *will* come, won't you?" she burst out despite herself. "It will be wonderful if I can tell my parents you're coming home with me. My father's a professor of physics at our local university. I've decided to take up my deferred studies there this coming term, and you did so well in your matriculation exams that the university administration might easily be very glad to have you. They could even give you a scholarship—"

I recalled miserably that my parents despised school teachers, just as they despised everyone else. Not only did my father say, "No child of mine could fail an exam," my parents would give me jobs to do whenever they caught me with school books open—jealous that I should want to obey anyone other than themselves. But schoolwork was a powerful escape, and I loved doing it. Just as I loved the promise of freedom and hope that Daisy now offered me. And there it was, mine to take. All I had to do was be strong.

Returning to the present, I demanded of Daisy, "Are you *sure* you should ask me?"

"Yes, I'm sure," Daisy reiterated firmly.

I began shaking with a combination of excitement and panic. If this were true, my life could change forever. I'd be freed from my parents and their outmoded view of life. But freedom couldn't be as easy as Daisy was implying—just going off to America with her and living happily ever after. I reminded her, "Once, in the Boboli Gardens, I said to you, 'If I stay here in Italy, I'll be stepping off a boat into the ocean; off the Earth, into the universe.

I'll be leaping into the Unknown, with nothing, no support, almost with no clothing.' And it will be the same if I go to your home now. I have no money. I have nothing whatever to offer in return for your parents' hospitality."

"Do you have any idea how greatly loved you are?" Daisy exclaimed. "I believe that America will one day lead the world not only materially, as now, but also spiritually, though we'll have to go through huge upheavals first. Your writing lyrics would surely simplify my life, and everything I want to do. As for money, my parents will work it out with you. When you finish at college and start earning, you can pay them back."

Could Daisy's parents really be as encouraging and loving as their daughter? But why imagine they weren't? The crazy thing she was suggesting was fast becoming a glorious possibility. And she was telling me I had all the support I needed at present.

"Would I need a visa?" I suddenly questioned. "How do I get one?" Ideas started tumbling out of me. "If I did come with you, I wouldn't like my mother or father to know where I was, not for a few years, anyway. I've been trying to work out how to go home to them without marrying Christopher. And I wrote them a letter, but every day I put off my walk to the Post Office. I'm not sure why I couldn't make myself mail what I'd said—"

"Was your letter dangerous?" asked Daisy. "I expect it was."

"Well, first I told them how extremely grateful I felt to them for this year overseas."

"Very good," she nodded.

"And I went on," the words burned in my heart, "that I believe all human beings have been created noble, and that no one should attempt to force his or her will upon another."

I paused, glancing at Daisy for response. "Was I wrong?" I checked.

"Oh no!" she answered, showing a hint of tears. "It's beautiful. How brave!"

I remembered my words further, "'Yet I cannot recall a moment of my life when I have not been terrified of you.' Should I go on?"

"What else did you say?"

"I begged for a new relationship, and added, 'Could we not meet with open hearts, as if for the first time, expecting to be friends? Could we even laugh together, and make each other happy?' And I ended, 'Hoping for a big change now I am almost an adult, your loving daughter'."

Daisy looked at me with soft sadness while, in the silence that followed, I knew what she was going to say, just as I knew I would move heaven and earth to travel to America with her.

Eventually, Daisy murmured, "I think it's good you didn't send it." I started smiling as she went on, "Your parents wouldn't understand such an emotional letter. But I'm really glad you wrote it. And you *will* need to write to them eventually. Just to let them know you're alive."

"But they can't know where I am!" I exclaimed.

"Absolutely not. Come to think of it, why not mail your first letter before you leave, so the postmark reads 'Italy'? Better make it short, I think."

"Yes, yes! And its main point should be that I want to stand on my own two feet—which means I'm not coming home!" I could hardly believe that I was saying this out loud but I was!

In an exaggeratedly innocent voice, Daisy then asked, "Your dad and mom would never guess you'd go to America, would they?"

"You're joking!" We burst out genuinely laughing, and hugged each other. "America is the country they jeer at the most," I admitted. "They say the men in high political office there look like overgrown schoolboys, and all the children are noisy brats. Anyway, I did right by not mailing to my family what I wrote."

"You certainly did. And you made that decision alone, before I even asked you to come home with me. You're one of the bravest girls I've ever known. And I mean that!"

I drew myself up to my full height, and told Daisy, "All right, I've made up my mind. I *will* run away from my parents one way or another. But with this proviso: after I've changed my name and tried to become a successful writer, after I've made my mark in the world and done my best to become a full human being, I *do* want to go back for a while when my frozen mother and bullying father have grown old and need to be cared for. When necessity will probably make them receptive to my love." I shut off the sad thought that my parents would probably prefer to kill themselves than have me, or anyone else, care for them.

"I hope you do go, are true to yourself in their presence, and that it works out," said Daisy. "Miracles happen."

"But I did have my brother, Kim. He taught me all about love."

Tears filled my eyes as Daisy reached to hug me once more. Hugging her back, I felt Kim's closeness. Not as I used to, but where he'd always been and would be—in my heart. It was because of him that I could trust Daisy. It was because of him that I could dare. We were both adventurers, Kim and I, and we were both starting on new journeys. *Be safe,* I called to him. *Journey well, as I know I will.*

I sighed. "Yes, Daisy, I'm coming with you—if you and your parents really want me."

Daisy flashed me a radiant smile, then glanced once more at her watch. "Oh, my God! See the time?" she blurted out.

Grasping my hand, she pulled me to the doorway, adding, "We're going to be late for my parents' call! But yippee!" She giggled. "I can't wait to share my mom with you."

The bumpy stone walls that narrowed the steps descending from my tower room slowed us, because we were two. But when we reached the corridor lined with bedrooms, we ran extra fast

251

along it to the next lot of stairs. Rapidly, I slid sideways down their bannisters, my beautiful skirt's sequins flashing occasionally. Daisy followed suit singing, to a rousing newly invented tune, "I am sliding home with Melissa!" No one was about. My friends would still be chatting and dancing under the brighter lights of the ballroom on the lower level, or venturing out to the garden.

The telephone was already ringing when we reached the little hall that gave access to kitchen, dining room, small sitting room and the Countess' office. Daisy immediately grabbed the receiver and yelled "Eeee!" into it. Then she said, "We only have three minutes. I'll give you Melissa. Love you mom, dad, everyone, Charlie."

Nervously, I said, "Hello?" as if it were a question.

"Welcome to our humble home, Melissa," enthused a throaty, amused-sounding woman's voice. "We've heard so much about you! I've been telling our friends, we'll have a real good party once you've recovered from your journey. The celebrations will go on for days—we won't sleep much. The thought of you coming made me remember—Daisy was always singing and dancing around the house when she and her brothers were children, and they'd compose songs and put on shows for us and the neighbors. She really has a lot to say to the world! She'll go far, we think, now she's got you. You don't have to worry about *anything. We'll* look after you. We'll put you in Daisy's bedroom for a bit, while we decorate our spare room to your liking. How do you feel? Would you like that?"

"I'd love to meet you," was all I could stammer. Daisy's words, "I can't wait to share my mom with you" were still making me tingle. They'd seemed strange when she said them but now her mother's sincere hospitality was giving them wonderful reality.

A tenor man's voice came on. "Daisy said 'Eeee!' to the operator!" he laughed. "She was hoping to get us right away. We always say that in greeting, as if we're hugging each other as tightly as can be. When I'm walking down the street here, I imagine Daisy as a little girl coming up behind me, flinging her arms around my legs and shouting 'Eeee!' And now I'll have two of you! That'll be great. A bit more laughter round the house."

I breathed deeply, remembering how Kasho had said "Eeee!" when he'd lain on his back and hugged me long ago in those wonderful sand dunes. It must be a natural human tendency to exclaim that way, I thought, even on another planet. But I'd never experienced it before that time outside time with Kasho. I recalled the fun we'd had when he'd changed shape from the old, scarred man to the young warrior and back again. No matter what form he took, I remembered, he still had the strength and surefootedness of a young tribal man working in open air, spearing fish for his family. I'd loved the way he moved, with the litheness of a big cat, either slowly or lightning fast.

But now Daisy's father's voice was bringing me out of my reverie, and I knew I'd soon have to answer.

"I never expected to visit America," I ventured, remembering my parents' conceited opinion of that country: *It's gone from barbarity to decadence without the intervening stages.* "Thank you so much." I gave Daisy back the telephone, whispering, "I think your parents see the whole world as family."

"They do!" Daisy laughed.

After a few words more into the receiver, she replaced it and turned to me. "You're going to share my room!" she giggled. "That's so exciting! We'll all take a camping trip to Yosemite National Park. It's one of my favorite places! So many animals! Picture it—towering cliffs and giant veils of water with lunar rainbows in them, under the full moon of spring or early summer and you never saw such trees!"

We embraced gleefully. "Come back to my bedroom," I said. "A plan is forming in my head. I'll write something very different to my parents now." Briefly, I glimpsed relief in Daisy's eyes.

But just then the Countess appeared at the top of the stairs that led up from the ballroom. As if no one were here, she was adjusting her pearls and straightening her dress at the waist. But she beamed on catching sight of Daisy and me. "Come in for a moment," she said, opening her office door and pulling two chairs to our side of her desk. "Sit down, my girls. Daisy, would you prefer chocolate or a *marron glacé*?"

Settling in her padded chair opposite us, the Countess opened her desk drawer and held out a colorful opened box in each of our directions. Expressing gratitude, Daisy took a strawberry-flavored chocolate, and I a praline.

"Melissa," the Countess asked, grinning widely, "Are you happy for me to give the Russian Count your address? Upon saying goodbye, and thanking me for inviting him, he asked for your details."

I said I was quite pleased. That I always kept my promises. "But my address in Australia is wrong," I added.

"Melissa will be living with me," Daisy cut in, with shocking sharpness. "I understand, though, that her parents won't easily let her go. They want to brainwash her and keep her under control. They believe their duty is to silence her, never let her loose on the world."

"I admit I've received that impression." The Countess' eyebrows descended in their middles. "You are much too young to extinguish your life and career before it has begun, Melissa," she pointed out. "I once asked you to laugh at society, because I could sense the big things I believe you are born to do. I teach my girls to grow up, which means making their own decisions." She went on, more dreamily, "I have seen how being here brings you joy, and a readiness to drink in life. So," leaning empathetically towards us, with her arms on the desk and her fingertips touching, "now you are about to embark on a great adventure."

I remembered how my parents had expected the finishing school's Principal to turn me into a heartless person who made empty conversation at cocktail parties. Though overwhelmed with relief that my Countess was not like that, I had to warn her about my father. "I have been infinitely lucky in your care, *signora*," I said. "People have been unbelievably loving since I left home. But I need to tell you, my parents have real power in Australia. They can prevent me from doing anything. A word in the ear of someone at my father's club—"

With her raised hand, the Countess cut me off. "Your parents may be big in Australia," she said, "but they have no power over *me.* And so, on Monday, I will accompany you both to the United States Consulate to discuss what, if anything, Melissa will need, if she is to enter and live in America. I'm on your side always." The Countess' eyes were upon mine with fierce love, her lips stretching horizontally, thin and closed. "I see you clearly, Melissa, as probably the only sane person to come out of your parents' immediate social circle. You can rely on me not to tell them where you are."

I reached for my *Contessa*'s hand, my anxiety gone. "I have my Australian passport handy, of course," I put in.

"I'm sure you'll meet all visa requirements," Daisy stated matter-of-factly. Turning, herself, to my Principal she said, "We both deeply appreciate everything you do. May I?"

Daisy lifted a pen and indicated a notepad on the desk.

"Of course," said the *Contessa.* "Yes, I will give your address to my friend the Russian fellow." She smoothed my fingers, patting them, and confirmed wistfully, "Naturally, Melissa, you are free to stay on at my school until you, or we, have everything worked out. Also, you are always invited back. I do hope I see you again.'"

"La mia Contessa," I returned, "you have been gigantic in my life. Once upon a time, all my hopes were secretly despair. But here they have been fulfilled beyond my wildest dreams.

255

That you, an older woman, should open your heart to me, giving me such precious advice… that you should care… I feel I have risen from a grave. Thank you so much for blessing our endeavors, *signora.*"

A gentle knock sounded on the closed door. The Countess strode around us and opened it.

Three Italian girls with similar faces stood outside. One small, with a confident air, dark-haired and vibrant, seemed to be chaperoning her taller, shy younger sister and possibly a cousin.

"We want to thank you a million times, *signora,* for having your driver bring us and wait for us," the small girl said. "We've thoroughly enjoyed ourselves tonight."

"Any time, Fiamma," the Countess replied warmly. "Whatever I can do for your lovely family, I will. Daisy," she stated firmly, "would you like to share my car with my young friends? Sergio will be pleased to drop you off where you are staying."

Daisy and I walked with the girls to the car. When they'd climbed in, she threw her arms around me; then I followed her lead as we both pulled apart, twirled, stamped and sang from Rock 'n' Roller Jerry Lee Lewis:

"I cut my nails and I quiver my thumb;

I'm really nervous 'cause it sure is fun.

Come on, baba! You drive me crazy

Goodness gracious, great balls of fire!"

Back in my tower room, in a trembling voice hoarser than usual, Kasho remarked, "Greater love hath no woman than one who tries to give up, for the sake of her soulmate, her own best hope of eternal, infinite happiness. But I can wait for you." He reassured me, a huge relaxing smile coming into his voice, "I have time, and so have you. I can wait for you forever. This is the way it was supposed to be. We'll get our work apart done, then come together to perform miracles."

"What if I fail you?"

256

"Whatever happens, you cannot fail me. You in your galaxy, I in mine, will serve as best we can, without attachment to worldly gain, or even to benefit in life after death. We'll see my planet and your Earth as training grounds, where we can develop love, compassion, faith, courage, and other qualities of the soul that will be needed ever more strongly after death. We will become true human beings, who sacrifice our personal interests for the sake of the tribe. And your tribe will be your whole world. Then, after we die, our unity will be such that even the spiritual realm will marvel at it. We will be a great pair! While in utter bliss, you and I will work without rest, alongside other spirits, to help your world make her transition to becoming heavenly. If you and I serve well in this life, we'll have a thousand times more power after death to help people create artworks and discover wonders in your world. God willing."

I could almost feel Kasho's arm around me, and was taken by a greater commotion than ever in his presence. "Listen to me, my darling Little Mystery," he said. "Your life will be over in a twinkling of an eye. But it is important, precious. I *want* you to have a human life, and I'll have mine with my people. Of course, you'll bear scars. But they'll be battle scars, honorable scars. And I'll often be with you. As I've said before, if we were not meant to be together, God would be contradicting Himself.

"And now let us turn to more immediate matters," he went on. "Tell me, my sweetheart, are you scared to leave everything you have ever known, and go to the United States?"

"Yes," I said simply. I was very scared.

"Your moving from one country to another will change things a bit for me too. But do you remember how we felt when, for the first time on Earth, you actually *saw* me? Sitting in a tree? When we were spirits together?"

"Yes, terror at a whole new world opening."

"What followed, for us both in the sand dunes," Kasho reminded me, "was, at least for me, the best time of our lives.

257

And I think the change to America will be similar. When you come to understand that country, it will bring you color and life. Yes, I'm pretty certain America will be like that for you.

"I see you and Daisy riding bicycles outside," he continued so comfortingly that, again, I was sure his arm must be around me. "The weather feels warm, with a light breeze. Soulful music emanates from Daisy's house, and everywhere else on the street. Daisy remarks to you from her bicycle, 'What could be better than this? Realizing we have so many weeks ahead here?' A Chinese woman on the street corner is playing the violin, accompanied by a black man on the guitar. Wearing rainbow-colored shoes, an elderly couple get up from a bench to dance. They are joined by passersby. And I notice a lot of dads playing with their children. That's never happened in your experience. But the scene will be something like this. Doesn't sound too bad, does it?"

I smiled.

"Of course," Kasho went on, "if you eventually prefer to relate to me as a granddaughter, sister or friend, I will still wait for you, and we can still enjoy a deep spiritual bond whose glories are beyond description. I certainly love you enough, and that love can tip into loving you in any way you allow me to. On your planet and mine, you and I have moved beyond pain and gained tiny glimpses of the eternal bliss to come. Yet it is really only one aspect of you, your soul-state, that I know. And I think you felt similarly inside my spirit. But the ecstasy of union after death will be a million times greater, because then we will be strong enough to bear feelings with infinite power."

I drew a deep breath. "Before I left Australia," I pointed out, "I thought that no one could really feel with me. Also, that I could not get inside other people. That this was the fundamental loneliness all of us had, a yearning to belong that we'd experience forever."

"Now you know differently," said Kasho, his tone expressing even more tenderness.

I sensed him caressing my hair like a lover. I moved my body, with faith, to nestle into his, and, to my surprise, my partly exposed back could feel his chest, warm, solid, hairy. What I felt in my body at that moment was certainly stronger than anything I'd felt with the Russian Count.

Like a blind woman about to be parted from her lover forever, I turned and walked my hands all over Kasho's solid face that I had seen among the sand dunes, so fierce yet compassionate, and containing all the beauty and gentleness of the universe. Of course, we would not be parted. I would be with Kasho forever. And now I truly felt the warmth of his relaxed arm around my shoulders, so I nestled into him again.

"I am but a man like others," he said, "though more downtrodden than many. I know hunger, thirst, imprisonment and torture. But what majesty lies in the soul of a single human being!"

"And yet you and I will never, never truly meet physically in this life," I lamented, "though we travel a thousand million miles. Can't we invent a bigger word than love for what crosses such an immense distance?"

"One day, in a greater dimension, I believe we will be spiritually husband and wife. But I do not want to act selfishly. Please always be aware that you are free to change your mind at any point, depending on what life does to you." Kasho's apologetic but infectious laughter, ringing, singing around my bedroom—laughter which I believed I would remember forever like a confident promise—took on a life of its own.

"We who laugh last laugh last last!" I shouted. Then I, too, began laughing uncontrollably.

Kasho joined in my merriment, and we roared out to the universe, like drunken people: "We who laugh last lars lars lars!"

After he'd calmed a little, Kasho added wryly, "She who laughs lasts."

"To think that I wanted God to contradict Himself!" I exclaimed through my tearful laughter. "To think that I would ever want to sacrifice eternity with you!"

Acknowledgments

My gratitude to all those who have helped me out of the most massive writer's block of all time, especially Emily Hanlon.